'You don't know anything about me. Why don't you go away? Leave me alone.'

It was horrible to feel this upsurge of panic. She was shivering, but when he put his hand on her waist and worked it up under her sweater to find her breasts, she stopped, filled with a sense of completion. Bone of my bone, flesh of my flesh. The words dropped, unbidden, into her mind.

'I could show you a good time. You'd love the places I'd take you to.'

'Well, maybe it can be arranged. When we go abroad next, you could come with us. I think Oliver's planning to visit Florida.'

'That isn't what I meant. Just you and me, Kim. No one else.'

His hand warmed her lace-covered breasts. She wanted to lean against him and have him continue that soft, insinuating caress. What's the matter with me? she thought, panicking. I wouldn't still be sitting here if anyone else had tried it on.

'Look,' she said, pushing his hand away and sliding further along the bench, putting a decent space between them. 'This is silly. It can't happen. Nothing's going to happen. We can't. I'm married. Besides, you're my brother.'

'Only half.'

The Ties That Bind

TESNI MORGAN

Black Lace novels contain sexual fantasies.
In real life, make sure you practise safe sex.

First published in 1999 by
Black Lace
Thames Wharf Studios,
Rainville Road, London W6 9HT

Copyright © Tesni Morgan 1999

The right of Tesni Morgan to be identified as the
Author of this Work has been asserted by her in
accordance with the Copyright, Designs and Patents Act
1988.

Typeset by SetSystems Ltd, Saffron Walden, Essex
Printed and bound by Mackays of Chatham PLC

ISBN 0 352 33438 X

Chapter One

*S*atan stood in the doorway.

'Hello. You must be Kim,' he said, and his voice was seductive, just as she had always thought the devil's voice would be. It curled round her ear like a secret caress.

'That's right,' she answered, wondering why Jenny hadn't heard the bell. Unlike her imagination's dark devil, this one was blue-eyed, almost angelic, apart from the little pair of horns springing from tawny, spiked hair.

'Trick or treat?' he asked.

This question always flustered her. When children appeared on her doorstep in covered sheets and gruesome face paint, she was never sure what to answer, usually going for her purse and doling out coins.

'It depends what you're offering,' she said guardedly.

'Anything you want,' he replied, and stepped over the threshold.

The entrance hall was full. Everyone wore masquerade costume. Rock music blasted from stereo speakers suspended from the beams. There were black balloons featuring witches on broomsticks, and red ones adorned with imps. Ivy decorated the beams. Plastic spiders and

1

bats jiggled on strings and a realistic skeleton leant on the carved banister rail, leering at the crowd below.

And now the master had arrived to join his followers on Halloween.

Kim didn't know him. Was he one of Oliver's business associates?

She glanced round, but her husband was deep in conversation with Flyte Reynald. Jealousy bit deep. It always did when she was in evidence. Flyte looked stunning, wearing a Queen-of-the-Night costume, a Hathor headdress on her fiery, crimped hair. She was showing a lot of bosom and leg. Kim was acutely conscious that she could have made more effort with her own costume instead of settling for the trite Dracula victim outfit: white, lawn nightdress; ghastly corpse-face with black, rimmed eyes; crimson-streaked teeth and lips.

Oliver. She melted at the thought of him, a fresh surge of dew dampening her panties. They'd had sex while getting ready for the party. A shared shower, the warmth of their room, the intimacy of the soft bed, his hands, his mouth. His upward-tilting cock; she knew it so well, every inch of smooth skin, every throbbing vein, the silky helm, would have recognised it out of a dozen by feel alone. Like everything else he did, Oliver made love with panache and artistry.

He revelled in gatherings like this. She never had done; she was far too self-conscious. And now she was being scrutinised by Satan in red leather pants so tight that his butt, the hollows in his flanks, and the impressive package behind his fly were all clearly defined.

'Are you on the guest list?' she said stiffly, falling into her wife-of-an-important-man role.

'No,' Satan answered, and his quirky smile did not reach his eyes. His mouth was beautifully shaped. She couldn't stop looking at it. How would it feel to run her tongue-tip over that sensual lower lip or to let that mouth play over her most intimate places?

2

'Then do you mind telling me who you are?' she asked, making little signals to Oliver, who looked across, raised an eyebrow, and began to saunter towards her.

The conversation dipped and, into the sudden hush, Satan said, 'I'm your brother.'

She stared at him blankly. 'My what?'

'Your brother. Illegitimate, and only half, but it's better than nothing, I suppose. We had the same father.'

He focused on her and his smile faded, replaced by a serious, intent look. There was an element in his ice-blue eyes that she couldn't fathom. Was it mockery, envy, lust, or a mixture of all three?

'You're joking,' she said, making a frantic bid in her mind for sanity. Her brother? She felt instantly guilty. She had been fantasising about kissing him.

He shrugged. His shoulders were broad under the red jacket, his bare arms tanned and muscular. 'It's true. I'm Jack Loring.' His gaze switched to Oliver and he held out his right hand. 'And you must be my brother-in-law.'

'So it appears,' Oliver answered, his tone questioning and slightly ironic, taking the hand and shaking it.

They were mentally stalking round one another. Had they been cats their tails would have been fluffed out to twice normal size. Kim guessed that Oliver was wondering whether to call security and have them deal with Jack. Very discreetly, of course. Glen House contained too many valuables to have unauthorised persons roaming around. Not that Jack looked like a thief, but then, what do thieves look like? she asked herself. A stocking over the head? Carrying a cosh?

'If it's true, then I'm glad to meet you, Jack,' she said, more confident now Oliver was there.

'It's true,' Jack answered blandly, and continued to subject her to a searching appraisal.

A slow burn began at the base of her spine, travelling upwards and manifesting itself as a blush that spread over her face and neck. It was embarrassing. She wanted

3

to end this uncomfortable encounter, and get back to being Oliver Buckley's much-envied wife. He was so good-looking and talented, such a catch, as other people called him. She didn't see him like that. She loved him. She had everything she desired. Their two years of marriage had been blissful.

Steady! she said inwardly. Who are you trying to convince? Then, she thought: Hell. I don't need this.

'You want proof that I'm really who I say I am?' Jack offered nonchalantly. He fished in a back pocket and brought out a business card. 'There you go.'

Oliver took it and turned it over in his thin fingers. 'Now I remember,' he said. 'Loring, the architect. I accepted your designs on behalf of Transglobe. You're going to oversee the construction of their new site on Aldermar Street. Forgive me. How remiss. If I'd known you'd already arrived in London I'd have made sure you were invited.' His eyes narrowed as he added, 'I had no idea you and Kim were related.'

'Neither did I till recently. My mother told me after she'd read James Millard's obituary in *The Times*.' He made a rueful grimace and added, 'It's a long story, Kim, and I'll tell you later. If you want proof of that, too, then I've plenty back at my hotel.'

'I'd like to see it,' Oliver said. 'In fact, it's essential that we do. Don't you agree? Such a claim can't be taken lightly. Meanwhile, what would you like to drink?'

'A shandy, please. I'm driving.'

'OK. Please help yourself to food.'

Logs blazed in monumental fireplaces set each end of the fifty-foot long Victorian Gothic hall. The night was cold and rain thrashed the curved bay windows. The bar ran along one side, and Kim wedged herself against a marble pillar, waiting for Oliver to return with the drinks.

'I like those,' Jack said, nodding towards two grotesque, grinning pumpkins shining in a darkened corner. 'Reminds me of America. Halloween's big there.'

'I carved them, with a bit of help from Jenny. She's the housekeeper. Is that where you come from, America?' she asked, thinking: he doesn't have an American accent, only British public school, rather like Oliver's. My brother. This man is my brother? She struggled to get to grips with the concept but it still didn't gel.

'I did some studying there: New York, San Francisco and L.A. But I was born in the West Country. Bristol, to be exact. Have you been to the States?'

'Never. You've travelled a lot?'

'Oh yes.'

'How old are you?'

'Twenty-five.'

'So I was two when you were born. I've always wanted a baby brother.'

'And now you've got one.'

Why is Oliver taking so long? she fretted, aware of the flimsy nature of her nightdress, the bodice now raised into two sharp points by nipples which were as hard as cob-nuts. She didn't want to be left alone with this disturbing individual, relative or not. He was too sure of himself, too smug. She wasn't sure that she liked him.

'Care for a cigarette?' he asked, smiling down at her from his six-foot-plus height. As he drew a pack from the waistcoat which was laced over his chest, crisp hair sprung from firm, sun-browned flesh, and poked between the thongs.

'I'm trying to give them up. I was doing really well, until tonight,' she said, wanting to add, until I set eyes on you.

'Have another go tomorrow,' he advised with that trace of mockery in his voice. Little flames sparked in his pupils as he lit her cigarette. 'We've got to get to know each other, Kim. Think of all those wasted years. Think of the Christmases we could have had together, and bonfires and fireworks and nights like tonight.'

'I've survived very well as an only child,' she replied,

5

trying to avoid his eyes. Outlined with a kohl pencil, they were compelling. She always had liked make-up on men. Something to do with her passion for the ballet. An erotic world of athletic dancers effortlessly lifting their partners, a world of fantasy, where bodies made graceful patterns, a world of strong males and fragile-looking yet steely-muscled girls.

'I've survived, too,' Jack said. 'But it's going to be better with the two of us. I feel like we've met before. Do you feel that? It must be blood calling to blood, old man Millard's blood.'

She looked at the scarlet leather, devil horns, bare arms, studded wristbands, a naked midriff and those lean, ultra-sexy hips. He was enough to tempt a saint into sin.

'You knew him?' she floundered. It was as if an abyss were yawning at her feet. She found herself smoking furiously, welcoming the nicotine hit.

'Never met him in my life. I was his guilty secret. Loring is my mother's name. He supported me though, through boarding school and university. She didn't marry. She preferred her independence. She owns a hotel, and makes money from the tourist trade. But I think she still carried a torch for our father. Would you like to meet her?'

'I don't know. Not yet. Let me get used to this first.'

Kim was chilled to the bone. The house was centrally heated and fires were roaring up the chimneys, yet old, unhappy memories touched her: her father conducting a life apart from her mother and herself. He hadn't been the upright, moral man he pretended to be. All this time he had been keeping a woman and her son, deceiving his wife, and hiding it from his daughter.

Kim had loved her father, but this revelation had turned her world upside down. I'm glad he's dead, she thought bitterly. I kid myself I'm open-minded, but this is too close to home. Thank God mother never realised. Or did she? The horrible thought struck her that maybe she had known, but had kept quiet about it. And now I'll never be able to ask her, or either of them. They can't give me answers from beyond the grave.

'It's been a shock. I'm sorry. I should have called you,' Jack said, and moved a little closer.

Don't, she wanted to scream. Keep away. But she could feel his body's warmth through his clothes.

He took the cigarette butt from her and ground it out, then enveloped her cold, pale fingers in his large, tanned hands. 'I had hoped you'd be as excited as I am. We should stick together.' He reached up to touch her loose, ringletted hair. 'Wicked. Just right for a vampire's bride. Viv told me that my father was dark. You obviously get this from him. I take after her.'

'Viv?'

'I always call my mother that. Everyone does. It's short for Vivien.'

'I know what it's short for.'

Vivien. Her father's mistress. Had he stayed at her hotel during a business trip? Is that when it had happened? And what kind of a woman was she?

'Oliver's dressed as a vampire, too,' she stammered, as if his name was a talisman against her father's secret life and the fair woman he had slept with, and the child resulting from this union. 'But not the Hammer House of Horror kind,' she rushed on. 'More the Anne Rice, elegant gentleman sort. Very sexy.'

'He is, and so are you,' Jack agreed, and lifted her hands to his lips.

His mouth barely grazed her skin, but the heat of his breath seemed to scorch. Her nipples tightened and her belly clenched. She was aglow with nerves and unwilling arousal. She trembled. He straightened up and slowly stroked the mock blood on her lips, tracing the soft curves with his thumb. She opened her mouth, her tongue flickering out, wanting to lick his fingers and draw them into the warm, wet cavity.

He made no attempt to do anything other than caress

7

her lips, but she was unable to stop herself from leaning into him. Her breasts chaffed against the supple leather, and her pubis lifted towards the pronounced fullness between his legs. She'd only had one glass of wine, yet she felt intoxicated, her body urging her into a rash course of action, her mind struggling to maintain control. No man had ever made her feel like this before, not even Oliver.

'Who's the guy in red?' Flyte said, leaning her firm breasts against Oliver's shoulder as she reached for a gin and tonic.

'Jack Loring,' he said, handing it to her, ice tinkling in the glass. 'He's come from the States to work on the Transglobe project. A brilliant architect by all accounts. Odd thing is, he says he's Kim's brother, one of Jim Millard's indiscretions. She'd never even heard of him. I'll get to the bottom of it, investigate his background.'

'Intriguing,' Flyte murmured.

She could tell he was agitated. Having been his lover and friend for over a decade, if anyone could claim to know him, then it was her. Life had dealt her a cruel blow on the day that Kim had applied for a post at Oliver's office. She hadn't got the job, but had got him instead.

'She's the one, Flyte,' he had said. 'I'm going to marry her.'

Flyte had shed her tears in private. She later found that she liked Kim. She was a serious young woman, and very beautiful. Her mass of dark hair surrounded a heart-shaped face, and with clear grey guileless eyes and a slim, straight body, she had an air of vulnerability that had appealed to Oliver.

Oliver was outstandingly bright and had always been surrounded by clever people. He could have had his pick among any number of highly eligible women, but had chosen Kim. Flyte knew him to be bossy, but never unpleasantly so. He liked to organise his life and those

8

in it. She sometimes chided him for taking Kim over so completely.

'She's much younger than you. Be careful you don't make her feel small,' she had warned.

'What d'you mean, small?' He had reacted so violently that she knew she had hit the mark. 'There's so much I want to show her.'

'Teach her?'

'Well, maybe,' he had conceded.

'She's a woman, not a little girl.'

'I know, but she has led a rather sheltered life.'

'She went to college, took a degree, and had boy-friends before you.'

'She's never touched the seamy side. She's not at all streetwise.'

Tonight Flyte felt again that same raw sense of loss. The gracious, old-world ambience of the recently pur-chased, riverside house in Richmond suited Oliver to perfection, as did his outdated evening garb of a vam-pire. His only concession to being one of the Undead was the black cloak lined with red satin swinging from his shoulders. His mid-brown hair straggled around his collar, one untidy lock falling forward to meet those peaked eyebrows and lupine eyes.

Flyte always thought of them as wolf's eyes. Amber flecked with green, slanting slightly at the corners where tiny lines, sharp as incisors, radiated outwards. He was as lean and agile as a wolf, too, and his body, though spare, was strong. His appetite for sex was that of a sensualist. If it could be said that Flyte loved any man, then it was Oliver Buckley.

Now she walked with him towards Kim and the stranger who claimed to be her brother. Flyte perused him with an experienced eye.

Oh, yes, he was a hunk, all right, and he knew it, she concluded, glancing over him appreciatively. Hard-faced, hard-eyed, hard-bodied. Young, but not too young. Age differences never bothered her. She was firm-bosomed and supple-hipped, and worked hard to keep herself that way. She took herself off to health farms, went to yoga classes, dieted, worked out, watched every inch and every pound.

She met Jack's eyes as they were introduced and read volumes. His glance flicked over her breasts which were tightly encased in a silver bustier, and went lower to where the shadowy triangle of her pubic mound could be seen through her black, chiffon skirt. Here was no innocent, he thought. He'd been round the block a few times. He knew about women, though maybe he didn't exactly like them very much.

A warning frisson prickled down Flyte's spine, coupled with instant animal attraction. Jack was potential trouble.

'So, Mr Loring, Oliver tells me you're Kim's brother,' she began, while a waiter in formal attire proffered the drinks on a salver.

'That's right. And won't you call me Jack?' he replied.

He was polite and perfectly controlled, but Flyte decided he didn't like being interrogated. She refused to play ball, asking, 'Have you been to London before?'

'Only on short visits. Now I'm going to settle here for a while. I'm house-hunting. I was hoping Kim would help me.'

'Why yes. She must,' Oliver insisted, politely but insincerely. 'What sort of property are you looking for?'

'Something unusual and challenging. An old church, perhaps, or a warehouse. They make fine conversions.'

'They're also sold for astronomical figures, if you can find one,' Oliver reminded him, leaning languidly against the pillar and sipping his drink. He was relaxed on the surface but like coiled steel inside.

Flyte noticed that Kim was jittery. Well, wouldn't you be, she thought, if a handsome young man had turned up out of nowhere and announced that he was closely related to you?

Jack smiled knowingly at her, as if daring her to say or do anything that might spoil his story.

'It's close on midnight, the witching hour, when water and bread are placed around the house for ghostly visitors and mirrors are covered so the dead don't have to look at themselves,' Oliver said dramatically. 'But we're not yet fallen to the Grim Reaper so let's dance.' He led Kim away.

'That leaves us,' Jack said, following them with his eyes.

'It appears so,' Flyte answered dryly. 'Come on then. Let's see what you can do, Jack.'

In the reception room, now a ballroom, the carpets had been removed and the floor waxed. Strobe lights punctured the gloom and the crowd swung to the rhythm of salsa. Their costumes were weird and wonderful. Spectres, werewolves, zombies and *nosferatu* partnered witches, banshees, hell-hags and succubi in a macabre dance.

'They love it, don't they?' Jack murmured, his breath tickling Flyte's ear. 'These middle-class straights can't wait to embrace evil. But do they know what it really is?'

'Do you?' she countered, as he led her into the writhing, sweating crowd.

'Perhaps,' he answered. 'You do, too, I think.'

'Not evil. Depravity, maybe. As some might call it.'

'The uninitiated, you mean.'

She did not reply, refusing to be drawn. This man had the power to wheedle secrets from your soul and she had no intention of giving him any hold over her.

He held her tightly, and she could feel his cock pressing into her thigh like a fleshy finger. To start with, his hand was at her waist, then it slipped lower, and dragged her skirt into the crease of her bottom, mapping out the line of her G-string and the swell of her buttocks. The tip of one finger went even further, working into the tight pucker of her anus.

11

He smelt of expensive perfume, male sexuality and the feral odour of leather. He felt good. Strong and virile. He was in his prime, and so was Flyte. She speculated on how many orgasms she could extract from him. More than him, she reckoned. If he knew his stuff, that was.

Jack was exciting, a new stud on the scene. She liked to think she'd be the first to fuck him.

Above the low-cut bodice, her nipples rose, café au lait circles crowned by erect, pink tips. As they danced, these sensitive points rubbed against his leather-covered chest. She could feel his hot body, and a prick that was growing larger by the second. Flyte smiled, getting his measure.

He lowered his head and nibbled her ear, then her throat, sucking and biting. She gritted her teeth, refusing to let him know that he was arousing her. But he gave her no respite, no time to regain control. All she could sense was the music, the dizzying lights and plunging darkness, her hunger and him; nothing else.

His erection was nudging her belly, and she gyrated her hips against it. Not yet, she said to herself, not tonight. You'll dance to my tune, boy. You've disturbed Oliver, and I want to know what this is all about.

Almost as cunning as her, he reached a hand between their bodies, and rucked up her skirt. He cupped her mons and, parting her petals with a finger, found her hard nub and rubbed it until she was wet. He uncovered it, his thumb pushing the Lurex to one side, and his finger stroked her cream over the pearl-shaped node, sending tremors through her entire body.

The crowd around them were oblivious to what he was doing, blinded by the strobes, absorbed in their own amusements. Jack did not stop, stroking her firmly and bringing her to a quick climax.

'Jesus Christ!' she muttered.

Someone tapped Jack on the shoulder. He half turned, still with his fingers buried in her folds. Flyte looked up and recognised one of her clients from the Harlequin Gallery.

'Hello, Flyte,' he said. He was a large man, made larger by his hunchback costume. 'Can I have the next dance?'

She disengaged herself from Jack, and said breathlessly to him, 'Catch you later,' then slid into Quasimodo's hot, sweaty embrace.

Jack inclined his head, his face distorted by the whirling colours. 'You certainly will. I'll be around for a while yet.'

The music was deafening, yet even through the noise Flyte picked up on a tone in his voice that gave her goose bumps.

It was two o'clock in the morning, and Kim was dozing in her bed. Lily-shaped pewter lamps provided subdued light. The sheets were cool and fragrant, the pillows frilled with lace. It was like being in the heart of a flower, the foot and headboard alive with stylised leaves and stems.

Kim shared Oliver's love of art nouveau, so feminine in essence, expressing fertility and growth and life. They had been ecstatic to find this house filled with such perfect examples. Nothing much had been changed since the 1890s, except the heating system. Of course, these valuable items had pushed the price sky-high, but Oliver could afford it.

She dozed, but something kept dragging her back to reality: the disturbing announcement made by Jack Loring. She hadn't yet talked about it properly to Oliver, and this didn't seem to be the right moment.

He was wide awake, hyped up. He didn't need drugs to make him fly; all it took was stimulating conversation, the exchange of ideas, the companionship of intelligent people and the adrenaline rush he got from entertaining. Not exactly a party animal, he did, however, adore playing the host, making sure his guests enjoyed their visit.

He couldn't relax when the last of them had gone, though there were a few – Flyte included – who had decided to stay. The new drink-driving laws had turned even the most informal gathering into a house party.

'I like house parties like this,' he announced, emerging from the en suite bathroom, a towel looped round his hips. 'It must have been like that when this house was built: weekend parties, people being driven from town in their carriages, or in those wonderful, early motors. Convenient little brass plaques on bedroom doors, so that everyone knew where everyone else slept. Frightfully naughty, but utterly discreet. No sex scandals making the headlines. I wish I'd lived then.'

'You might have been killed in the Boer War,' Kim reminded him.

'True. You're always so sensible,' he said, and dropped the towel and walked towards the bed, his erection bobbing. She wanted to feel him inside her.

'I thought you were the sensible one,' she teased, watching his erection's progress. It was long and thick, with his heavy balls swinging, one slightly lower than the other.

She glowed with satisfaction. The party was a job well done. Everyone had said how much they had enjoyed themselves. Now she needed to rest, though it was Sunday and she had no reason to get up till noon.

She had showered, too – just a quick one – and her skin felt soft under her hands. When she combed her fingers through her pubic bush they came away smelling of soap and the faintest whiff of her own personal essence. She was ready for Oliver.

'Yummy.' He drew in her smell approvingly, folding back the duvet and climbing in beside her. 'There's nothing quite like the scent of a woman in one's bed.'

'Any woman?' she asked, squirming against him, as he cushioned her head on his shoulder.

'Stop fishing. Not just any woman. You, darling.'

'But you've had other women. Why don't you ever talk about them?'

'I'm sure you don't want to hear details of my sordid past,' he replied with a chuckle, one hand cradling her breast, his thumb revolving around on the hardened nipple.

'I do. I do,' she answered eagerly, and fastened her palm round his cock, then moved it up and down, the foreskin sliding back over the swollen end. 'Tell me about your first time.'

'You want to know how I lost my cherry?' His voice was low, his touch on her teat sending fiery darts down to the hardening sliver of flesh crowning her slit. His cock jerked in her fist. 'Good God, can I remember? It was so long ago.'

'Of course you can. Everyone always remembers the first time. Go on. Please. I love it when you tell me stories.'

'All right, if you insist. Well, I was eighteen; late to lose my virginity, but I'd dabbled here and there.'

'Go on,' she whispered, and wriggled down his body, lipping over his chest, lingering on the discs of his nipples, then circling his navel and burying her nose in the crisp, brown hair that coated his underbelly.

His bare thighs were warm against her breasts, his cock a smooth bar brushing her cheek. She turned her head and ran her tongue up its length, as if she were licking an ice-cream. It tasted even better than ice-cream, especially when she reached the tip and worked her tongue's point into the single eye, extracting a drop of pre-come juice.

'Oh, darling, I think I've died and gone to heaven,' he murmured, his fingers clenched in her hair, holding her to him.

She lifted her lips away from his cock long enough to demand, 'The story.'

'How the hell am I supposed to concentrate when

you're doing that?' he growled. 'No, don't stop. I'll give it my best shot. I was staying with friends in New Orleans and had gone into the French Quarter on my own. It was a hot night and Royal Street was crowded. They were celebrating Mardi Gras, and there were carnival floats and jazz bands, bead necklaces and flowers thrown from the balconies, and the wonderful smell of Cajun cooking. They certainly know how to party down South.

'A group of whores stood outside a bar. Music blared from the open door. Two were white with blonde hair, skirts so short I could see their pussy lips, and big tits that strained against their T-shirts. Another was a Creole in jeans that fitted so tightly round the crotch that the seam disappeared between her slit. She was scrawny, and her little breasts were supported by a scarlet bra. Her nipples rose out of the cups.

'I was so hard it was difficult to walk. I was used to wanking – in fact, I couldn't leave it alone – and had touched up girls back home, but I was serious about my studies at Oxford, and didn't spend my time drinking and shagging like the other undergrads. But that night in New Orleans I was remembering the smell that had lingered on my fingers when I had tried it on with one of the barmaids, meeting her round the back of the pub and having a feel of her pussy. That smell seemed to be wafting from those women.'

'I can't believe you weren't always experienced,' Kim sighed, as Oliver dipped a finger between her legs, coated it with her juice and then lifted it to his nose.

'That's flattering, darling, but no, I was a shy boy, and she opened my eyes to pleasure.'

'Was it the Creole? I'm jealous. It should have been me,' Kim complained, reaching up to tweak his nipples.

'What typically female logic,' he teased, tugging gently at her pubic hair. 'Have I ever grumbled because you weren't a virgin bride?'

'I might as well have been. Neither Sam nor Jerry were much good in bed.'

'I don't think I want to be reminded of your former lovers,' he said edgily. 'Unlike you, I've no urge to hear the squalid facts.'

'It's exciting. And so is that,' she whispered, opening her legs to let his finger penetrate her slippery entrance.

'The girl was exotic, her hennaed hair falling in ringlets down her back, and her skin like olive velvet. I approached her nervously and her friends laughed. They called me names: "Pretty boy, baby doll". Their mockery made me harder still. I didn't know what to do. Whores were an unknown quantity and I was afraid of picking up a disease. But they looked at the aching bulge in my trousers, and the girl I wanted shrugged and moved closer to me.

'"You want to fuck?" she said, and grabbed my hand, holding it close to her breast.

'I couldn't speak. My heart was hammering against my ribs, my cock throbbing painfully, and any movement on my part threatened to topple me over the brink and make me come in my pants.

'I remember that she leant back a little, holding my eyes with her dark, predatory ones and saying, "What's the matter, little boy? You got a rocket there just waiting to be launched? You want to come in me?"

'"Yes, please," I stammered.

'"You got money? I don't turn no tricks for free," she said, and even her crudity was exciting.

'Close up I could see she was not much older than me, but she was wise in ways I would never be. My awe of her and my raging desire increased as her fingers moved across my face, tickling my ear, while the tip of her tongue licked across her full, red lips.

'My friends had warned me not to carry much cash, but I had about twenty dollars on me. Would it be enough to buy the favours of this sultry goddess? I had no idea of the going rate for a whore's services.'

'I wonder how it feels to be paid for sex,' Kim said, and pushed Oliver on to his back. Stretching her thighs wide and kneeling each side of him, she lowered her mouth to his sky-pointing cock.

She felt wanton, her breasts and clit tingling as she imagined herself to be the Creole girl. 'It must be great to have such power over men, to rouse them, tease them, get them so worked up they'd pay a fortune to be milked of their spunk.' Her crudity surprised her, but she was enjoying it.

'I can't tell you how she felt,' he said, almost purring with pleasure as she tongued the ridge of his foreskin. 'She didn't seem to find it degrading; she was enjoying her domination. All I know is that I had to have her. I was driven demented by the smell of her, the heat and my throbbing dick. If she had refused me, then I'd have had to stand there in front of them, expose myself and masturbate.'

Kim released her lips from him to say, 'But she didn't refuse you.'

'Oh, no. She took me into a dark alley and through a gate leading to a yard. It was cobbled and full of vines and flowers and the scent was overpowering. I could hear the clamour of the carnival close by, but couldn't think of anything but the pressure in my balls. We went up an iron staircase to a balcony, and through a door. The interior was dimly lit, one of those crumbling, once-splendid rooms typical of the Quarter.'

'And then? Tell me what happened next,' she begged, and cupped her hand round his bulky penis, working her fingers along its entire length. She went lower and felt his balls contract.

He reached between her legs, parted her swollen lips and rubbed back and forth over the rose-red bud. He started to speak again, and, despite the steadiness of his voice, Kim knew that her arousal added to his.

'She was a kind girl, and gentle with me. I just stood there, and she unbuckled my belt and tugged at the zipper tag. My cock sprang out like something possessed. I grabbed at her, wanting to plunge myself into her hot body.

'"Wait," she said, and I almost came as she rolled a condom up my prick.

'I tried to kiss her, and it was then that I learnt that whores don't kiss clients. She said a kiss was too personal, and that it was reserved for lovers or friends or children.

'She undressed for me, slowly, unfastening her bra and letting it fall away from her breasts. Her nipples were large and dark, set in wide, brown circles. Then she pulled her jeans down, and between her legs was a mass of black hair that almost hid her crack. I could smell her sweat and her pussy, warm and sensuous, in contrast to her cheap perfume.

'She kicked off her shoes, got out of her jeans and then lay back on the tumbled bed. Her eyes were heavy-lidded, her body stretched out with a natural grace. In all my turmoil, I remember wishing I was a painter, able to capture that moment on canvas.'

Kim closed her eyes, visualising the dusky room, the bed, the naked whore, and the young Oliver, wanting, needing, his rampant cock a thing quite apart from himself.

'Tell me how you felt when you put your cock in her,' she said, holding and caressing it.

'I couldn't slow down. Once she had me between her legs, and my dick at her hole, that was it. She guided me in, I think. It's a blur, and I'm afraid it didn't last long. A couple of thrusts and I was there, coming into the condom violently.'

'Like this,' she murmured, and breathed on his cock, sucking it into her mouth. It swelled, filled her, and butted against the back of her throat.

He gasped, and grabbed her closer, his hips pushed upwards to meet her. She held him firmly at the base with one hand, the other hand caressing his tight, full

19

balls, and swirled her tongue around his glans. His balls contracted, his shaft stiffened a little bit more, and he started to come, flooding her with his rich-tasting semen. It spurted from him once, twice, three times, and then he pulsed in her mouth before slipping his penis out and slumping down on the mattress, sighing deeply with relief.

'Darling,' he said, totally relaxed. 'Give me a moment, well, more like a half hour, and we'll do it again. You didn't come and that's churlish of me. I hate men who are bad-mannered in bed.'

'That's all right,' she said, knowing that Oliver wouldn't fall asleep beside her, snoring, as less considerate lovers tended to do. He would make sure she was satisfied. She could afford to carry on with the game a little longer.

'Did you pay her, Oliver?' she said, wiping his juice from her lips and chin.

'All I had. Twenty dollars.' He looked up, surprised.

'Will you pay me?'

'If you like. How much do you charge?' He was indulging her, entering into the fantasy.

She pretended to think it over, then said, 'How much have you got?'

Oliver reached for his wallet on the bedside table. 'Ten quid for a blow-job?' he offered.

'That's tight,' she fenced, feeling foolish.

'It's about right.'

'How do you know?'

'I don't. I'm guessing.'

She gave up then. It didn't seem natural to be bargaining with her own husband. 'Oh, Oliver,' she said. 'You know I love you, don't you?'

'Of course I do.'

'And do you love me?'

'Of course I do.' He ruffled her hair.

'Why d'you put up with me?'

'I've just told you why.'

'What are we going to do about him?' she asked, making patterns in his fine chest hair with her nail.

'Who?' Oliver sounded sleepy.

'Jack Loring.'

His arm tightened around her. 'Don't worry. I'll sort it.'

'Do you think he really is my brother?'

'Could very well be. You didn't know, darling, but your old man put it about a bit.'

This cut like a knife. Damn, she thought, it's going to hurt for ages.

Sensitive to her bruised feelings, Oliver soothed and petted her, playing with the wet warmth of her pussy, sucking her nipples, making her forget everything in the urgent need to reach her own climax. She came, crying out in a single, sharp gasp, her body racked with acute pleasure.

Afterwards she lay cuddled in his arms, her fingers in his hair, safe in that warm intimacy which she though was the best part of marriage. But even as she caressed him, sleepily and fondly, she was thinking about Jack, speculating on this man who had so unexpectedly walked into her life.

Chapter Two

*T*hree in the morning. Lights burned over the empty London streets, reflected in puddles. It was cold and quiet. Jack reached Bloomsbury and turned his car into the car park of the Byron Hotel.

Elsewhere clubs would be buzzing and he was raring to go, but no: Oliver had invited him to tea at Glen House. 'Proper English Sunday tea at four p.m. precisely. Earl Grey and muffins, cucumber sandwiches and scones,' he had said in an irritatingly patronising way.

You asked for it, old boy! Jack thought sardonically, and ran up the steps to the Byron's entrance.

A manager was on duty. 'Can I get you anything, sir?' he asked from behind the reception desk.

'Send a pot of coffee to my room, scalding hot and black,' Jack said, picking up his key from the mahogany counter.

'Yes, sir,' the manager replied, then called across to the white-coated young man lingering in the foyer. 'Coffee for Room 30. See to it, Andy.'

'Yes, Mr Baird,' Andy said, glancing at Jack.

He's about nineteen, Jack thought. I noticed him when I checked in. Short and dark, nice body, neat tush, possibly Greek extraction. He's got bedroom eyes and that unmistakable sexual aura that makes women cream their knickers, and gets men of a certain persuasion going, too. He knows what his cock's for without a doubt.

Jack nodded, then made for the elevator. The Byron reminded him of his mother's hotel, which dated from the last half of the eighteenth century. There were many similarities: spacious rooms with lofty ceilings; red velvet drapes; crystal chandeliers; gilt-framed mirrors. It reeked of gracious living.

Room 30 was on the second floor, identical to the others linked by a corridor. It was functional and pleasantly furnished. Reproduction stuff, he had noticed earlier. Fakes, but quality fakes. Viv would have approved. But Jack was sick of hotels; he couldn't wait to get his own place. Oliver had promised to advise him over tea.

As he washed off the eye-liner, he speculated about Kim, surprised by the forceful feelings she had evoked in him. It had started out as a totally selfish venture, but might well develop into something else, still self-orientated, but perhaps taking another turn.

He scowled at his reflection and thought of Flyte. Warning bells had rung when they were introduced. Not that she wasn't desirable, but he had sensed opposition. It was obvious that she adored Oliver, and was fiercely protective. Definitely one to be watched.

Kim would be a challenge. She was wary of him, but fascinated. Was she really the happy housewife she appeared to be? His hunter's instinct told him she had hidden depths. He intended to dive down and explore them.

He peeled off his waistcoat, then his boots, and wriggled out of his red trousers. Naked, he stalked back into the bedroom. His cock was semi-hard, stimulated by the silk lining of his trouser leather and his contemplation of Flyte and Kim. He caught a glimpse of it in the dressing-table mirror. It rose higher as he looked, almost brushing his navel. A thick brown stem, with an angry, purple helm. He took it in one hand, an ache gathering in his groin as he worked the loose foreskin back and forth. This slippery rubbing doused everything except the urgent need to reach his pleasure and discharge his come.

Plenty of time, he mused, dipping a finger into the clear pre-come. He spread it over the head and his wrists and ankles tingled with the remembrance of manacles, while his mind recalled the delirious feeling of helplessness. Flyte would be into bondage, he was sure. He could imagine her striding around in black thigh boots with six-inch heels, wielding a whip. Did Kim know anything about these adult games? He doubted it. What about Oliver? Had he been dominated by Flyte, or did he like to be the master? His cock stretched a further inch and excitement crawled over his skin. He couldn't wait to find out.

He shrugged his shoulders into a short, towelling robe and lit a cigarette. Sitting on the side of the bed with his legs wide apart and bare feet flat on the carpet, he continued to keep his cock aroused, using long, smooth strokes and concentrating on the tender spot under the head. He worked himself up slowly, holding off when the cock stiffened to its limit and he could feel the beginning of that tumultuous rush towards release. Then he pressed down hard round the base, avoiding the sensitive crest, letting the feeling die back down.

When he was sure of his control, he gradually eased his grip and ventured upwards again. He stroked his thumb over the top and pulled the foreskin back with his fingers. Kim fuelled his fire, and he thought of her watching, and of her small hand masturbating him. She would be curious, but guilty because of Oliver, though mostly concerned about their close kinship. The idea of corrupting her was so exciting that Jack gasped and almost came. A tap on the door brought him back to earth.

'OK. It's not locked,' he shouted.

Andy walked in, carrying a tray. The smell of freshly ground coffee seduced Jack's sense of smell. He folded his bathrobe over his erection; no need to be too blatant about it. Besides, he may have misread Andy's signals.

'Shall I pour for you, sir?' Andy asked, and the way he looked up under his eyelashes convinced Jack that he hadn't been mistaken.

'Please,' Jack said, and lounged on the bed, adding, 'I thought you'd be cruising the clubs tonight.'

Andy shook his head. 'I would have been, if I hadn't been on duty. They'll be going for it at Thrashers or Billy Budd's.'

'Is that where the action is?'

'Depends what you're into,' Andy replied, adding with a grin, 'I like your fancy-dress costume, sir. Leather's a right turn on.'

'Yes,' Jack agreed, thinking: he's clued up, no shrinking violet. 'Perhaps we could have our own party here,' he suggested. 'There's some booze in the fridge. How about a slosh of whisky in the coffee?'

'You'll get me into trouble, sir,' Andy said archly, but he moved to the built-in fridge and brought over a couple of miniatures and a polystyrene cup. 'Mr Baird's a right old Scrooge. Hates anyone enjoying themselves. He'll have my bollocks for earrings if he knows I've been hanging about up here. We're not supposed to fraternise with the customers.'

'He won't know,' Jack assured him. 'Come on. Drink up.'

Andy half-filled the cups and topped them up with whisky, then handed Jack the china one, standing closer. 'So, there must be some perks to the job. How much do you earn?' Jack asked softly.

'A hundred and fifty a week before tax. All found, of course, and I'm getting trained. I want to manage a place like this one day.'

'I may be able to help you. How would you like to work in Bristol?'

'I don't know,' Andy said cautiously. 'I've never been away from London.'

'There's a lot going on there and I could get you a job in the family hotel.'

'You own one?' Andy sounded impressed.

'My mother does.'

Jack stood up and took a bundle of notes from a drawer, peeling off three twenties. He tucked them into Andy's breast pocket, feeling the young man's heart pounding against his fingers.

'That's a generous tip, sir,' Andy murmured, still as a statue.

'I can afford it,' Jack answered, thinking: I'll make damn sure I get my money's worth.

'Thank you,' Andy said, waiting Jack's lead, then blurted out, 'I'm not one of those bloody rent-boys.'

'I shouldn't have been interested if you were. Do I look as if I need to pay for sex?'

'No, sir. You're too handsome.'

'Yes. I could have anyone I like, man or woman.' Jack was pleased by the compliment, though doubting its sincerity.

'I'm sure you could. Then why me?'

Lust and opportunity, Jack wanted to say, but instead subjected Andy to the full blaze of his smile. 'I took to you right off,' he replied.

Then Andy reached out and, opening Jack's robe, closed a hand round the cock jutting aggressively from its nest of coarse hair. He used a hard, deliberate motion of the wrist, and Jack grunted at the feel of that knowing, male touch.

Andy was standing in front of him, between his thighs, and Jack opened up his jacket and shirt and placed a hand on his warm chest. Andy's heart thumped, and Jack felt him quiver. He found Andy's nipples, circled and tweaked the hard tips, then let his hand drop down, his fingers lightly tracing over the

26

zipper of the black trousers, squeezing the stiff cock through the fabric and cupping the ripe balls.

His excitement surged up abruptly, and he freed himself from Andy's clasp. He wanted more than a hand job; he could provide that himself. Andy dropped to his knees, spread Jack's thighs with his hands and lowered his face to his crotch. Jack closed his eyes and imagined himself buried in Kim's pussy as Andy took him in his mouth. His tongue worked sweetly under the ridge and down the veined stem, but then Jack said huskily, 'Drop your trousers.'

Andy obeyed and unfastened his belt, after removing his black shoes and socks. The pouch of his white briefs nursed his burgeoning erection. He ripped off his jacket and held his shirt up out of the way as Jack eased down the boxer shorts and appreciated the circumcised cock framed by dark curls. It was as ready as his own, flushed from base to tip, the exposed helmet a deep, plum red.

Jack looked up into Andy's face and read acceptance in his smile, and eagerness, too. He wasn't doing it entirely for the money. Jack returned the smile, feeding his passion with images of woman flesh, and memories of other adventures with men. He was lucky to swing both ways, and had never denied himself pleasure. He stood up, his robe falling away from the angles and planes of his superbly fit body.

Andy stared at him admiringly, while Jack fondled the younger man's prick and rubbed his own against him. Then Jack commanded, 'Bend over,' and, putting a hand on Andy's shoulder, turned him and pressed down hard, forcing him to his knees.

'I won't do it without a johnny,' Andy said sharply. His rump was already presented, his palms braced on the floor.

'Neither will I,' Jack said, and produced the little coil of rolled-up latex. He put it on, then lubricated the thin rubber. It glistened in the lamplight, stretched taut over Jack's needy flesh.

He greased his fingers and positioned himself between Andy's thin legs, massaging the oil into the amber crack dividing his buttocks, and finding his puckered anal opening. It felt warm and smooth and silky, and the sensation in Jack's fingers was fired to his groin. He dipped lower, sliding across Andy's scrotum, and found the rigid penis. As Jack's hand encompassed it, Andy moaned.

Jack could smell their mutual odours: heat and sweat and male arousal. There was something crude and basic about men gratifying their lusts together. Jack could think no further than pushing his penis into the nearest available hole. He thrust an oiled finger past Andy's tight ring. Andy lifted his arse higher, widening his thighs and sinking down submissively. His muscles relaxed, taking the whole of Jack's finger. Jack ventured another, then a third, before feeling the muscles close round them.

His cock pulsed, and he held it up to Andy's arse, and worked the glans round the slackening ring. He felt Andy shudder and heard his strangled cry as he suddenly removed his fingers and thrust hard with his cock, forcing it into that confining place. The orifice was tight, and for a second he feared the condom might split. Then Andy sighed and, as the pain of penetration was superseded by pleasure, the passage softened and relaxed.

Jack pushed in further, fire licking through his loins, his balls hard and tense. He held Andy close, kneeling behind him, his hands gripping his hips, while Andy rubbed his own penis, matching the strokes to Jack as he moved in and out. Jack's head snapped back and his eyes slitted. He withdrew, then thrust in, pulled out and plunged back, testicles tapping against Andy's perineum. He breathed gustily as he felt his orgasm coming, the aching need in his balls turning to boiling, bubbling pleasure, as his seed pumped out with the force of a geyser.

Andy yelped, and his body bowed as come jetted

from him, spattering his fingers and dripping on to the carpet.

Jack slowed down, then withdrew, before pulling off the condom and wiping his cock on his discarded robe. He wanted the lad out of his sight as quickly as possible now his lust had been appeased. He poured himself a cup of lukewarm coffee and went to take a shower.

When he came out later, Andy had gone. Jack settled himself in bed, picked up the phone and rang his mother.

'What the hell time do you call this?' Her voice hammered against his eardrum.

He held the instrument away, saying, 'Give over, Viv. You never sleep. I'll bet you're not on your own. Who is it this time? The newest waiter? The page-boy?'

'Bloody cheek!' she responded smartly. 'Do you think I'd be telling you? You'd only come along and screw him. Anyway, what's been happening? Did you see Kim?'

'Yes.'

'And? Come on. What's the gossip?'

'She's better than her photo.'

'That was only a press one taken at the wedding. Oliver Buckley looked dishy. Is he?'

'He's an arrogant, pompous twat.' Putting it into words made Jack sharply conscious of how much he disliked Kim's husband.

'But you won't let him know that, will you?' There was a hint of anxiety in Vivien's voice.

'Not yet. I'll reserve that pleasure until a later date,' Jack promised grimly.

'You do that. Don't blow it.' His mother's tone brooked no argument.

'OK, OK. I know.'

'How did Kim react when you told her?'

'She was shocked. Didn't have a clue that her father was a womaniser.'

'He wasn't,' Vivien declared indignantly. 'I won't have

you saying nasty things about him, and the poor man unable to defend himself.'

'All right, Viv.'

'What's the next stage?'

'I'm going to tea with them tomorrow. Today, actually, at four. Kim's definitely interested, and I don't think Oliver's fulfilling her, somehow or other. I'll try one or two little things. Leave it to me.'

'Oh, I will, darling. You won't let me down.'

'Would I dare? By the way, there's a waiter here who could be persuaded to work at the Rockburn.'

'What's the catch? Have you a vested interest in him?'

'I might have. Actually, I was thinking of you, dearest mama.'

'Cut the crap, Jack.'

'Bye, Viv. I'll keep you posted. You can go back to fucking your toy-boy now.'

'Say that to my face, next time we meet,' she challenged.

'I wouldn't dare,' he said, grinning into the phone.

Contrary to her son's belief, Vivien Loring was in bed alone. She often preferred it that way.

Here she could relax, read, work on her accounts or pamper herself as the fancy took her. She had been snoozing when Jack phoned, the room lit by apricot-shaded lamps and the flicker of the television screen. The sound was turned down and a weatherman was pointing to a map of England. He was attractive, she noted almost automatically. Well-dressed, too. She had always fancied men in pinstripe suits. They smacked of wealth, control and power, all qualities she admired.

She sat in the middle of her four-poster bed like the captain of some proud ship. It was purple-draped, ostentatious, even vulgar, but she loved it. Here, she worked out menus, consulted her bank statements, and plotted her deepest mischiefs.

Jack had sounded cheerful. She could read him like an

open book, even when they were miles apart. It was her guess that he had been up to something, or more likely into someone. This waiter he'd mentioned. Had he been screwing him? It was more than just possible. But she didn't care who he fucked, as long as he kept an eye on the main objective.

From where she sat, Vivien could see herself in the pier-glass on a mahogany stand. She collected antiques, and was a regular visitor to auction sales. She fluffed up the sides of her hair, warm brown with gold streaks that hid a sprinkling of grey and, stretching her neck, patted firmly under her chin. In such gentle light she looked much younger than fifty. The aubergine silk of her nightdress and negligée was flattering. Like Jack, she had blue eyes and her skin turned gold at the smallest exposure to the sun.

Of course, their plans had brought all the memories back; her meeting with James Millard and Jack's birth. For years she had been able to keep her anger down, accepting James's terms: support for her child in return for her silence. They hadn't met again after she'd agreed to the terms, but money had come in regularly, and she'd been able to have whatever she needed for Jack simply by contacting James's solicitor.

She could have made big trouble for him, had she been so inclined. But what good would it have done? He would never have divorced his wife; he was too concerned about his reputation. Now he was dead, and Vivien was free to do whatever she felt necessary to redress the balance.

She leant over to the bedside table and took out a photograph in a silver frame. A snapshot taken in her twenties, wearing a flowing Laura Ashley dress, a wide-brimmed straw hat perched on her long Afro curly-perm. A Flower Child. James was with her, more conventional, of course, but the fashion had been for flared trousers and waisted jackets with wide lapels. How outdated and comical they looked now, and how

31

full of dreams in those days. He was a young, ambitious politician, sure that he could change the world, and she'd just inherited the Rockburn from an elderly hotelier who had been her lover and, in gratitude, had left it to her in his will.

God, you were a handsome beast, James, she whispered, running the tips of her mauve-lacquered nails over his face. But what an unfeeling bastard!

Desire warmed her loins, that well-remembered ache which only James could satisfy. No virgin when she met him, Vivien had started out as a call-girl and then gone into partnership with a brothel madam. The brothel was where she met James, but their relationship had developed further than a purely sexual business arrangement.

'I loved you, James, you sod,' she whispered, and held the photo to her breasts, pushing aside the satin, baring her nipples and grazing them with the frame. They peaked, the areolae crimping. She feathered her fingers over them, reliving the feel of James's mouth and that of her suckling babe. There'd been many other lips since, young men, older men, but nothing and no one had given her the thrill she had experienced with James.

'You're a sentimental bitch,' she chided herself wryly. 'You enjoyed being in love. Or was it really that? You've always wanted what you can't have, and you couldn't have James.'

She'd never felt such emotional pain and passion as he had aroused in her. The worse he treated her, the more she desired him. It still had the power to wound. In the early days, when she had first realised the extent of his callousness, she'd felt as if she were dying inside.

'And now it's you who are dead,' she went on, addressing his ghost that surely must, she thought, be wandering in limbo. 'But I'm alive, and so is our son and your daughter. There's nothing you can do to stop me.'

I'm sinful, she thought, thrilling with triumph as she rose from the bed and moved closer to the mirror. She stood the photo on the dressing table, turned towards her so that James could watch. She unfastened her robe and let it drop to the thick pile carpet.

She admired her figure, lifting her breasts in both hands and rubbing her thumbs over the nipples protruding through the slippery satin. Spaghetti straps were the only thing between her and complete nudity. She untied them. The nightdress slithered, caressing her body all the way down, to concertina into a silken puddle round her feet. She stepped out of it.

No one to see but herself and James. No one to criticise hips that were too broad for today's fashions, a rounded belly and the solid thighs of a mature woman. Once she had been waif-like. Now the years had added bulk, but she could still pull the men. Her voluptuousness promised heaven.

She stood with her legs slightly parted, and her eyes were drawn to her triangle. Her bush, darker than the curls on her head, betrayed her true colour. She walked her hands down over her navel and mons, parting her slit to reveal the pink lips. Her clit appeared between them, red and swollen. Exerting willpower, Vivien refrained from touching it.

Instead, slowly, and with great deliberation, she opened a drawer and took out a carved, sandalwood box. It was oblong, tooled with gold, and about the size of a vanity case. Holding it almost reverently, she carried it to the bed. An anticipatory thrill coursed down her spine, making her womb ache and her nipples tingle.

My Big Boys, my Beauties, she thought. An avid collector, she included them in this hobby. They were far more fulfilling than Spode, bronze figurines, fans or perfume bottles. Setting the casket down, she turned the little key in the elaborate brass lock and lifted the lid.

It was lined with bottle-green velvet. Resting in moulded hollows lay a collection of dildos. Vivien smiled at them fondly, her fingers hovering as she decided which should be her lover tonight.

She picked up a black one, twelve inches long and made of synthetic material. She rubbed it against her cheek, thinking of the West Indian chef who had run her kitchen until he was spotted by a TV scout and given his own cookery programme. His cock had been thick and long. She had secretly called him 'Donkey Dick', finding such an enormous organ a disadvantage during straight intercourse; nice to play with and suck, but painful when rammed into her pussy, and she never had been able to take it up the arse.

This rubber replica had proved to be a more gentle playmate, the smooth ball of the head bringing her off in a matter of seconds. Maybe it would be this one. It was certainly among her favourites. Then she picked out an ivory lingam, a two-hundred-year-old artefact from a rajah's court, possibly used to break in virgins for his pleasure. She remembered how its cool surface warmed when it came into contact with her hot fanny.

She was spoilt for choice, and familiar with every one. Finally she settled for a small, slim plastic wand. It started to buzz as soon as she switched it on. Standing by the bed, she teased the head over her bush and her clit jumped as the vibrations tingled through every pubic hair. Her hips rose involuntarily, chasing the sensation, and she allowed the curved, white tip to flutter over her like a breath of ecstasy.

She sat down, opened her legs, held her lips apart with her left hand and guided the wand to her epicentre. Climax was a few seconds away. Pleasure shot through her, so intense that she cried out.

'Yes, oh, yes. That's lovely. So lovely. I want – I must have it.'

Giving herself a moment's respite, she stroked the dildo down her cleft. It roamed over the moistness, embraced by her swollen lips. Then, driven by over-powering lust, she held it to her throbbing clitoris again. It seemed to rule her, like a demanding little tyrant, and she was eager to please it.

No holding back now; just pure, unalloyed bliss. This was better than any man's cock. It was almost too much. Continuous vibrations sped from the machine. What would have taken a finger incessant rubbing to achieve now happened like lightning. She came against the humming head with a force that made her sob as she reached euphoria.

With tingling toes and trembling legs, she stabbed at her vagina, spasming as the sensation shocked through her. She withdrew the wand, now slippery with creamy juice, and rammed it against her clit again, intent on a second orgasm. Painfully sensitive, her little organ recoiled, then tingled and fattened. Waves washed over her, and through her thighs, her lower back, and her belly, until she exploded into another shattering climax.

Still she wasn't fully satisfied. This was so good that she settled down to see how many more orgasms she could muster, only laying her busy friend aside when she became conscious of grey dawn smudging the windows, and sounds from the hotel below telling her that the night shift was going off duty and the day staff taking over.

'A pity it's not summer,' observed Jenny Colby, busy at the pine table occupying the centre of the large, stone-flagged kitchen. The table had been scrubbed so often down the ages that the surface was white.

'And why is that?' Liam asked, looking across at her. His eyes were blue-green, and Jenny thought their shape and dark lashes typical of an Irishman.

'Tea parties are better outside. Remember the ones we had in July?'

'It was bloody hot.'

'Yes, and there was a marquee, and some of the ladies wearing Edwardian frocks and using parasols. It was elegant. I liked it.'

'Strawberries and cream and all that malarkey,' he

observed and, coming up behind her, slipped a hand under her buttocks.

Jenny blushed. 'Get off. I'm working. And so should you be,' she scolded.

'I am,' he assured her, running his tongue round the velvety edge of her ear, tantalisingly exposed because her chestnut hair was confined by a bandanna.

'Oh, yeah? Barry's done the baking, I've cut the sandwiches and you've done sweet FA.'

'Ooh, that's right, tell me off. I love it when you're angry. I can't resist bossy women,' he said, pretending to cringe, then seizing and kissing her full on the lips.

He was black-haired and beguiling. At first, as the housekeeper in charge of the Buckley's property, Jenny had been cool, feeling her responsibility keenly. But Liam had succeeded in smashing her defences, not brutally, but with unbelievable subtlety. He was helpful, always good-humoured, dealing with difficulties with the minimum of fuss, and not altering in his attitude once they had slept together.

His position was ambivalent; he was a sort of butler crossed with secretary and sometime chauffeur. There were other members of staff: a gardener; a handyman; and a woman who came in daily. Apart from these, Liam and Jenny ran Glen House between them, with Kim giving a hand sometimes, and Jenny giving Liam head. She was willing to have him a dozen times a day. It was useless trying to fight it: just thinking of his strong, compact body made her wet. How could she concentrate on anything when he was around, let alone prettifying plates of sandwiches?

'Go away, you bugger,' she gasped, freeing her mouth from his.

'Can't,' he declared, insinuating his denim-clad thigh between her legs. Her sensible, calf-length skirt was little protection against that hardness pressing against her aching pubis. 'I can't leave you like this. How can I serve tea with my cock as stiff as a broom-handle?'

She thought she might die of need as he rubbed his leg up and down, but she wasn't going to give in that easily. 'There's no time,' she reminded him. 'Someone might come in at any minute. Barry's only slipped out to fetch more cream.'

'He's broad-minded. If he catches us at it, he'll want to watch,' Liam said, trying to dismiss her fears about the chef.

'I don't want him to watch,' she protested, but his words made her wetter still. The smell of him, the feel of him, the whole, desirable sexiness of the man brought heat to her genitals. It was no use trying to be reasonable.

She was very conscious of her professional position. The kitchen was her special domain, where light from the cobbled yard outside gleamed on ancient copper pans and Le Creuset equipment, on the Willow Pattern dinner service lining the shelves and the alcove where a red, enamelled Aga had replaced the black range. Yet Liam had the power to make her risk everything; her job, her future prospects, all meant nothing when her body yearned towards him, feverish with the desire to have his wonderful dick stroking inside her.

On the table lay duty: the peeled cucumbers; the grated cheese; the egg mayonnaise; the paper-thin curls of ham and finely sliced bread. But her wanton self was whispering, 'Go on. Have him. Let him lift you on to his prick. You know you want to. Why else did you wear black stockings and a garter belt and no panties?'

She wanted to grab him by his pony-tail and drag his face down to her crotch.

He released her momentarily, and, his hands under her skirt, he pushed it up, warm palms exploring the silk-covered thighs and finding the patch of trimmed russet hair. 'No knickers,' he whispered. 'And such a wet little snatch. Stop pretending to be Miss Prim. Just look at what you've done.'

He unzipped his fly and she watched his cock emerge.

It was upright, the veins pulsing on the underside, the knob glossy. 'How on earth do I get all that inside me?' she exclaimed, always amazed by this mystery.

'No problem,' he chuckled, wagging it at her.

His fingers parted her lower lips, sliding into the cleft, and then anointed her with her own juice. Jenny opened her legs wider, her lower back braced against the table's edge, as he frigged her, lightly at first, flicking over the bud. Her knees were trembling, a fine film of sweat breaking out on her skin.

'What is it you want me to do, darling?' he whispered, kissing her mouth gently.

'You know how I want it,' she gasped urgently.

'Like this?' he asked, and stroked the length of her clit, then commenced a luscious motion over the head.

'Oh, God, I can't stand it. Do it, Liam, do it, do it,' she wailed, as he brought her to the top of her pleasure.

She came in a series of small explosions, her body shaking, then relaxed against him. He lifted her with his strong hands under her buttocks. She guided his cock into position and with an easy push it sank into her. She tightened her thighs around his waist and levered herself up, savouring the silky-wet joining of their bodies, then lowering down with sensual slowness on to his erection.

His searching fingertip found her anus, and she wriggled, grabbing him round the neck and planting wet kisses all over his face. He growled with pleasure, his cock swelling inside her as he inserted his finger into her tight little hole.

The feeling was incredible; strange but familiar, too. And she wished he had three cocks to plunge into her; one for her mouth, one for her pussy, and another to penetrate her forbidden place. It was a shame they had to hurry. Excitement was pounding through her, and she wanted to come again, her nipples hard against the lace of her bra. She would have liked to pace herself for the second time, letting the feeling build slowly and inexorably, rising like flood-water smashing against a dam, until it gushed over and drowned her in a welter of pleasure.

He didn't want to wait. He sped up his strokes, lifting her up and pulling her down again with a thrilling urgency. She thrust with him, gasping into his wide, open mouth as he fountained his ecstasy into her, his hips jerking convulsively.

Jack has decided to give it a miss, Kim thought, unsure whether to be pleased or sorry, experiencing disappointment and a forlorn kind of emptiness.

The conservatory was light and warm, an ideal place for tea in late autumn. Plants leant towards the curved windows and creepers swarmed up to meet the glass cupola. There were rubber plants with huge, shiny leaves, exotic orchids from a tropical rain forest, and fecund creations with unpronounceable names and a plethora of fleshy, white blossoms from which protruded phallus-shaped crimson stamen.

Feathery palms stood in ornamental pots, and cacti with lethal spikes were a hazard to the unwary. The air was perfumed with a rich mixture of odours, mostly pleasant ones, some sickly. The sound of a Brahms string quartet added to the tranquillity.

'It's my Garden of Eden,' Oliver commented, lounging in a padded wicker chair near the table. 'I'm still waiting for the serpent.'

'Lovely,' twittered Polly Ashe, one of their neighbours. She had arrived with her husband and three curly-headed moppets who looked cherubic but behaved atrociously. 'They must be free to express themselves,' she had once said when Oliver dared complain about their vandalism. 'I don't want to give them a complex.' Her husband, Keith, had very little say in the matter.

'He's just the sperm donor,' Oliver had commented privately to Kim. 'She's like a female spider, deadlier than the male.'

'She seems harmless enough, and means well,' Kim had replied in mitigation.

'You wear rose-coloured specs, my love,' he had answered, 'and see good in everyone.'

This wasn't true, but she hesitated to shatter his illusion by mentioning her gut-wrenching resentment of Flyte.

Polly admired Oliver greatly, perhaps because of his work. There was a great deal of money in business analysis. Certainly she cultivated the Buckleys, and Kim was sure it also had something to do with James Millard having been a leading light in the Liberal Party. Polly was left wing, naturally, but what Oliver referred to as a 'champagne commi'.

Oliver liked having the neighbours in, and there were several other couples and an elderly brigadier present. When he bought the house he had worried that he and Kim would be out of place. The area had a snobbish reputation. But it seemed that those who owned properties up and down the river were bankers and brokers who wanted to be artists or writers or work with stained glass, while their wives dabbled in aromatherapy or candle-making or pottery. They fitted in very well: Kim with her interest in interior decorating, and he with his intellectual pursuits.

Now Kim looked at their neighbours restlessly. It had been one of those nothing days, when they had got up late, had lunch, said goodbye to Flyte, and then watched a classic version of *Jane Eyre* on Channel Four, the wobbly scenery redeemed by the acting of a young Orson Welles.

No one had bothered to dress up for tea. It wasn't expected, and she wore jeans and a loose sweater, her dark hair teased into that unkempt look that Oliver liked so much. Oliver smiled over at her and kissed the tips of his fingers to show that he loved her, while engaging the brigadier in conversation about the state of the economy in Hong Kong.

'We would have loved to come to your party last night. Had a babysitter lined up, but Harry had earache and didn't want me to leave him,' Polly breathed, pushing back a strand of mousy hair. She was so thin that it seemed to Kim that her brood were consuming her like baby piranhas.

The recalcitrant three-year-old Harry – a sturdy boy who looked as if he'd never had a day's illness in his short, indulged life – stared at Kim solemnly from the safety of his mother's lap.

'Is he better now?' Kim asked, trying not to flinch as Gemma, aged five, deliberately placed a sticky hand on her knee.

'Oh, yes. Say, "I'm all right now, thank you, Kim,"' Polly prompted brightly. She believed in children addressing the adults by their Christian names. Harry ignored her, stared into the middle distance and stuck his thumb in his mouth.

'Jeans and jam,' Kim said through gritted teeth, reaching for a paper napkin. 'I suppose it makes a change from scones and jam. Why not try a dollop of cream, too?'

'Careful, Gemma, dear,' Polly chided, so tentatively that it sounded like approval. 'Say sorry to Kim.'

'I want a cake,' Gemma demanded, and snatched a chocolate eclair from the plate, then changed her mind, put it back and took one smothered in pink icing.

'Do you plan to have children?' Polly the earth-mother asked, gazing at her daughter adoringly.

Oliver raised a quizzical eyebrow at Kim who was scrubbing at the jammy patch, and replied, 'Later. I don't think you feel you're ready yet, do you, darling?'

'No,' she answered firmly, and that itch of rebellion and unease increased. She had the urge to jump up and behave as badly as Polly's children. Maybe she would join the eldest, Anna, who was wilfully tampering with the hothouse plants, or take off all her clothes, leap on Oliver and ravish him, then run riot, ending up in the

41

swimming pool. She guessed he'd find this mildly amusing. What would it take to shock him?

Liam came in. Jack was with him.

'Sorry I'm late,' Jack said.

'The food's nearly all gone,' Oliver observed quietly, and Kim compared the two men; her husband with his untidy hair, sloppy sweatshirt, jogging pants and bare feet, and Jack, equally casual but with a designer label difference; black leather jacket, black shirt, beige combats and suede Dr Martens.

He was introduced as her brother, recently returned from the States and he had an immediate effect. The children turned from monsters to almost human. Polly shed years and positively simpered. The other women came to life and the men were suddenly galvanised. The conversation sparkled.

He is Satan, Kim concluded. He casts a spell over everyone he meets. The conservatory was too hot. She was too hot.

'I'm going for a walk,' she announced, and headed for the door.

'I'll come, too,' Jack said, freeing himself from the clambering Harry.

'Show Jack the boat-house,' Oliver suggested, pouring himself another cup of tea. 'I'm too lazy to move.'

Something in his voice caught Kim's attention, but only momentarily. She couldn't quite put her finger on what it was.

It was a crisp afternoon, despite the sunshine, colder today, and a frost was forecast. 'You should have brought a coat,' Jack said. 'Here. Have mine.'

She was enveloped in supple calf-skin, remembering a French perfume her mother had once worn. It was warm, seductive, musky, and the jacket smelled of him, too.

They crossed the garden in silence, the River Thames gleaming in the distance. The wide lawn sloped to the riverbank. There was a landing stage and, nearby, a boat-house.

'Here we are,' she said unnecessarily. Any idiot could see what it was.

It was damp inside, and quiet, except for the occasional drip of water. The boats had been tucked up for the winter; a punt, a rowing boat and that broad-beamed craft with an awning which Oliver insisted in taking out on hot days, fishing – or so he said – but really as an excuse for elegant lounging.

They sat on one of the side benches. She was acutely aware of Jack, her stomach churning and her fingers hungry to touch him. He opened the jacket and she started, bracing herself to rebuff him, but he merely slipped an envelope from a pocket, saying, 'I've brought these to show you. You want proof? Here it is.'

A colour photograph. Her father, younger but instantly recognisable, and a woman. She wore suede hot-pants and tightly laced boots with stack heels and platform soles, and a skimpy Indian crushed-velvet top. She had long, blonde hair and a lot of make-up; spiky lashes and pencilled brows. She was staring at Kim's father with an adoring, besotted expression.

'My mother,' Jack said simply.

'And my father.'

'Our father. And I won't add, "which art in heaven", for I very much doubt that he's there. Oh, here's a letter from his solicitor. It mentions something about my school fees.'

'So it's true.' Kim was numb; no pain, no hurt, nothing.

'Aren't you glad?'

'I don't know what I feel.'

'This isn't really you, is it?' he asked, his eyes shining in the dimness.

'What isn't?'

'This house, the grounds, those people, everything.'

'You've got a nerve,' she shouted, suddenly angry. It

43

was easier to whip up anger than fend off that driving compulsion to be touched by him, to have him explore her and penetrate her, physically and mentally. 'Are you saying that Oliver isn't right for me either?'

'Maybe,' Jack murmured. 'He's older, and knows a hell of a lot. Do you really share his interests? What are they? Books, art and music?'

'And the Stock Exchange and world markets.'

'That, too. He's a smart cookie. Don't you ever feel like saying to hell with it, packing a bag and getting out? Never mind where, just travelling?'

'I did some of that before I met him,' she said, hugging her arms round herself. She felt as if all the heat in her body had been drawn into her sex, leaving everything else freezing.

He chuckled. 'Oh, yes, and what was that? Neatly arranged package tours to foreign holiday resorts? Safe and sanitised. No chance that you'd come in contact with the natives.'

'You don't know anything about me. Why don't you leave me alone?'

It was horrible to feel this upsurge of panic. She was shivering, but when he put his hand on her waist and worked it up under her sweater to her breasts, she stopped. She was filled with a sense of completion. Bone of my bone, flesh of my flesh. The words dropped, unbidden, into her mind.

'I could show you a good time. You'd love the places I'd take you to.'

'Well, maybe it can be arranged. When we go abroad next, you could come with us. I think Oliver's planning to visit Florida.'

'That isn't what I meant. Just you and me, Kim. No one else.'

His hand warmed her lace-covered breasts. She wanted to lean against him and have him continue that soft, insinuating caress. What's the matter with me? she

44

thought, panicking. I wouldn't still be sitting here if it was anyone else who had tried it on.

'Look,' she said, pushing his hand away and sliding further along the bench, putting a decent space between them. 'This is silly. It can't happen. We can't. I'm married. Besides, you're my brother.'

'Only half. And just imagine, this is going to happen to a lot of other people in the future. All these frozen sperm and ova waiting to be implanted. We won't be the first. People are bound to meet and sleep with one another, without knowing their origins.'

'That doesn't mean we've got to. Anyway, it's different with us: we know.'

'You can't turn off feelings, just like that.'

'We have to. We shouldn't meet again, not alone.'

Then, as if she was already saying goodbye, Kim leant across and ran her hand over his hair, tawny as a lion's mane, short and spiky, but soft.

He grasped her hands and pulled them, using them to drag her against his chest. Then he kissed her, in a long, slow exploration with his tongue which she couldn't resist returning.

She hadn't been kissed by anyone else but Oliver for years. This was exciting and new, spiced with that deep sense of sin. Jack's lips were firm, and his jaw was silky and close shaven. Oliver sometimes didn't bother to shave at weekends, excusing his laziness by saying that he thought she thought designer stubble was sexy. Maybe it was, but it felt uncomfortable when his bristles rasped against her.

She moaned into Jack's mouth, and he went on kissing her. She felt his fingers between her legs, rubbing over the tightness of the jeans, and the seam dug into her crotch. She moaned again, but as a token protest this time, as he knew, for he didn't stop that agonisingly sexy motion. Delicious sensations swamped her, but she struggled and fought, twisting her body and crying out.

'Hush,' he said. 'Be still. It's all right. Here. Feel what

you do to me,' and he took one of her flailing hands and placed it on the hard swell of his cock. He held it there and moved it up and down.

'It's not all right. Oh, God. Stop, Jack. Please stop.'

The door opened with a crash and daylight streamed in. Polly's children were suddenly everywhere, in the boats, balancing on gang-planks, swinging on ropes over water, a danger to themselves and everyone else.

'Ah, there you are,' Oliver said. 'And what do you think of our fleet?'

'Fine,' Jack answered, recovering his cool with a speed that amazed Kim.

'You must come and see my cars. Do you like vintage motors?'

'Oliver has a Bentley and an early Silver Cloud,' Kim babbled, her clit still thrumming from the memory of Jack's finger, the narrow gusset of her knickers wet.

Jack smiled and looked suitably impressed and Kim was relieved to see him so controlled. She linked her arm with Oliver's as he said, smiling at her puckishly, 'I suppose you two have a lot of catching up to do.'

'He's shown me a picture of his mother, with Dad,' she said, wondering if her face was as fiery as it felt.

'That's it then. You've got yourself a brother. I wish I could get rid of mine,' Oliver remarked, patting her bottom. 'Now, what say we go in and have more tea? Jenny's brewing up again.'

But Kim was trying to see what Jack was doing without appearing to be the least bit interested. The brigadier's daughter, Sandra, had made a beeline for him. She was a willowy, doe-eyed girl, several years Kim's junior.

He gave her his full attention, and Kim heard him asking, 'And what do you do?'

'I'm a model,' Sandra said, in her fresh-from-girls'-college accent. 'At least, that's what I want to be. I've been tested for a commercial.'

'You should do well, with those legs,' Jack said, bend-

46

ing his head closer to hers, but holding Kim's eyes at the same time. 'I know someone who is an agent. Would you like me to fix up an interview?'

'Would you?' Sandra looked ecstatic, as if she was about to have an orgasm on the spot. 'Here's my address. Daddy has a place in town and I use it when I want.'

Kim didn't like her air of availability and the way she was rubbing herself up against Jack under cover of exchanging business cards. But, of course, he should have girlfriends. It was essential. She would welcome them when he brought them to visit her and Oliver.

But as they were leaving the boat-house, walking back through the fading light, she was aware of Jack beside her, his breath on her cheek as he whispered, 'I'll be in touch. Oliver wants you to help me find a house, doesn't he? Here's my mobile number.' He pressed it into her hand, his thumb tickling her palm in a gesture so intimate that she felt its reverberation in her core.

She couldn't have denied him had her life depended on it.

Chapter Three

'*A* mysterious brother! Bloody hell! That's a turn up for the books,' exclaimed the sleek-hipped woman poised at the top of the stepladder.

Palmer's Emporium, her select warehouse showroom, had once been a factory. Iron girders supported the high ceiling. It was impressively spacious, with little to clutter it except a few blow-ups of some interiors that Elaine Palmer had designed hung at intervals on the red-brick walls, a shelf unit stacked with bales of material, and several extremely modern examples of statuary on moulded, metal plinths. At the rear were further shelves holding everything the wealthy DIY fanatic could desire. And beyond this were her living quarters: one massive room containing a lounge and dining area, kitchen, bedroom and bathroom tucked away behind a dividing wall. The whole was extremely fashionable and had cost a lot. Elaine could afford it. Her name was synonymous with style.

She was folding a length of amber, brown and yellow cotton into an elegant swathe when Kim started to tell her about Jack.

'I know it sounds far-fetched, Elaine, but it's true.' Kim braced herself against a display stand, trying to appear nonchalant and failing miserably. 'I've seen the proof. Dad had an affair with a woman in Bristol and Jack was the result. For all I know, she might not have been the only one. Maybe there are others scattered about.'

Elaine jumped down from the ladder, then stood back, her head to one side, eyes narrowed as she scrutinised the fall of the material. She appeared to be absorbed in this, but Kim guessed her keen mind would be ferreting away at what she had just told her.

She swung round, smiling at Kim, her beautiful, dark eyes carefully emphasised by mascara and liner, her complexion enhanced by toning base, a touch of blusher and poppy-red lipstick. 'Always put on the slap before tackling the day,' was her motto.

Of around Kim's age, she was petite and looked chic in her working gear, a belted safari suit, the pants tucked into tan, suede boots. Kim and Elaine had shared a house as students at art college. At the end of the course, Elaine had pursued her career with single-minded determination, founding this prestigious place, where she was cashing in on the vogue for innovative room changing inspired by popular TV programmes. Kim had dithered, unable to make up her mind what she wanted to do with her diploma. It wasn't till she married Oliver that she had taken her lazy talent from cold storage and, with Elaine's guidance, refurbished the kitchen and staff quarters of Glen House.

'You're good. Don't waste it,' Elaine had advised. 'Come and work with me.'

'Oliver says there's no need for me to work,' Kim had said, almost shamefaced, for Elaine was so independent, without the need of a man, either out of bed or in.

Now looking at the boldly striped hangings she had just blended so skilfully, she asked, 'What d'you think?' The wall looked like a Bedouin tent.

'It's striking, and unusual,' Kim commented, eager to

49

change the subject, yet longing to pour out every last detail of her meetings with Jack.

'Mrs Denise Wilson is coming in this afternoon. She's new money and no taste. Thinks the more it costs the better. They've just paid a million for a house in Surrey and I've been commissioned to tart it up. Nice little number. Should net me a few grand. I'll need your help, if that husband of yours can spare you.'

Kim shrugged off the last remark. Elaine and Oliver kept a wary distance from one another. She respected him, but thought he was old-fashioned and too controlling. He gave her credit as a clever designer and shrewd businesswoman, but it was plain they would never be bosom buddies.

Elaine straddled a high, rush-seated stool, coiled her thin calves round the beechwood legs, and reached for a cigarette. She pulled a face. 'I can't kick the habit. How about you?'

'I was doing well until Jack appeared.'

'He's really rattled your cage, hasn't he? Why?'

Why indeed? Kim thought in that split second before she replied, 'He's too full of himself. I've got a feeling he's up to something.'

'Is it to do with money? He's putting in a claim on your father's will, perhaps?'

'He can't,' Kim replied, and poured out the whole story, right from the moment Jack had turned up on her doorstep. She left out one important factor though: the heavy, dirty lust that possessed her every time she thought about him.

He inspired obscene images. She found herself brooding on fantasies that had never troubled her before, and couldn't stop wondering what would have happened if, as he had urged, she had run away with him somewhere exotic, foreign, utterly different. Perhaps a place where her moral standards would go out of the window.

Jack! To whisper his name made her wet between the legs, guilt, shame and passion warring within her.

Elaine flicked back her burgundy bob and said, 'I'd like to meet him.'

Kim fidgeted, laved with heat, even though the showroom was at a comfortable temperature. She hadn't had a moment's peace for days. She was uneasy in Oliver's company, hoping against all hope that he didn't suspect the cause of the desire quickening her orgasms.

'I don't know if I want him to meet you,' she said to Elaine. 'He's nosy, prying into my life, and I'd like to keep this bit of it secret.'

Elaine cocked an eyebrow, and studied her through a blue-smoke haze. 'What's he look like? Is he handsome?'

'Oh, yes.' The words were out before Kim had time to temper their enthusiasm. 'He's tall, a graceful mover, with a boy's tight bum and a man's physique. His body's strong and agile; maybe he's a sportsman. Even if he's not, he gives the impression of power.'

'Mm, and is he fair, or dark?'

'Fair hair, cut short, and blue eyes. He's handsome all right, quite devastatingly so, if you like that type.'

'And you don't?'

'I'm married,' Kim answered frostily. 'And in love with Oliver.'

'Of course,' Elaine agreed, her lips twitching. 'And Jack's your brother.'

'Precisely.'

'Does he have a big cock?'

'How should I know?' Kim fired back, her cheeks flaming, horrified by the memory of Jack moving her hand over his surging bulge.

'I just wondered,' Elaine said and slithered from the stool, going into the kitchen and returning with two gin and tonics.

'Why are you interested in his cock? You're not usually interested in male appendages, are you?' Kim responded tartly.

Though at ease with Elaine now, there had been a time when she avoided her. She had been scared of her

51

own response to Elaine's sexuality. She recalled that it had happened after a student party when they had arrived home a little drunk. Sitting together on the sagging sofa, Elaine had leant forward and kissed her full on the lips. Kim would always remember the mixture of surprise and excitement that had shivered through her. When Elaine followed this up by putting her hands on Kim's breasts and toying with her nipples through her dress, the sensation had been like an electric shock. It was the first time she had been touched intimately by a woman, and she hadn't known what to do. As she felt herself spiralling into Elaine's embrace, she suddenly struggled free, ran from the room and slammed her bedroom door behind her, throwing the bolt.

This incident had put a strain on their friendship. The course finished shortly afterwards and they had gone their separate ways, not meeting again until Kim's wedding. Neither had ever mentioned that moment when they had hovered on the brink of a deeper relationship. Kim had accepted that Elaine was gay, and since they had become close again, Elaine had openly discussed her love affairs which seemed as complicated, ecstatic or downright hurtful as anyone else's between the sexes.

Now Elaine stood in front of Kim, put the glasses down on the table and looked into her face, saying, 'Do you want to know what I think? It's my guess you find Jack disturbing and arousing. You don't like the feeling. It upsets your preconceived notions of how a nice girl should behave, and you, my dear, have always striven to be nice. Not only are you being unfaithful to Oliver – '

'I'm not,' Kim protested.

'Perhaps you haven't actually fucked Jack yet, but the thought is father to the deed and, oh, delicious added sin, he's taboo, too close by blood to make it acceptable.'

'You're wrong. I don't want to fuck him, I have no intention of fucking him,' Kim blurted out, putting space between them. 'He's just a nuisance and I wish I'd never seen him.'

'Bring him to meet me so I can suss him out,' Elaine suggested, then consulted her watch. 'Nearly time for Mrs Wilson.'

Jack spread the plans of the Transglobe project on the wide, glass-topped desk in Oliver's office suite. It was flooded with grey November light coming from wide windows that looked out over the water and a view of Tower Bridge.

Oliver studied the plans, saying, 'I'm already familiar with this. The foundations were laid three months ago and its up several levels. My client forged ahead. He couldn't wait for you to arrive. I trust everything's in order?'

'Yep. I've talked to the foreman. I told him I expect an exceptionally high standard, and had a look at the work in progress,' Jack answered, stabbing a sideways glance at that supercilious individual who had the right to fuck Kim whenever he wanted.

With a finger on fashion's pulse, Jack knew that Oliver's brown suit had been tailored by Ralph Lauren, and that his white shirt probably came from the same collection. Yet Oliver still managed to look vaguely rumpled, even in working conditions. But he was the boss, without a doubt, and he had a secretary whose eye Jack had caught as he entered.

He had registered swinging honey-blonde hair and a pair of opulent breasts straining against a tight-fitting jersey dress. The short skirt ended above deliciously shaped knees in seal-grey stockings, and the curves of her legs were exaggerated by platform-soled shoes.

With his sixth sense in all things carnal, he knew she fancied him. He imagined her escaping to the rest room as soon as she could and locking herself in a cubicle, pushing aside her panties, and parting her pussy lips to play with herself. As she fondled herself, she would sit on the lavatory seat with her legs wide apart and her back pressed against the tiling. She would dream of him, on his knees between her thighs, his tongue flickering in and out of her moist folds, then lapping at her clit and bringing her off.

Jack smiled his quirky, knowing smile, and she blushed, confirming his suspicions.

'Coffee, Mr Buckley?' she enquired, flustered but feigning efficiency.

'Thank you, Lara,' he nodded, without looking up.

He made one or two suggestions which Jack had to agree were sound. There was no doubt about Oliver's grasp of essential details. Jack thought with a flash of regret that had it not been for circumstance, they might have become business partners, even friends.

Oliver was to be envied in his shining empire. He took the swivel chair and indicated that Jack should be seated. Lara returned with two cups of freshly ground coffee, cream and sugar, and a plate of chocolate digestive biscuits.

Jack noted her quick, hot glance in his direction, and the way her hips swayed invitingly as she sashayed out of the door. He could feel his cock rising against the silk of his boxer shorts, luckily hidden by the fall of his loose-fitting trousers. Had he been wearing jeans, the shape of his erection would have been on full display. He considered asking Lara out to lunch, then decided that a quick shag would be sufficient for him. He had more important fish to fry.

Oliver sipped his drink and Jack grew wary under his sharp scrutiny.

'Found anywhere to buy yet?' Oliver asked, and pushed the plate towards him. 'Have a biscuit. Bad for the waistline, full of additives and all sorts of naughtiness, but I love 'em.'

Jack declined, then said, 'I've seen several places, but nothing that's appealed.'

'You might be interested in this.' Oliver rummaged in

a drawer, then handed him an estate agent's brochure across the table. 'I know this place. Considered buying it myself, as an investment, you understand. The area it's in was once prestigious, then it went downhill, and turned into a slum. But now trendy people are beginning to buy there. Soon the property prices will go through the roof. It needs a fortune spent on it, but you could save by doing it yourself. Employ your own builders. See the whole thing through. It'll be magnificent when it's finished.'

Jack looked at the colour photograph and read the theatrical specification. A church of moderate proportions. Early Victorian, maybe late Regency, as Gothic as a creepy Edgar Allan Poe story. He could almost hear the voice of Vincent Price intoning his chilling version of the agent's blurb: 'Fine example of ecclesiastical building. St Edwin's-on-the-Marsh. Deconsecrated C of E. Stained-glass windows. Original features. Vacant crypt, former occupants removed to other lodgings. A small portion of the surrounding graveyard still in use for plantings. The rest well fertilised and producing a splendid crop of vegetables and flowers, particularly deadly nightshade and mandrake. The growth of garlic strictly forbidden by certain aristocratic, foreign individuals who have a particular interest in the vaults. Early viewing advised. To savour the ambience, a night visit is recommended, preferably by moonlight.'

It was all that, and more. A tall, sombre house of worship, complete with bell-tower. Its gloomy aspect pleased Jack. He had been invited to a gig at a place like this following its restoration by a rock-star. It had been superb; a great venue for parties and as eerie as a horror movie set.

'"Offers invited in the region of one hundred thousand pounds,"' he read slowly. 'It says it stands on half an acre of land.'

'Haggle. You'll probably get it for ninety. As you can see, it's going to cost a bomb to restore. All that lead on the roof needing replacing, crumbling masonry, broken guttering, and that's just the outside.'

'I'll take a look,' Jack said. He folded the leaflet and put it in his pocket. 'I'd like Kim to see it. I could use her expertise. Will that be OK?'

Oliver hesitated fractionally before he answered, 'I suggested that she should help you house-hunt, didn't I? Why don't you take her out tomorrow evening, dinner or something. I'm going to an exhibition opening at Flyte's gallery and it isn't really Kim's thing. She's been invited but has refused to attend.

'She may not want to come out with me,' Jack said, thinking, of course she will. She won't be able to resist it. Oliver's a fool.

'Give her a ring. She's at home now. Actually, I will. Hang on a minute.'

He slipped the cellphone from his breast pocket and was soon engaged in conversation.

'Hello, darling,' he said, nodding across at Jack. 'I've got your brother here. I've just shown him a picture of that derelict church. You know the one, St Edwin's. He's keen but wants you to go with him. We did say you'd help him house-hunt. Remember?'

Jack heard her terse reply, tinny but quite clear. 'You did.'

'What's the problem?' Oliver asked placidly.

It seemed that she was reluctant, and Jack smiled darkly, visualising her face, with that little worried frown drawing her brows together, her eyes anxious, fingers tugging at her dark hair. His thoughts wandered. Were her pubes dark, too? In his experience, brunettes usually had thick, bushy triangles. He doubted that she would have trimmed or shaved it. She's too unsophisticated as yet, but I'll soon change all that, he promised himself.

The one-sided telephone conversation continued. She'd be dying to come, he knew it, but was still fighting to control herself. The thought of her torment made his balls clench. His penis fattened, moved up across his belly, the end brushing his navel, a dribble of pre-come wetting it.

He sat upright in his chair, hands loosely linked between his knees, hiding his arousal. He let his eyes roam the room, checking out the carpet, the furniture, the fittings, the carefully chosen antiques rubbing shoulders with state-of-the-art computer equipment. One day, not too far ahead, he'd have an office to rival Oliver's.

'She has my number,' he said into a pause. 'Ask her to ring me.'

Oliver relayed the message, then mouthed a kiss into the mobile and folded it away. 'I expect she will,' he said carelessly. He stood up and stretched. 'I must go. People to see. Things to do. Catch you later.'

He saw Jack to the door, and they arranged to meet at the site in a couple of days. The phone trilled and, with an apologetic gesture, Oliver went back to answer it.

Lara was at her desk in reception. She looked at Jack as he stared at her. 'Is here anything I can do for you, sir?'

'Yes,' he answered promptly. 'Mr Buckley has asked me to pick up some papers to do with the job. He says you'll know where they are. After finding them, you can give me head.'

Jack's pulse was racing. Taking risks was meat and drink to him. It was just possible she'd get all indignant and cry sexual harassment. He didn't think she would, but you could never be quite sure.

Her china-blue eyes widened, and her nipples were hard against the beige, jersey-knit dress. Was she wearing a bra? If not, did she leave it off in the hope that her boss would notice and tweak those prominent tips? Jack rather hoped so and hoped that Oliver responded. It would certainly make it a lot easier for him if the damn man was a seducer of secretaries. There would be something to convince Kim that she owed her husband nothing in the way of loyalty.

Lara's lips parted. They were coated with aubergine gloss that accentuated their sensuous shape. The thought of them closing over his cock was enough to make him rock hard, and it pressed against the top button of his waistband.

As he had surmised, she didn't leap up and create a fuss. Instead, she rose slowly to her feet, smoothed down her minuscule skirt, and walked towards the cedar panelling behind her. 'I believe the documents you want are in here, sir,' she replied calmly.

She pressed a button and part of the wall slid back smoothly, revealing a small room lined with filing cabinets. A strip-light sprang on automatically.

Jack stalked behind her and partially closed the gap.

Lara perused the labels on the files, straining up to see those at the top. Her skirt slid higher and he saw the flash of white, lacy suspenders crossing the backs of her pale-skinned thighs. He didn't offer to help.

The atmosphere in the confined space was heating up. His sensitive nostrils told him that she was wearing Samsara perfume, but this did not disguise her own personal odour, that smell of an aroused woman, which made his spine tingle.

'Oh, dear. It doesn't seem to be here,' she sighed, seemingly unaware of his hungry eyes on the tiny line of gusset that covered her mound and pushed into the crease between her buttocks.

Like a cat stalking its prey, Jack was silent.

Lara pulled forward a small set of steps, then lifted one leg and placed it on the bottom tread. Her skirt wrinkled up higher. He could now see the whole of one bare thigh, the stocking top, the satin and elastic suspender. He reached down and rubbed along the length of his cock behind his fly fastening.

Two steps up, she bent over, still searching, though Jack was convinced this was all show. She knew he had a monumental erection. Women! he thought cynically, they are randier than men under all that pretence. His own mother had taught him that. He wanted to run his hands up Lara's legs, slip his fingers into her knickers, expose the feathery fringe edging her lips, and bury his mouth, and then his cock, in her juicy crack.

'Where are the wretched things?' she murmured, then turned and smiled at him. 'Silly me. They must be in that desk over there.'

He held out his hand, and she placed hers in it and climbed down. She passed close to him to reach her objective, and her breasts brushed against his chest. Years of practice in self-control prevented him from seizing her round her pliant waist and dragging her against his hardness.

She picked her way across to the desk and bent over. About to pull out a drawer, her legs were apart, balancing her weight. In a single stride he was behind her, unzipped, his cock jutting out fiercely. He grabbed her by the hips, held her fast and forced her face-down over the desk. She didn't cry out or protest, simply opened her legs wider and arched her bottom up towards him. With one hand under her, he found her breasts. No bra: he had been right. Her nipples were pronounced, and getting bigger as he rubbed them through her dress. With his free hand he pushed aside a knicker leg, and glanced down to make sure he had been correct about how ready she was.

Her lips were pink and swollen, her juices glistening in the harsh strip-light. He couldn't remember ever seeing a quim more ready, willing and eager. He nudged his cock up her crease, passing her vulva and heading for the tightly closed anus. But not the back door this time. He had recently taken his fill of Andy's. He wanted to feel the muscular contractions of a slippery, wet pussy closing round his dick, caressing it, kissing it, sucking it inside, absorbing it into the deep cavern where a woman's magic lay.

She opened under him, moaning quietly, and he drew back a little, then thrust into her with full force. She jerked, and gripped the edge of the desk with frantic fingers, lying prone beneath his rapidly thrusting pelvis. He slowed down, reached round and found the clit between her thickened lips. She gasped, moved up and down on his finger, while she rammed herself up to meet the downward thrusts of his cock. He swooped into her, a hand on her rump, his nails digging into her flesh while he squeezed and pinched her sensitive, rigid crest.

She came, convulsing and trembling. Jack pulled out sharply, seized her by the shoulders and rolled her over on to her back. Her thighs spread on the desk top, and her legs were bent at the knees. Her sparse, light-brown bush parted over her cleft to reveal a slick, hungry pussy. Jack poised over her for an instant like a falcon about to strike. Then he plunged, impaling her with a savage thrust that forced a yelp from her throat.

He was riding her now, letting go, encouraging the raging fire that ran down his spine and flooded into his belly, his balls, his cock. Up it surged, his orgasm peaking, ready to pour over. At the ultimate moment, he pulled out, and come jetted from him in creamy spurts, spattering her garter-belt, her pubic hair, her thighs. He slumped, but only for a moment. Then he stood away from the sprawled and satiated Lara, dried his cock on her skirt and returned it to his trousers.

As he buttoned up, he looked down at her and said, 'Never mind the papers for now. I'll be in again soon. You can give them to me then, and the blow-job.'

'Bastard,' she hissed, staring up at him, eyes sparking.

'That's right. I am a bastard,' he said quietly, and left her lying here.

'I refuse to have anything to do with him. Damn him, and his bloody house-hunting,' Kim said to her reflection in the bathroom mirror.

Why had Oliver rung, almost insisting that she help her aggravating brother? What was Jack trying to do? She could see the green, cordless phone glinting, almost enticing her to phone him.

She had placed it by the bath before trying to drive out all these evil and disturbing thoughts by a long hot soak. It hadn't worked. Even adding lavish aromatherapy oils had failed to relieve the stress and tension. All it had done was make her even more conscious of her nakedness. Her skin was yearning to be touched by his fingers; each and every one of her jet-dark pubic curls seemed to send electricity into her sex. Her nipples had risen through the bubbles, poking up hopefully, wanting to be fondled by a firm hand.

She had lain back, resting her head against the porcelain, and run her hands over her needful flesh. Dipping down beyond the floating pubes, she opened her lips and, using the bar of fragrant soap, massaged them gently. Such slippery friction had been too much to bear for long, and replacing the soap in the shell-shaped dish, she had allowed her passions to take over, using her fingers. No one – not even her beloved Oliver – could pleasure her like she could herself.

It was so simple and uncomplicated, a wonder she had stumbled across in her teens. She hadn't realised at that age that what she was doing was called masturbation. All she knew was that she could achieve the most incredible, achingly wonderful sensations by rubbing the little, fleshy point at the top of her lips. Once she had experienced this mind-blowing revelation, it had become a never-ending source of comfort and joy. Even when having full and regular intercourse, she still needed her own, totally satisfying caresses from time to time.

Oliver didn't know. He was so kind and considerate when making love that she didn't complain on the odd occasion that she couldn't climax with him. Instead, she escaped from their bed and sought seclusion to bring

61

herself to orgasm. It seemed unkind to let him know he had failed.

After climaxing, she rose from the bath, and, dripping on to the mat, wrapped herself in a fluffy, white towel. It was late afternoon, and she had plenty of time to prepare herself for Oliver's return from the city. She anticipated an evening in, just the two of them and, until recently, it was something she had looked forward to eagerly: her husband's presence, his wit and amusing conversation, or the two of them, just sitting quietly together, building imaginary castles in the fire.

Jack had ruined this.

She was almost afraid to be alone with Oliver these days. His mental antenna picked up on her every emotion. It was difficult to fob him off, or pretend to be light-hearted and at peace when this was far from the truth.

The phone winked at her, and though she tried not to look, her eyes kept returning to it. Would Jack be on site or at his hotel? She knew he didn't have an office yet.

'I suppose there'd be no harm in ringing him and saying that I'm too busy right now,' she said, talking to herself again. 'It's partly true, anyway. Elaine wants someone to hold the fort while she's at Mrs Wilson's place and I'll be in charge of the showroom every day for a while.'

Gripping the towel tightly round her body, she reached for the phone, withdrew her hand as if scalded, then picked it up resolutely and dialled the number, wondering how it was that she knew it by heart, when she usually forgot numbers if they weren't entered in her address book.

Seated on the side of the tub, she waited. Her pulse jumped madly. He's not there, she thought, dismayed but relieved. Then suddenly she heard his voice: 'Hello. Jack Loring here. Is that you, Kim?'

Damn him, she swore to herself, and almost rang off; almost, but not quite.

'Yes,' she answered, adopting the brisk tone she used at work.

'What do you want, Kim?' he asked, his voice creeping around her insidiously, heating her blood, making her nipples crimp, and sending a stab of lubricious longing through her centre.

'It's not a question of what I want,' she snapped. 'More what you want. Oliver phoned me.'

'I know. I was there. That was before I shagged his secretary.'

'You did what?' Kim went cold.

'Had a quick poke among the files. Do you know her? She's blonde with big tits, goes by the name of Lara.'

'I've met her.'

'Funny that Oliver likes big busted girls about the place. Yours are quite small.'

'I didn't ring you to discuss my measurements,' she replied acidly, astounded by the jealous spasm twisting in her gut.

'Where are you, Kim?'

'In the bathroom.'

'At Glen House?'

'Yes.'

'Ah, so it will be en suite and very private.'

'Yes,' she said, wondering where this was leading.

'Do you and Oliver have it off under the shower sometimes?'

'I'm not answering that. It's nothing to do with you.'

'Oh, but it is. I want to be sure my sister is being serviced regularly.'

'You've got a nerve! It's not open for discussion.'

'OK, calm down. So, what are you wearing?'

'A towel.' She was answering almost in spite of herself.

'Ah, you've just bathed. Did you play with yourself in the tub?'

'Mind your own business.' The question made her

63

breathless. It was as if, by some psychic perception, he knew exactly what she was doing and when.

'Everyone should wank in the bath. I do,' he said. 'Just thinking about it gets me stiff. I'm lying on the bed in the Byron Hotel and feeling my cock through my trousers.'

'Why aren't you working?' The picture conjured up by his words made her clit throb.

'I was, this morning, but I'm not a workaholic like Oliver. I gave Lara a seeing-to, then popped to the estate agent's and told them I'd be bringing a friend to view the church the day after tomorrow. I cruised round and had a quick dekko. Lots of land, yew trees, tombstones, masses of character. And you'll be with me when I first go inside.'

Now was the moment to make her position clear. She had rehearsed it over and over again, that speech of rejection, delivered in a cool, calm voice, but all that came out was, 'I'm not sure. I'm very busy at present.'

'I'll pick you up tomorrow night and we'll snatch a bite to eat somewhere, and talk it over. I know you'll be free. Oliver's already told me about Flyte's little bash.'

Jealousy nipped her again with serpent fangs, not of Jack, this time, but reopening the wound of Flyte's friendship with Oliver. They were so much closer in years, had so much in common. Her body was familiar territory to him and his to her. Both knew each other's erogenous zones and how to get the best result from penetration. He swore he hadn't touched Flyte since he met Kim, but Kim wasn't convinced.

She imagined Flyte hanging on Oliver's arm as she swanned about the Harlequin Gallery in Mayfair. She would be proud of her exhibition of the controversial artists and sculptors she took under her wing.

'All right,' she said suddenly. 'Let's meet. But I'll drive myself.'

'Come to the Byron. You know where it is?'

'I'll find it.'

'I'll reserve you a parking space and we can eat there. The cuisine isn't at all bad.'

'What time?'

'Shall we say around eight?'

What have I done? she mourned as she replaced the phone. She felt as if she had just made an adulterous appointment. But that was ridiculous. Oliver knew about it, had talked her into it, and practically arranged it. And Jack was her half-brother. There was nothing, absolutely nothing improper going to take place between them.

Jack grinned and pressed the remote control. The television screen lit up and he channel-hopped through the tea-time crap; kids' programmes or Australian soaps or the news. He lay for a moment watching it with the sound turned down, then propped himself up on one elbow and rang for room service.

Andy would bring it up.

Jack unzipped and freed his cock. He stroked the shaft. It juddered and jumped, expanding beneath his fingers. He began to pump himself slowly, images of Lara and Kim floating behind his closed eyelids. He'd like to see them together, the sluttish blonde and the genteel brunette. They would lie naked on his bed, kissing and tonguing one another, Lara's big, brown nipples brushing against Kim's tight, pink ones.

Kim would protest at first, looking at him with those distressed, shining eyes and saying, 'But I've never done it with a woman.'

'You'll do it now, for me,' he would reply, standing over them and trailing the thong of a black leather whip over her naked hip, belly and thighs.

Joys to come, he gasped, and felt the pressure in his balls intensify. He'd had Lara at lunchtime, so it was easier to control his urge. Fun, too, to see how far he could take it before he spurted. It required careful timing, and he was an expert.

He cupped his balls in both hands, relishing the sensual feeling of them rolling between his fingers in their hairy sac. Freeing one hand, he squeezed his cock and flipped it from side to side. It seemed to grow even larger, the head gleaming wetly from the retracted foreskin, and darkening to a deep, rich red. He rolled it, kneaded it, avoiding the sensitive tip, then drew the skin up over it and down again. The feeling was exquisite. He wanted to go on, wanted to stop, wanted to fountain out his spunk, wanted to hang on to it till his dick was fit to burst.

He gently released it, allowing it to jut up freely, stiff as a lance. He admired it for a moment; such a stalwart weapon pulsing with desire. And, in admiring his own, so he wished that Andy would hurry with that snack he had ordered.

Fixing his mind on the food – and not on Andy's nether hole – he succeeded in taming the beast between his thighs. It drooped a little, and he calmed it, softly caressing, slowing down when the pressure built, leaving it alone all together, and then returning to give it a hard, vigorous rub, and easing off when he felt himself on the verge of coming. He didn't want to waste it. Where the hell was that bloody Andy?

He didn't have to wait very long. Andy rapped on the door. Jack called him in, and as soon as the young man crossed the room and set down the tray, he grabbed him and pulled him on to the bed.

Chapter Four

'They're both out tonight. The boss said we could use the pool,' Jenny told Liam as they relaxed on the couch in the staff sitting-room. It was light and colourful, keeping to its traditional decor, but enlivened by the throws, curtains and cushions arranged by Kim and Elaine.

'And Barry's out, too. Gone to frock up,' Liam vouchsafed, lying full length beside her, his head in her lap.

'So, how about a swim?' she asked, looking down into his face and tracing over his strong features with an idle fingertip.

'Skinny-dipping?' he enquired, eyes twinkling.

He reached up and nudged his nose against her breasts. Full and lush, they swung forward as she leant over him, the top buttons of her shirt undone, the deep cleft, exaggerated by her bra, inviting exploration.

'Why not?' she whispered, smiling broadly. 'I'll show you mine if you'll show me yours.'

'I never get tired of looking at you. Your furry minge is enough to drive a man insane. I haven't seen it yet today,' he replied, his voice muffled as he tried to mouth her nipple through the brushed cotton.

He undid a few more buttons and opened the shirt to

get better contact. Her right breast swelled in the cream silk and lace bra. He ran a finger along the edge and pulled it down and her nipple emerged, erect and rosy.

As Liam wound his tongue round the nutty-flavoured, crimped flesh, he was thinking that perhaps it was time to make their affair legal. Employment agencies specialising in staffing big houses favoured husband-and-wife teams. It smacked of responsibility and maturity. He'd been lucky so far, landing this cushy job with the Buckleys and getting in with Jenny without preamble.

Jenny was a rare girl. Her fiery temperament, unquenchable spirit and animal appetite matched his own. Barry proved to be no sexual rival: chef's duties completed, he sought fulfilment in transvestite clubs. This suited Liam; if Barry wanted to spend his time off dressing up as a woman, that left the field clear for him. He had been able to woo Jenny and, horny under her super-efficient exterior, she had reciprocated beyond his wildest expectations. Together they ran the house superbly and, when the Buckleys were away on holiday or out, like tonight, they treated Glen House as their own.

He reached up and closed his palm round the back of her neck, stroking the sensitive skin there, and pulled her lips down to meet his, the bright fall of her hair screening them. Her lips relaxed. She moved them over his, slowly and sensuously, then thrust her tongue out, pushing past his teeth, dancing with his own fleshy tongue and filling his mouth with the sweetness of her saliva. Having fired him up, she withdrew and gave a low laugh.

'A swim first, and then we'll see what happens,' she teased. 'I may let you put it in. Then again, I may not. Depends on my mood.'

Liam slid a hand along her denim-covered thigh and found that gap between them which always enticed him. The jeans were stretched so tightly that he could see the division of her lower lips. She jumped when he scraped a nail up the double-stitched crotch to where the zip ended, just above her mound.

She pushed him away and struggled to her feet, and he followed as she headed through the house. He hurried to catch her, and put a hand under her rump, and she giggled, pulling her shirt off as she went. The warm tones of her skin contrasted with the cream-coloured brassière.

The pool had already been there when the Buckleys took over, but Oliver had spent money on improving it. A great deal of money, Liam thought appreciatively. Situated in an extension to the conservatory, it was used frequently. Oliver's alterations had included sliding doors which, weather permitting, gave access to a paved terrace, wonderful on hot days or warm, summer nights. No party went by without some guests ending up in the water.

The damp, sub-tropical heat hit Liam as he stood under the arched, glass-paned roof. He pulled his sweater off and laid it beside Jenny's clothing on a lounger at the pool's edge. She was already stripped to her panties, her hand slipped down the front, thumb hitched in the elastic, posing for him and teasing him, fronds of red-gold hair wisping over the top.

His cock was half erect, but now he could feel it rising higher and hardening. He reached for her other hand and guided it towards the bulge. 'Wait a minute,' she said. 'I'm not ready. I need to pee. Shan't be a couple of ticks.'

Her words enflamed him. The way she wriggled her pelvis as if in discomfort gave him strange ideas. He wanted to see her urinating. It was something he had always longed to do, watch a woman pee.

'Hang on,' he said. He dropped her hand and started to unbuckle his belt and run his zipper down. His jeans slid over his hips. His cock emerged from its nest of black curls, curving upwards. He stroked it, then sat on the lounger and slipped off his shoes and socks, and then his jeans. He stood again. He had that olive complexion of the swarthy man, his arms, legs and chest coated with dark fuzz. His excitement intensified as Jenny looked him over from head to foot, her eyes lingering at his groin. All they could hear was their breathing and the sound of a miniature waterfall trickling into an ornamental basin. Liam's throat was tight, his balls even tighter. Jenny wriggled again, giving a little moan. The sight and noise of the water must be adding to her desire to empty her bladder.

This was their playground for the evening. The feeling of being king in this solitary paradise gave Liam a dizzying sense of omnipotence. Jenny, as his queen, would obey him, performing any act he demanded, however perverted.

He stepped towards her, the underheated tiles warming his feet. Perhaps later he'd take her in the sauna or the Jacuzzi. But for the moment he intended to act out his wet fantasy.

Placing his hand alongside hers at the panty waistband, he held her gaze. She stood there as if transfixed by what she read in his eyes. Her hold on her knickers slackened and he eased them down, brushing over her pubes and sliding the fragile fabric beyond her thighs, knees and calves. She rested her hands on his shoulders, kicking the panties free. Her nipples brushed his chest, and his penis pushed against her, leaving a silvery trail across her belly. She tipped up her face to his and kissed him.

'Ah, that's grand.' He sighed, then looked down at her. 'I want you to do something for me.'

Smiling, wondering, she said, 'What is it?'

'I'll show you,' he answered and lay flat on his back at her feet. 'Now, stand over me, Jenny, open your legs, and piss on me.'

'I can't do that.' She sounded genuinely shocked, but Liam was sure there was a trace of excitement in her voice.

70

'Why not?' He reached up and ran a hand up the inside of her leg, then pressed hard on her lower belly.

'Don't!' she cried, distressed. 'I shan't be able to hang on.'

'Then do as I say and let it go,' he urged, running a finger into the hot, wet furrow dividing her mound, and tickling the clit poking out between the lips of her pussy.

'I won't. It's disgusting. I never go in front of anyone or anywhere else but in the toilet. This is so embarrassing! You can't want me to go all over you, surely?'

'That's exactly what I want,' he said huskily, the Irish lilt more pronounced. 'I want to see how you do it. Does it jet out in a stream, or just dribble?'

'Liam! You do talk dirty,' she protested, but was rubbing herself on his finger. 'It'd be messy. Pee all over the tiles.'

'Don't worry about that, they're easily hosed down,' he said, smiling at her. 'Now, come on, darling. Put a foot each side of me.'

Jenny stepped across his body, her legs braced on either side. Liam had a clear view of her inner thighs and the open lips of her pussy. Her breasts reared above him, the skin flushed, the nipples peaking. This, and the juice he could see glistening at her crease, gave her away. She was very nearly as aroused as him.

'Oh dear,' she said breathlessly, truly distressed. 'I'm desperate, Liam. We'd better stop this game or I shan't be able to control myself.'

'Good,' he murmured slowly, his palm tracing the curve of her stomach, the heel of his hand digging into her distended bladder so that she winced in discomfort.

'Oh – ow!' she whimpered, and he pressed harder on the swollen nub bulging shamelessly out of its fleshy, pink cowl. 'Please, please, Liam,' she moaned. 'Don't force me to do this.'

In answer, he made slow, circular motions round her clit, rubbing it artfully each side and avoiding the tip. His finger became warmer and wetter as she inadver-

71

tently emitted a few drops of urine. Her obvious torment excited him beyond belief, and he strained up to caress her damp, engorged sex with his tongue.

Without abandoning her, he continued to rub her clit with a skill that was sure to bring her to the point of no return. Meanwhile, he used his other hand to wank himself slowly. Mouth parted, eyes slitted, he watched Jenny, watched and waited as the inescapable orgasm started sending signals straight down his spine to his balls and cock.

He squeezed her clit between his thumb and forefinger and she screamed as her climax broke and she released her bladder. Liam arched his body in a juddering, shattering orgasm and slithered down under the golden stream. It gushed into his mouth and drenched his face and hair.

Suddenly losing all her inhibitions, she spread her lips wide with her fingers and squeezed out the last remaining droplets.

'Oh, baby! That was so good,' he groaned, feeling her rapidly cooling urine trickle over his skin. It puddled the tiles beneath him.

She stared down at him, her eyes unusually bright. 'Did I do it right? Is that what you wanted?' she asked.

'Perfect. It was just perfect,' he answered, and cupped his hand round her mound, her wetness and heat penetrating his palm. 'Will you marry me, Jenny?'

'What?' She stared at him incredulously.

'Let's get spliced.'

'Why? We're all right as we are, aren't we?'

'I love you, Jen. That's why,' he said. 'What do you say?'

'I'm gob-smacked.'

'Does that mean yes? Or do I have to use further powers of persuasion?' he said, though almost one hundred per cent sure of her.

He decided there was no harm in continuing his courtship and making his offer irresistible, and dived into the pool. He surfaced near her feet as she dithered on the steps. His hand fastened round her ankle, and she jumped down into his arms. With the water sloshing chest-high around them, he tangled his legs with hers. His penis stirred, hardening again. He pressed it against her thigh, and imprisoned it between his own. He smiled into her eyes through spiky, wet lashes, driblets of water running from his hair across his shoulders and down his back.

Water was his natural element. Every nerve responded to the sensation of a rippling mass buoying him up. It reminded him of water-holes and lakes he had swam in as a boy in County Wicklow. But never like this, never with a willing water-nymph ready to take him into her lithe, slippery body.

His hands sculpted her shoulder-blades, the throbbing in his groin increasing. The turquoise, translucent lights at the bottom of the pool gave Jenny's limbs a magical grace, that of the dryad of his imagination. He held her away a little so that he could feast his eyes on her nipples bobbing above the water, then looked down to admire the wavering outline of her belly and the silky fronds of her pubic hair.

He turned her and held her back to his chest, his hands under each full breast, fingers gently lingering on the tips, teasing them until they peaked. The breath escaped from her lips in a low moan, and she rested her head back against his shoulder. Every inch of her body seemed to show her desire, her need to have him plunge into her. He pressed the jutting prong of his erection along her buttocks and she rubbed against him, angling herself into a more comfortable position. As easily as slipping a hot knife through butter, his cock entered her. He heard her sigh, and felt her vaginal muscles contract round his length. She moved against him lazily and he felt the caress of warm water and the tightness of her sheath as he slid in deeper, until he could feel his helm butting her womb. He was proud of his large dick. She couldn't take every inch of him; it was the same when she tried to absorb him into her mouth.

Their feet were touching the blue and white mosaic tiles that covered the pool's floor. Spreading one hand wide so that he could maintain friction on both nipples, he reached down and imagined he could feel the liquid of her arousal mingling with the water lapping lasciviously against her clit. Holding her lips apart with two fingers, he stroked her with his middle one. She shuddered, and he rocked against her, his cock swelling as her inner muscles clenched round it.

'I want it,' she whispered, tossing her head from side to side, her hair brushing his chest, and floating on the pool's surface. 'I want it! Make me come, Liam!'

'I will, darling. I will. Now, like this. Do it. Do it for me.'

He felt the quiver that ran through her, and fastened his teeth at the back of her neck, as a stallion holds a mare. This tipped her over the brink, and she clawed at him, crying out her ecstasy on a high, keening note of absolute pleasure.

Liam surrendered to the pounding urge of his own body, pumping into her faster and deeper until his semen boiled up and he lost himself in the frantic maelstrom of orgasm.

Then he heard her voice, guttural with the intensity of the pleasure he had just given her, whispering, 'I'll marry you, Liam. Of course I will.'

Kim didn't like driving through London after dark. As soon as she left Richmond, she regretted her rash promise to chauffeur herself. But Oliver had suggested she took the tube and met him at the Harlequin Gallery after she had eaten with Jack, and the thought of seeing Flyte queening it over everyone had made her gorge rise.

She found the Byron Hotel. Jack was lounging under a striped awning at the top of the short flight of wide steps. He hefted his shoulders from a pillar and came down to meet her as she drew up at the kerb. She wound down the window, and he stood looking at her, making her very conscious that her long skirt had slithered above her knees. She wished she had worn her sensible velvet pants.

'Shove over,' he said. 'I'll steer her into the parking space.'

'Are you insured to drive my car?' she asked, annoyed with herself for obeying him.

'I'm insured to drive all sorts of vehicles, including heavy goods,' he said, smiling as he took her place. 'Wow!' he added. 'The seat's warm. Your arse heated it up for me. It feels squidgy and a wee bit damp. Were you thinking about cock as you drove in?'

'You've a one-track mind.'

'Maybe,' he replied, slanting her a glance as the vehicle swung down a side-street. 'Perhaps it's you who bring out the worst – or the best – in me.'

Kim ignored this leading remark, but however much she tried, she couldn't ignore him. Despite herself, she watched his hands on the wheel and wanted them on her flesh. She couldn't resist glancing at his profile, then down into that shadowy area at his crotch, and along the thighs that moved so smoothly under his trousers as he controlled the accelerator and brakes.

To her annoyance, she realised that she was sticky between the legs. The aroma of her body wafted up and her nipples were stiff under her bra. He manoeuvred towards a yellow-painted barrier at the entrance to a parking area. He leant out of the window and exchanged words with a uniformed man stamping his feet and shivering outside a sentry-box kiosk. The barrier lifted smoothly to let the car pass.

Jack steered into a space near some steps, switched off the engine and swivelled towards her. 'Nice car,' he said. 'I'd like a BMW. Oliver spoils you, doesn't he?'

This wasn't what he wanted to say, and she knew it. She could feel the layer upon layer of pretence and lies between his words and his real meaning. To get to the truth would be like peeling an onion. And what about her truth, too. What did she really want? Why was she there, sitting in a freezing car park with him? Why didn't she just tell him to get lost?

'It isn't a question of spoiling. Oliver's my friend as well as my husband,' she remarked frigidly, but her body contracted and she had to look away.

Jack chuckled, leaning back lazily and observing her. Then he moved with a speed that took her off guard. He seized the hem of her skirt and whipped it up over her thighs. She could feel the wintery air between her legs. Shock pinned her to her seat.

Jack's eyes bored into her, and she pressed her thighs together, partly in protection, and partly to bring pressure on her clit. 'As I thought. You're wearing tights under your panties. Barbwire protection for your pussy? Afraid of what you might do if it's easily accessible?' he said mockingly.

'I wear them for warmth. It's a cold night,' she squeaked, her pulse throbbing. Her heartbeat seemed louder than she could ever remember it. She couldn't help squirming, and pressing her crotch down against the leather seat.

'Nonsense. You're frightened, aren't you? Frightened that your big, bad brother will tempt you into something you're longing to try,' he said and prodded one finger, silk and all, into her wet cleft.

'I've never met anyone as detestable as you!' she hissed, fighting free and tugging her skirt down. 'What makes you think you're God's gift to women?'

'What if I am? It's you I'm interested in,' he answered calmly. He lifted his finger to his nose and sniffed, adding, 'The smell of your quim is like seasoned wine.' Leaving the car, he then came round to open the passenger door for her.

Her knees were trembling as she got out. The cold pressed against her face like a mask and she huddled into her fluffy, fake-fur coat. The full skirt of her wool dress covered her to the ankles, but she felt chilled to the bone.

'You should wear real fur, not that synthetic crap,' Jack said, taking her arm and hurrying across the concrete to a lit door. 'I'd like to see you nude except for leopard skin.'

'I couldn't do that. Leopards are an endangered species.'

'Yes, but knowing this would make it doubly exciting. You'd be doing something reprehensible, even sinful. And you want that, don't you, Kim?'

'No,' she shouted, turning on him, shaking with rage. 'I like my life just as it is. This was a bad idea. I'm going home.'

His hand gripped her arm, and his fingers felt like talons, even through the thickness of fur. 'You'll have a drink with me. OK, you're driving, so we'll make it non-alcoholic. But I'm going to talk to you about the church, and about us.'

He hustled her through the door and into a passage connected to the hotel lobby. It was comfortable, even luxurious, with a deep-pile carpet and damask, upholstered chairs set at small tables in the reception. A mock fire, set in a mock Adams fireplace, popped. Porters were coping with new arrivals. A group of evening-suited businessmen on a night out were waiting to be shown to their private dining room. A gaggle of American women who loudly proclaimed that they were on a literary tour of London, lugged carrier bags full of shopping and demanded cups of tea.

Kim managed to extricate herself from the gaggle and Jack led her up a curving staircase to the second floor and into a bar. 'Are you sure you won't eat?' he asked her.

'Quite sure,' she said, quivering with nerves and confused arousal. 'Let's get this over as quickly as possible.'

A young, dark-haired waiter approached and Jack

77

said, 'Whisky for me, and Perrier water for the lady, Andy,' then sank his virile body into the chair opposite hers.

'Why don't you ask Sandra's advice? Take her over to the church,' she said suddenly, clutching her bag in her lap like a shield.

'Who?' He stared at her blankly.

'Brigadier Clifford's daughter. You were chatting her up when you came to tea.'

'Oh, her,' he said carelessly.

'Haven't you met her since?'

'Sure. I've fucked her a couple of times, but she's a model and always wanking her ego. She bores me.'

Pain knifed through her. He'd been to bed with that vapid creature, despising her as he joined his body with hers. Kim was relieved that Sandra bored him, hurt because he had even bothered to waste his sexual energy on her, and desperate because she couldn't control the torrent of emotion pouring through her.

All over the bar women were staring at him, mesmerised. She felt a tiny twinge of pride. He was so beautiful. She wanted to go to them and say, 'He's mine. My beautiful, beautiful brother.'

'Calm down,' Jack said, and she could feel herself drowning in those ice-blue eyes. He reached over and put his hand on hers, radiating confidence, making her feel safe and as if nothing else mattered but being with him. She had the odd sensation of sinking through his clothes, nestling into his bare flesh. She was strongly aware of the smell of him, the malt whisky and after-shave and cigarette smoke.

'I am calm,' she replied.

'You worry too much. Life's a ball, isn't it?'

'Is it? For you maybe, for me, possibly. But for a lot of people, no.'

'Oh dear, are we about to get into a deep and mean-ingful discussion? That isn't why I'm here.'

'Why are you here, Jack?' she asked, knowing why,

but somehow wanting her worst fears confirmed. It was like sucking on a nagging tooth.

He smiled sardonically, and caressed her full lower lip with his thumb, just as he had done the night they met. She couldn't resist the urge to draw it into her mouth. She felt certain that soon she would be licking his cock.

'I'm here to ask my sister's advice on buying a property,' he said blandly. 'Why else?'

But even as he spoke, she felt his foot pushing between hers under the table, prising her ankles apart. 'Jack, stop it. I've already made my position clear –' she began.

'Oh, sure. Like when I kissed you in the boat-house,' he said, his eyes brimming with mischief.

'We must forget about that,' she stammered.

'Kim, stop being silly. We're going to have sex, so you may as well accept it. I'll give you a choice. The last one you'll ever have with me. We do it here, or outside.'

'Here? In the bar? You can't be serious.'

'It can be done, I assure you. This is a dark corner. If I came and sat on the banquette beside you, I could lift your skirt and roll those ridiculous, passion-quenching tights down below your bum and slip my length into your pussy without anyone seeing. We'd be covered by the tablecloth.'

Kim swallowed hard, her hand between her thighs, so excited by his words that she couldn't help manipulating her clit through her clothing. He eyed her shrewdly, and repeated, 'The choice is yours.'

I should simply get up and leave, she thought, though any sensible ideas were slipping away fast. Instead, she said, 'You want to have sex with me, now?'

'Don't you want it?'

Later, she could not recall answering or choosing, only that he held her hand as he took her through a door. The corridor was a long one and she heard her heels tapping on wood and the sounds of laughter and voices coming from the bar. With a hand at the back of her waist under her coat, Jack guided her. The passage took a sharp turn right and a stone stairwell yawned at her feet, illuminated by a dim, yellow light.

He flipped her round and pushed her against the wall. It scratched her cheek. She was thrown off-kilter, disorientated by his force and her willing humiliation.

He ripped at her tights, dragging them and her panties down about her knees. She felt him grab her bare arse and felt the pain as his nails dug in. Then he ran his fingers over her rump and whispered, 'Have you ever been whipped?'

The question terrified and bewildered her. 'No, never,' she replied and clenched her buttocks tightly together.

'You mean to tell me that dear old Oliver hasn't caned your backside for being a naughty little girl?'

'He wouldn't hurt me. He loves me too much.'

'No? Sometimes pain is a demonstration of love. Didn't you know that?'

'I didn't. I don't know about such things.'

'High time you learnt, my sweet,' he murmured into her ear, his breath bringing her out in goose-bumps.

She felt the cold air sharp on her pussy as he opened her legs as far as the tights would allow. 'Get them off,' he growled impatiently, giving her buttocks an open-palmed slap.

She yelped, then hurried to obey him, stepping out of her court shoes and rolling down her tights and knickers. She turned towards him.

'Put your shoes back on,' Jack commanded, and she imagined him sneering, but when she dared look at him he was staring at her intently.

His breathing was loud, and she knew he was hot for her, his erection tenting his trousers. He jerked her arm and she stumbled down the stairs, reaching the litter-strewn floor, the cracked window pane, the heavy door with the word EXIT glowing above it.

'This will do,' he said, his voice expressionless, without approval or disapproval, lust or love.

'It's too public. Someone may see us.'

'So what? It's perfect, Kim. You suit dirty stairs and dingy alleys.'

'You mean I'm a slut?'

'Aren't all women? You need to be shafted away from the sanctity of the bedroom. Live a little, Kim. Let danger heat your blood up. Like this,' he said and he pressed her back against the wall, his arms like a cage around her.

There was no escape; not from him, not from her own lust. Looking up into his eyes she knew it was hopeless to object. His single-mindedness melted her resistance. His thinly veiled violence found a savage response in her. Had she been unconsciously seeking this? She had never had a clear idea of her identity. One moment she was a woman who knew her own mind, and the next she was shy and lacking in confidence. Jack had picked up on this insecurity.

He unbuttoned her dress and flicked open the front fastening of her bra. Her breasts swung free and her nipples tightened as he rolled them in his fingers. She ached with longing. A quivering sensation rose in her clitoris. Jack's hand moved down, tucking her skirt up into her belt, and found the pathway to her mound. She told herself she wanted to close her legs, but his touch was so seductive, so tender now, with no trace of cruelty. Without realising it, she was sliding her thighs apart, offering herself to his caress.

Such wantonness alarmed her. She was defenceless, giving herself to this man who claimed to be her brother. If she yielded completely, he would own her for the next few minutes. Maybe he would own her for the rest of her existence. He tugged at her pubic curls and then, without warning, plunged his fingers into her wet sex.

He held her arms behind her back so that she could not hang on to him. There was only his arm to lean against, and the firm grip of his fist keeping her upright, as he fucked her with three fingers, in and out, finding her G-spot.

She closed her eyes, blotting out the sordid stairs, the grubby walls and harsh, yellow light. Focusing her thoughts, she pretended to be in her bedroom at Glen House, or his room in the hotel, somewhere where she could forget the crude, brutal fact that she was allowing him to use her. Only Oliver should be able to do this. He was her husband, her love, her partner for ever. Not this tawny-headed, blue-eyed devil who was getting his kicks by embarrassing her.

It was impossible to kid herself. She felt the cold air on her bare skin, smelt the alien smells, and heard the rumble of traffic passing the Byron. The cold wall against her back contrasted sharply with the liquid fire in her sex. Wrenching her arms free, she held his wrist, guiding his fingers back to between her legs where she throbbed with unsatisfied need. The moistness of her juices made the touch intoxicating, but he was teasing her, rubbing at the side of her little organ and not touching the thing itself, delaying her orgasm.

Crazy for release, she lifted her hands to her breasts and pinched the erect nipples between her fingers so that a current of wild pleasure coursed through her. Now she was going to come. She tingled from the feet up, a spasm building and building as Jack excited her clit with every movement of his hand.

'Oh, oh,' she groaned, as she climaxed in a shattering welter of sensation. 'Oh, oh,' she gasped, as she convulsed round his fingers.

He pulled his hand away, and pushed her to the ground by his feet. She looked up into that saturnine face, the mouth grim, the eyes blazing. 'Suck my cock,' he growled.

Sensing her reluctance, he wound his fingers in her hair and forced her forward. She yielded; there was nothing else to do in that moment of primitive pleasures and needs. Reaching up, she gripped the tag of his zip and drew it down. His cock escaped, too swollen to remain in captivity. It was larger than Oliver's; the shaft was thick and pale, the helm wet and fiery. Holding it firmly, he pushed it to her face. She opened her mouth and suddenly he was inside it. She tasted the hard flesh as he moved the stalk between her lips. She gagged, tried to draw back, but he jammed himself in hard, his nails digging into her scalp to prevent her rejecting him.

Kim opened wide, afraid she would choke, but he slid in easily and moved slowly, with less force than if he were using her sex or anus. Drawing away, she remembered what turned Oliver on, and teased the head with her tongue-tip, dragging it down the sensitive underside. Then she sucked and slurped, running her lips over it. It was easy now; she was getting into it, loving the individual flavour of him, so different to Oliver's, closing her eyes to better appreciate the velvety feel of his glans, the rougher surface of his stem.

He stood there with his legs spread, his head up and his eyes closed. His mouth was slack and he moaned as she rubbed him vigorously. His grip on her tightened and she expected him to shoot over her face, spattering her with a stream of come. But he moved quickly, standing her on a step, and lifted her to the right angle. He opened her legs and plunged into her to finish. The energy of that driving cock made her hips gyrate and her inner self contract. But she never could come that way, with a prick inside her. Wriggle and squirm as she might, there was never enough contact on her clitoris to bring her off. Jack wasn't aware; he was solely intent on his own pleasure. He rammed the last inch into her and she felt that final swell and spasm as he climaxed.

Kim held him, arms tight around his body, feeling him rock in his final throes, and feeling him slump, his head against her shoulder. But only for a moment. He recovered swiftly, stood back from her and tucked his prick inside his trousers. The zipper done up, it was as if there had never been any intimacy between them.

Something dragged her gaze back up the stairs. It was a shadow, no more, nothing but her imagination, yet for an instant, she thought she saw the waiter, Andy, looking down at them. She blinked, and he was gone.

'Get dressed,' Jack said from out of the gloom.

'Aren't you coming with me?' she asked, losing her tenuous grip on the moment of madness they had just shared.

'No. The car park is through that door. You can't get lost,' he replied.

Sitting on the stone step, she drew on her tights, eased them round her hips and felt the gusset grow instantly wet. Her panties followed and warmth permeated her legs. She huddled into her fur coat and stood up.

'Goodnight, Jack,' she said, lost for any other words.

'Goodnight, Kim.'

She felt abandoned, afraid of the darkness outside. 'Won't you come with me, to the car at least?' she asked, hating herself for begging.

He was halfway up the stairs but looked back at her. 'No,' he said. 'I'll see you tomorrow. Be at the church at three o'clock.'

Chapter Five

'*I* think that went rather well,' Flyte said, slipping off her bead-embroidered black cloak as she stepped into the hall.

She always dressed the part; the gallery owner and entrepreneur, glamorous, slightly eccentric, a force to be reckoned with at auction sales. A patron of artists, too. She preferred them young and pretty, but recognised real talent when she saw it.

'Your exhibitions always go well,' Oliver answered, and she saw the appreciation in his eyes, not only for her achievements, but her appearance, too.

She knew she had chosen wisely for tonight. The full, rustling taffeta mantle with its jewelled yoke said it all. It had been made for her by Jason, a new star in the fashion firmament, and had been well worth the cool thousand she'd paid for it. Jason was worth it, too, showing his gratitude in a novel way. She had quickly discovered his weakness, or maybe his strength. Strapping young man though he was, he wanted to be her slave. That was fine by her.

Now she preceded Oliver into the sitting-room of her large, detached, period house in north London. The alterations were almost finished, and the proportions, simplicity of style and interesting textures gave it a timeless look.

'It's great to have money,' she remarked apropos of nothing, as Oliver settled his rangy figure on one of her latest finds, a *chaise-longue* re-covered in gold brocade. 'And I didn't have to marry to do it. Call it a slice of luck that my godmother was well-heeled and left it all to me.'

'You've not wasted it, Flyte. I've rarely met a woman with more business acumen,' he answered, and she knew he was paying her a big compliment.

'And knowledge,' she reminded him. She was aware of how the light shone through the 1930s Nile-green chiffon gown that undulated round her limbs. It was low-backed and cut on the cross and all she wore under it was a thin, silk slip.

Do you hope to tempt him? she brooded, as she poured red wine into crystal glasses. Don't kid yourself, girl. Of course you do, but Oliver's a lost cause. He's such a romantic under all that bluff. When he met Kim it was almost like the novel *Rebecca*, him playing the hero, Maxim de Winter, the older man to her sweet innocence. Oddly enough, there was a Jack in the book, too, who had tried to seduce her.

She put on a CD, and soon the exotic sounds of an Argentinian tango filled the room. She moved her hips to the sensuous rhythm.

'Ace recording,' Oliver commented. He was critical when it came to such things. 'Is it new?'

'Yes. The music of Astor Piazzolla, recorded in Buenos Aires by Latin American musicians and a famous cellist who usually plays classics. It's unusual. I wasn't sure if I liked it at first, but it's grown on me.'

'We haven't been to a concert or the opera together for ages,' Oliver said. 'Kim's not too keen on opera, though she likes ballet. I'm trying to educate her.'

'Well, you either like it or you don't. It speaks to you

immediately, or leaves you cold. I'm not a Mozart fan personally, but I adore Puccini and Verdi.'

'And Wagner,' he added. 'Every facet of human emotion is there, isn't it? Tremendous stuff. Let's go again soon.'

'Won't Kim mind?'

'I don't think so. She's out with Jack tonight.'

'So you said earlier.'

'He said he would amuse her while I was at the exhibition. He's going to look at a converted church with view to buying. Wants her to go along with him tomorrow and give her opinion.'

He said this coolly, but Flyte wasn't convinced he was easy in his mind. She took a cigarette from her antique gold case and immediately he was there with his lighter, his fingers brushing hers. He's a gentleman, she thought, smiling at him as she inhaled. You don't get that kind of treatment from many men today; no opening of doors, or standing up when a woman enters a room, or walking on the kerbside to protect a woman from traffic. It's a shame.

I miss him. Things haven't been the same since he married Kim.

'Are you still faithful to her?' she asked, sinking down beside him and crossing one leg over the other, the rasping of silk stocking causing a pleasant sensation deep in her loins.

He looked at her quizzically. 'You'd like me to say no?' he suggested, then touched her hand and added, 'The answer is yes, my dear. By the time I met her I was ready to settle down.'

'Oh, Oliver. I can't see you in a rocking chair with slippers and a pipe. You're too wired.' She leant towards him, her unfettered breasts pressing against the silk, nipples puckering at the gentle friction. 'What good times we used to have. Not only galas and ballet and Covent Garden but parties, too. Remember?'

'How could I forget?' he answered gallantly, but she guessed he almost wished he could.

'Do you remember that party we went to in Cannes during the film festival?'

'Which one? There were so many,' he said, smiling and stroking her arm, not with passion, she noted regretfully, but with friendship.

She was getting tired of containing her feelings, weary of acting the part of self-sufficient, successful woman; she was even sometimes sick of her lovers and the games she played with them. As for biting her tongue when it came to Kim? This was difficult. And, since she had met the brother and watched them together, hope had struck root again. Maybe Jack would take up some of Kim's time and leave Oliver with more for her. It seemed he was already considering this.

She refilled her glass, but he placed his hand over his, shaking his head. He was driving home. There was no chance of him changing his mind and spending the night with her.

'I was thinking of that party in ninety-four,' she went on, the wine suffusing itself into her blood, adding to the warmth of recollection.

'I remember. It was on Charlie Random's yacht. He'd produced and directed one of the films up for an award, and he filled the boat with starlets; male, female, and those in between.'

'He never could decide which he liked best,' she said with a low-pitched laugh.

'So he had them all. And he wanted you, Flyte.'

'I know. We decided to tease him, didn't we?'

She could see it so clearly in her mind's eye; the splendid sailing vessel at anchor alongside a score of motor launches, cruisers, sloops, all toys for the rich. The lights were reflected in the dark blue water, and more were strung like diamonds round the curving bay of Cannes. Charlie's boat overflowed with celebrities, reeking of wealth and ambition and that compulsion towards fame that sent the hopefuls to the festival in their droves.

And then there had been Oliver. She'd already known that she was lost. Her hard exterior was melting, her need for him so great that she had been willing to do anything to keep him.

It had entertained him to see her flirt with that mountain of a man, Charlie, huge in body, personality and reputation. And she had recognised that Oliver didn't love her, at least not as she wanted to be loved and not as he had later loved Kim.

'You said, "We'll give Charlie the thrill of his life,"' she began.

'And we did.'

'Oh, yes. Remember how we got ready that night in our cabin? I wore a purple, satin corset, laced very tight, my nipples poking over the rim, and you took my lipstick and coloured them carmine. Remember? We were so excited that we did it twice, right there on the wide double bed. We could hear the band playing on deck, and the party was in full swing, but we couldn't stop fucking.'

The CD was still playing, the South American music like that on the yacht; the rumba, the samba, the tango had been an accompaniment to their love-making.

'Jesus, you've got a good memory,' Oliver exclaimed, and, like a creature with a mind of its own, his penis swelled, spoiling the cut of his trousers. 'All these details. I'd forgotten, until you mentioned them.'

'Anyway, I eventually finished dressing; mesh stockings, stilt heels and a simple black number with bootlace straps at the shoulders. I was ready for anything. I didn't wear panties, and you had shaved my pubes. You took the lipstick again, pulled up my skirt and rubbed it over my clit, making it ruby-red.'

'Did I? I must have been pissed,' Oliver said, shifting in his seat. The bulge at his crotch hadn't gone away.

Flyte's fingers tingled with the need to touch it, but

she kept her fists tightly closed, saying, 'You got a kick out of shaving me. Have you ever done it to Kim's bush?'

'No. I'm sure she wouldn't be into that sort of thing,' he answered, but his thin, sun-browned face was flushed about the cheekbones.

'So, you have a terribly normal sex-life with her, do you? The missionary position with the lights off, and nothing else?'

'Flyte, darling, please. We're very happy as we are. I've grown out of experimenting, and I don't believe she was ever into it. She's never mentioned wanting to try anything unusual.'

'Or perverse?'

'No.'

'Or even the smallest bit rude? Haven't you watched her masturbating? You were always urging me to play with myself in front of you.'

She wanted to do it now. The underslip clung to her thighs and the urge to press her fingers into her naked cleft was almost unbearable. Oliver used to lean over, wedging himself between her legs, a dark, intent look on his face as he saw the feathery, light movement of her fingertips over her clit.

Sometimes he'd insisted on helping.

'Let me do it. Let me touch you,' she could almost hear him saying.

'You were talking about the party.' His calm voice brought her back to reality, though she could smell her juices underscoring the sharper notes of French perfume wafting from her skin.

He didn't want to enlighten her further about his intimate moments with Kim. And why should he? she thought wryly. There are many secrets shared only by husband and wife. I've no right to pry, even though we were once almost as close.

'Ah, yes. The party. It was hot in the saloon and we went outside. Charlie had been watching me like a hawk, never mind that he was surrounded by nubile bodies of both sexes. The deck was deserted. I remember how pretty the fairy lights were, slung between the spars. We leant over the iron railing, and looked at the sky. It was dusted with a million stars. They were so clear above the ocean.'

'You were dazzling,' he said softly. 'You outshone every woman there. And you're still lovely, Flyte.'

He feels safe to say this to me now, she thought angrily. So secure in his marital status. Well, I'll make his dick throb, even if it does mean an extra portion for Kim when he gets into bed with her.

'We had plans for Charlie. My dress was so discreet that no one guessed what I was wearing – or not wearing – underneath.'

'He was already foaming at the mouth for you. Ah, Charlie Random,' Oliver sighed, reminiscing. 'He didn't give a damn for convention. A mighty bull of a man, completely bald even then, and while everyone else was dolled up to the nines he wore loose pants and an Arran sweater. As for the paparazzi? He told them to go screw themselves.'

'You started to fondle me, your hand toying with my backside, then pushing my legs apart and slipping under me to rub my bare pussy. I bent forward, so that you could reach my clit. "In the mood?" you asked me. "I've arranged for Charlie to join us. Promised him a surprise." That's when I pulled my dress off over my head. The corset underneath was painfully tight, but I liked the feeling of restraint as it squeezed my waist. I was ready for anything. A hundred cocks wouldn't have satisfied me that night.'

'My dear girl, that's an overstatement, surely?'

She curled her fingers into her palms, the green, lacquered nails like daggers. She welcomed the pain; it stopped her from grabbing him, pulling his face down to hers and kissing him. The memories of that long-ago night made her stomach knot and her body quiver.

91

'You can't have forgotten, can you, Oliver?' she murmured. 'I was always ready. Never could get enough of sex. Unlike your recent bedmate, perhaps?'

'Kim's keen,' he responded, and she wondered if she was pushing him too hard and too fast. Patience, she counselled herself.

'Naturally she is. She loves you,' she said soothingly, and didn't add: and I loved you once, but even you weren't enough to cool the frantic, desperate need in me. She had found ways of being satisfied since, discovering a secret world where all her most fantastic, dark and shameful desires had been met by others of the same persuasion.

Charlie had only been the beginning. Though it had torn her apart, in a way she had been relieved when Oliver finished with her. Now she could do as she liked, be depraved and licentious, and abandon herself to endless pleasure.

'I want another drink,' she said, sweat gathering under her breasts and trickling down her body into her pubic hair. She was trembling with the need for release, certain that Oliver only had to touch her to bring her to orgasm.

With her skirt sticking sweatily to her buttocks, she got up and went to the chiffonier, a large piece with a mirror in a carved frame. Flyte saw her face reflected, eyes bright, the pupils huge under the sooty lashes. Her Titian hair was a tribute to Topknot, the hairdressers where Mario always attended to it, coaxing it into a shaggy mane that, at its longest, reached below her shoulder-blades.

She was pleased with her body. It was in fine shape, and she posed briefly, then touched the tips of her nipples poking up under the chiffon. This wasn't a sensible thing to do; the pressure was building up inside her, seeking an outlet. She filled her glass, and returned to Oliver, but she didn't sit down. Instead she paced the carpet, feeling the tops of her stockings caressing her

92

thighs, the taut suspenders tugging on the belt, the high heels firming her calf muscles. Every inch of clothing was like a subtle caress against her skin.

Always hyped up after a show, she had taken the precaution of telling Jason to be on call. All she had to do was pick up the phone, if – and she suspected there wouldn't be any other outcome, Oliver returned unsullied to his wife. Flyte despised herself for these thoughts for, underneath it all, she couldn't help but like Kim.

'You'd really got me going by the time Charlie came out,' she said, her voice husky. 'You held me from behind. I could feel your hard prick wedged between my cheeks, the tip rubbing against my arsehole. I wanted you to ram it home, take me up the bum, force it into me. And you didn't, not then. You just kept on rubbing me and pulling at my nipples.'

'There was a guy on the deck just above us. He'd seen you, and was standing there transfixed,' Oliver said, and she could see his hand was unsteady as he lit his cigarette. 'The view must have been superb; your naked fanny framed by the corset hem and suspenders, your breasts spilling out over the top. What an eyeful! I didn't care about Charlie any more; I was just frantic to enter your body. And then, suddenly, I heard his voice behind me.'

'And you displayed me to him, and to the guy on the upper deck,' Flyte said, her voice uneven. 'I was on the point of coming, and the shock as you removed your finger made me scream. But Charlie was on his knees in an instant, licking me with his thick, wet tongue. You held my outer lips apart so he could see everything, and pinched my nipples with your other hand. Your mouth was at my neck, nibbling and sucking, and the guy was wanking as he watched the three of us. It was the most erotic moment of my life.'

'You pressed back against me. You were heavy, I remember, and I supported our weight on the rail,'

Oliver went on, agitatedly dragging at his cigarette. 'You shuddered as you came. It was delicious. I could see your wetness on Charlie's face as he went on ploughing your crack.'

'Till I pushed him away. It was too sensitive to take any more. I was still reeling from that orgasm when he stood up and let down his pants,' Flyte said.

'The voyeur on the deck above had shot his load. I saw a flash of white as he wiped himself on his handkerchief. The next time I looked, he had gone. But I had other things to think about; I wanted to see Charlie inside you.'

'You weren't disappointed. He had a big one,' Flyte recalled, wriggling a little, remembering taking that huge, forceful organ into her narrow opening.

'He did indeed. Even I was surprised when he got it out. It was a thick, beefy cock, with a circumcised head that almost matched the colour of your corset. It stuck out like a truncheon, seeking your pussy, and even at that point, he had the presence of mind to put on a rubber.'

'I should think so, the number of people he'd fucked,' she exclaimed indignantly. 'You didn't let go of me. In fact, you held my thighs open and guided Charlie in, though he was oblivious. His only thought was how to keep grinding away at my pussy.'

'He was cursing and muttering something about your little waist, the ripeness of your hips under the tight satin, the smoothness of your honey-pot. That was the word he used for it. Maybe he thought he was taking part in one of his own porno films. I don't know. Whatever, he couldn't stop pumping, his forceful movements shaking the both of us, until he gave a grunt and slowed down.'

'He didn't withdraw straight away,' she said, thinking of that enormous man. 'He wanted to look at me; he was fascinated by the bustier, poking his fingers between the suspenders and my skin, and then tweaking my tits over the lace edging.'

'He should've been a Roman emperor, Nero or Caligula or someone, who could indulge his appetites to the full. He really was larger than life. His death was such a loss to the movie industry.'

'He was kind to me,' she said with a sigh, setting down her glass and pausing in front of Oliver.

'You saw a lot of him?' Oliver sounded a little surprised.

'Oh, yes. He bought me the Harlequin Gallery and my first Claude Monet,' she said and nodded towards the gardenscape hanging over the mantelpiece. 'Of course, that was before the artist became as popular as he is today, but even so it cost him a bomb.'

'Generous,' was Oliver's only comment.

'He was.'

'So our performance proved beneficial?'

'I didn't realise how much at the time.'

In vain, Flyte sought for some sign that he was the smallest bit jealous that she had been Charlie's mistress. She didn't tell him; there was no need for him to know. Charlie had enjoyed playing the submissive. Like so many powerful men used to having people jump at their every command, he wanted a woman to dominate him. Flyte could almost feel the whiphandle in her hand and hear its song as it whistled through the air.

Oliver rose to his feet, stretching and saying, 'Time to go. I expect Kim will be home by now.'

'She'll be asleep, won't she? Or will she be waiting up for you?' Flyte clasped her arms round her body, suddenly cold.

He smiled and his eyes were amber pools, the pupils inky. 'I expect so.'

'Can't you stay a little longer?' Flyte asked, furious with herself. She never asked anything of a man.

'Better not,' he answered seriously. 'It's no use trying to turn the clock back.'

'I guess you're right,' she agreed, but linked her arm with his as they went into the hall.

'I'm still very fond of you,' he insisted, shrugging his shoulders into his overcoat. 'If there's anything you want, anything at all, just let me know.'

'I will. Goodnight, Oliver.' She reached up to kiss his cheek.

When she had closed the door after him, she went to the hall table, lifted the phone and dialled Jason's number. By the time he arrived she had changed into a sleeveless black PVC catsuit that moulded every curve and angle of her body. A zip ran from the pit of her throat to her mons, between the legs and up her crack. It was open, straining back so that her breasts were exposed, and excitement thrilled through her as she glanced down at the wicked-looking strap-on cock standing proud between her legs.

In her bedroom, she stalked to the mirror, hands coasting over her breasts as she admired herself in all her horny glory. The latex phallus was lifelike, a battery-powered godemiche, displaying considerable craftsmanship and artistic detail. Flyte couldn't help switching it on. She squealed, the electric shock of its bristly base thrumming against her clit, and, coupled with the throb of the ben-wa balls she had slipped into her pussy, it immediately brought on climactic sensations. She clicked it off.

Custom-made for her, the black leather harness fitted perfectly. No amount of thrusting could dislodge it and it fulfilled Flyte's dreams of having a cock and being able to fuck someone. The feeling of power was exhilarating.

'Come in, the door's open,' she said into the intercom when Jason spoke from below.

She heard his light footsteps and swung round, challenging him with the jutting vibrator. Jason wasn't gay, but he couldn't resist the pleasure of anal penetration. They didn't speak, and he started to remove his clothes;

draped jacket, Armani sweatshirt, wide-legged jeans of his own design.

Flyte watched him, almost licking her lips in anticipation. He had angular features, broad shoulders, and his short hair was bleached. He was no pretty-boy fashion person but a tough East End trader who had started out on the market stalls and worked his way up, first in a shop selling end-of-range goods, then an atelier where he produced his own stuff. Flyte had encouraged him in those early days. Now he was famous, but he was still at her beck and call.

Completely nude, apart from a spiked dog collar around his neck, he waited for her orders meekly, head bowed, hands clasped behind his back. Chains stretched from the collar across his muscular, hairy chest, their clips fastened to rings in his pierced nipples. A wide belt banded his waist, with further straps that passed under his balls and hoisted his cock high. Another chain linked the ring in his foreskin to that in his navel.

'On your knees,' she said at last, pacing round him with slow deliberation, the metal tips on the thin, spiky heels of her boots clacking against the polished floorboards.

Jason dropped down on all fours, his bare arse exposed, his cock stone-hard, a dribble of moisture seeping from its eye. Flyte strolled to the Chinese urn containing an assortment of sticks, rods, whips and other instruments of chastisement. Aware that he was peering at her through lowered lids, she took her time selecting one.

'Which shall it be? How about this?' she mused, and lifted out a short-handled whip with a dozen or more thongs, each knotted on the end. 'Or this?' and she gripped a silver-mounted riding crop with a razor-like lash. 'Or maybe a rod for naughty pupils? What do you think, Jason?'

'It's not for me to decide, mistress,' he murmured,

crawling towards her. 'You're my goddess, and the choice is yours. I'll accept it and thank you for it.'

'I should think so,' she replied haughtily. 'You're nothing, Jason, nothing. A mere boil on the bum of humanity. Isn't that so?'

'Yes, mistress. If you say so, mistress,' he answered humbly, grovelling and pressing his face to her instep. The buckle on her boot gouged into his cheek.

Flyte ignored him and selected her weapon, a pliable paddle covered in white leather. She made a few practice strokes across her palm. Jason shivered and moaned, his cock leaping. Forbidden to touch it, he wrung his hands together at his back.

'You're naughty tonight,' she remarked in that hectoring voice she reserved for her dominating role. 'I can see I'm going to have to use the cuffs. Can't have you rubbing that disgusting thing, can we?'

'No, mistress,' he whimpered.

Flyte took up a set of handcuffs that she'd persuaded a besotted police sergeant to give her, clamped them round his wrists and snapped them shut. Jason almost came, but she gripped his cock at the base and squeezed hard.

'Not yet!' she ordered, her lips curling in disdain. 'Don't you dare come!'

He panted and groaned, but she kept up the pressure till the spasm had passed. 'Thank you, mistress,' he whispered.

'That's better. We don't want it to be over, do we? Lots of things to enjoy first. You'll have to satisfy me, and then, just maybe, I'll permit you to jerk off.'

Walking round behind him, she lifted the paddle and brought it down smartly across his left buttock. His breath rushed out in a gasp, but he didn't move. Flyte stood back, noting the red blotch forming and spreading on his pale-skinned rump. Swimming shorts had kept that part of his body white and the kiss of the paddle had produced an interesting fiery contrast.

She struck him again, this time on the other side, and he was unable to stop himself from shifting forward on his knees, instinctively seeking to avoid the pain. Flyte permitted him to creep, but didn't stop raining blows, the thwack of paddle on flesh resounding satisfyingly, his backside reddening all over, and his cock in a fearsome state of arousal.

Judging his control to a nicety, Flyte threw the paddle aside and took up a tube of lubricating jelly, and smeared it liberally over the vibrator. She could hardly wait; her sex was burning with need. The earlier stimulation during the evening had made her hungry for completion.

'Kneel on the bed,' she commanded.

He hurried to obey her, and she knew he was eager to experience in some measure how a woman felt when she was penetrated by an erect cock. She knelt behind him, remembering the sensation when she was entered from the rear. Charlie had been well into that but Oliver hadn't, not with her at any rate. He needs to try it, she thought, as she oiled her fingers and inserted them past Jason's sphincter, preparing the way for her fake dick.

He grunted with pleasure and hunched his bottom higher, taking her three fingers and obviously wanting more. Flyte positioned herself, guided the godemiche to his well-greased hole and pushed hard. There was a moment's resistance, and then the toy slid in easily. She switched it on, closed her eyes, and pretended to be a man. She felt virile, in charge. Thrusting into that tight, slippery orifice was incredible, the buzzing bristles chafing her clitoris and her lips.

She had used both sexes in this way, but somehow the pleasure was that much sweeter when she could stab aggressively into a male, giving him a taste of the force with which he drove into a female partner. Jason's arousal added to her triumph. He strained towards her, the vibrations making him swing his hips from side to side while Flyte withdrew and plunged in again. The dildo was so cunningly made that her clit was stimulated with every movement, the ben-wa balls shifting in her vagina. The intensity was driving her mad. It was too much, too harsh, but impossible to resist. It was coming. She was coming. A huge roller-coaster wave was sweeping her up and she gave a harsh cry as she exploded, thrusting and pumping, just as a man would do when he reached his climax.

Jason yelled, too, and she reached round and grabbed his cock as it gave a final jerk and shot creamy white spunk into her hand.

He collapsed under her and she slowly disengaged the dildo from his arse, pulled away from him and stood up. Now the manufactured penis looked ridiculous on her, and she couldn't wait to get it off and slide the balls from her pussy. She showered, washed the equipment thoroughly, and put it away till next time.

Oliver tiptoed into the bedroom. Kim was curled up in the heart of the flower that formed their nuptial couch. His heart contracted at the sight of her, so perfect, so peaceful, with her night-black hair spread over the pillows. He felt a twinge of guilt because he had been talking about sex with Flyte. But was it so wrong to reminisce with an old friend? It rather depended on the tenor of the conversation. He was too honest to deny that he'd been aroused.

He undressed, showered, then slipped into bed beside his wife. He was still hard, and he wanted her. He passed his hands over her naked body, relishing her perfection. The perfume of her skin was like roses, the scent of her hair a mixture of jasmine and honeysuckle. He wanted to cover her in petals and rare gems, imagining a rope of pearls trailing down her body, along the division of her thighs, their glowing purity contrasting with the dark, pubic bush and disappearing into the shady crevice between.

Sentimental idiot, he told himself, but the notion

delighted him. He wished she'd wake up. He wanted her to turn languidly in his arms and coil her limbs round him, her fragrant sex parting to take him inside. The bedside lamp threw its mellow light over her face. She looked younger than her years, as yet unscarred by life, yet she had known sorrow: the deaths of her parents; the disappointment of earlier loves. Oliver ached to take care of her for ever.

In spite of his efforts, he was hardening even further, titillated by the memories pouring through his brain: the boat-deck and Flyte and the surging bulk of Charlie's cock. He had to control himself. To wake Kim would be pure selfishness on his part. Yet he could not help cuddling against her, and cupping one of her breasts in his hand.

She stirred, sighed as if in the coils of a troubled dream, then turned away from him, curling on her side in a foetal position. With a shock in his bones, Oliver realised that this was the first time ever she had rejected him, even in her sleep. Normally, kitten-soft, she would snuggle in his arms, and together they would relax into the world of the subconscious, going deeper and deeper, to wake up refreshed.

His erection subsided and he lay on his back, staring up at the ceiling, trying to figure out why her withdrawal into her own private dream bothered him so much.

Vivien took Jack's call as she was preparing to leave the van.

'Viv, where are you?' he asked bossily. 'I tried the hotel but Reggie said you were out and to try your mobile. What's going on?'

'I've gone shopping, dear. To the Cash and Carry. We need to stock up.'

'Shopping? But it must be gone twelve.'

'It stays open all night. Shopping for the hotel's a

101

drag. Doing it at night makes it more of an adventure.'
She answered with a smile, thinking: if only he knew.

'I'm not sure about that,' he said, sounding cross and
anxious. 'Is it safe? Bedminster's a rough part of town.'

'I know it like the back of my hand. Don't forget, I
was born here,' she reminded him. 'Anyway, why are
you phoning me? Is something wrong?'

'Oh, no. Far from it,' he answered, and she could tell
by his tone that he'd been up to something. 'I had a date
with Kim tonight. We went to the hotel bar and I fucked
her on the back stairs, close to the toilets, a really grotty
spot.'

'Did you indeed? And?' Vivien said, sitting in the
driving seat staring out at the wet tarmac and the lights
of the huge warehouse.

'And, she put up a struggle. She was feeling guilty as
hell, but she couldn't resist me, Viv. I've got her, and
what's more Oliver's encouraging her to be with me. He
trusts her; he doesn't believe she might fancy someone
else, especially her brother.'

'Half-brother,' she reminded him, suspicious of his
excitement. 'And keep him thinking that way for the
time being. Don't let it get out of hand, not yet.'

'I won't. I've got the perfect excuse. I'm house-hunting
and I think I've found the place I want. It's an old
church. Spooky isn't the word. You'd love it.'

'Not if it's cold and draughty. I like my creature
comforts.'

'I'm going to see it tomorrow and Kim's coming with
me.'

'What? Shagging among the gravestones? I always
knew you had peculiar tendencies.'

'Like yours, Viv, like yours. You were my role model,
you know. Anyway, it's had some work done on it, so
the agent tells me – an upper floor partially put in and
the central heating pipes in place – but the owners ran
out of money. That's why I'll get it for a song, if I can
come up with the cash. I don't want a mortgage. Can

you help me out if it gets too much, what with paying builders and all? I want to take over as soon as I can. This hotel is costing me.'

'We'll see,' Vivien answered slowly. She liked to keep him dangling, just to prove who held the purse-strings. 'Ring me again when you've been over it, and send me the details.'

After tucking the mobile into her pocket, she swung down from the van, then aimed the locking device. Maybe it was foolhardy to roam around alone at night, but she wasn't afraid. She felt at home there; she was born and bred in this sleazy part of the city. She had attended the mixed secondary modern school, a breeding ground for trouble. There she was forged into a tough cookie, well able to fend for herself; there, too, she had her first encounter with sex, in the form of a gang-bang with half a dozen sixth-form yobs taking her virginity. They had left her with an appetite for inter-course that refused to be appeased and a hearty distrust of anyone with a penis.

Perhaps you're not distrustful enough, she told herself, as she started to walk across the car park, deserted now, though so crowded in daylight. You fell for James's sweet-talk, hook, line and sinker.

She drew in a lungful of dank air blowing from the River Avon that flowed through the smelly old port of Bristol. The Cash and Carry was on an industrial estate, built slap-bang over the street where she grew up in a terraced house with her mother and sick, alcoholic father. The area had been cleared years ago and designated for trade. The tobacco factory where her mother had packed cigarettes for a pittance had gone, too.

'Forget it,' she had been told bitterly when she pleaded for a brother or sister. 'We can't afford to keep you, let alone any other kids.'

They had existed on her mother's meagre wages and a tiny army pension. Her father had been injured during the war and drowned his sorrows in drink.

'I don't know why I'm letting myself think about it,' she muttered, entering the warmth and bustle of the store's interior. It was the size of an aircraft hanger. 'Thank God things got better when they had a win on the football pools.'

Still no siblings came her way, and she realised later that her father's disability had probably left him impotent, which may have accounted for her mother's bad temper. However, this windfall enabled them to purchase a boarding-house near Arnos Vale Cemetery. And, once her father was dead, his insurance money facilitated a further move – upmarket this time – to the prestigious area of Clifton. Elocution lessons had rid her of the ugly Bristolian accent, and she was confident she could pass as a member of the upper-middle classes.

The Rockburn Hotel. Vivien's monologue continued in her head. It's mine, all mine. Now, I'd better stop wandering down memory lane and concentrate on the shopping list. Lord, it's as long as my arm. Reggie, do we really need all this?

Reginald Arkwright, to whom she mentally addressed the last question, had been her faithful assistant and devoted dogsbody for years. He'd never married and she knew that he wanted her to be his wife, not only because of the flourishing business, but also because he lusted after her. She occasionally gratified that lust, when there was nothing better on offer. However, she refused to commit herself.

She found a substantial trolley and cast her eye round the aisles lined with shelves. They were stacked with a multitude of commodities and seemed to go on for miles. A few nocturnal shoppers like herself meandered along, looking slightly dazed.

Vivien acknowledged one or two shoppers, fellow hotel-owners and the like. Her confidence soared. She knew she was still a handsome woman and was wearing a trench coat, calf-length and buttoned down the front and belted at the waist. She liked to think she looked a little like Marlene Dietrich, though it did rather date her.

Who cares? she thought. I can still sing 'Lily Marlene' in the bath. I've got fine legs, too, and I'm in the mood to show them off, and what's between them. Let's see; who's about tonight?

As she sought her victim, she selected giant-sized jars of pickle, tins of jam, boxes of canned baked beans and tomatoes, packs of cereal and catering jars of instant coffee.

Then someone said at her elbow, 'Can I help you, madam? Here, let me put that into the trolley. I'm sure it's too heavy for a lady like you.'

Vivien looked up into a pair of twinkling eyes set in a cheeky young face. He was tall, and wide-shouldered under his white overall, and the curls escaping rebelliously from his regulation hat were a pale shade of brown. Eighteen perhaps, Vivien thought, and interested in football, I should imagine. Yes, football and sex. I bet he masturbates every night before he goes to sleep, and when he wakes up, too. There's bound to be a heap of top-shelf porno magazines under his bed, just like Jack used to have in his room.

Cradle-snatching again, Vivien, she chided herself, but felt totally unrepentant. 'Thank you,' she said, giving him the full benefit of her smile. 'I could do with some assistance. Darren, is it?' she added, reading the name tag pinned to his left lapel.

'That's me. Just say the word, madam, and I'm all yours,' he replied, grinning as he showed off, hauling the heavy boxes on to the trolley. 'Where next?'

'Toilet rolls by the gross, kitchen towels, cartons of soap –'

'Meat and vegetables?' he asked cheekily.

'No. I've a greengrocer and a butcher who deliver.'

Soon the trolley was piled high and she was glad she didn't have to push it. She preferred to admire Darren's strength and the ease with which he manipulated it round corners.

'Now for the cold room,' she said. 'I need butter, margarine, lard, bacon and sausages.'

'Over here, ma'am,' he said.

'Lead on, Macduff,' she answered gaily.

She liked the way in which he was looking at her trim ankles and small feet in their black court shoes, and she felt glad that she always took care with her appearance. You never knew when an occasion such as this would arise. 'Be prepared' was the only Girl Guide motto she had ever put into practice.

She followed him to the far end and through the door into the freezer section. 'Oh dear,' she exclaimed. 'It's always like the Arctic in here.'

'Has to be, madam. It's one of the rules,' he replied knowledgeably.

He's trying to impress me, she thought, icy fingers of air creeping up her legs and cooling the heat at her crotch. The gusset of her French knickers was already damp, her body responding to his proximity.

They were standing close together and, as she bent over to examine a large tub of butter substitute, she was aware of his hand touching her backside. Excitement darted through her, but she carried on sorting through the freezer's contents without giving any sign that she had noticed his advances.

The air around them seemed to warm, and she felt the exploring hand go lower, drifting down the backs of her thighs to creep under the trench coat. Still she gave no hint of the thrill racing along her nerves. Emboldened by her silence, he stroked her stocking-covered flesh and eased round the suspender attached to her garter-belt. Then, hesitantly, as if expecting her to scream in protest, he worked a finger into the wide leg of her satin knickers and rimmed the fuzz-fringed edge of her pouting lips.

She could feel the wetness of her arousal, and couldn't stop pushing back a little, parting her legs and angling

106

to his fingertip so that it rested on the underside of her clit. The sensation was beautiful.

Reaching back, she pressed the palm of her hand against the front of his linen jacket. Even through this, through the jeans he wore under it, she felt the hardness of his erection.

She heard voices and from the corner of her eye saw a couple push through the plastic curtain that covered the doorway. The trolley partially hid Darren and her, but even so, a frisson of excitement shot through her at the thought of discovery. She rubbed her palm over his cock and it surged. His finger stroked and stroked her stem and brushed over the head of her clit.

'Where can we go?' she whispered urgently.

'Out the back. In the loading bay,' he gasped and, when she disengaged herself from his fingers and looked at him, it was to see a look of utter disbelief and delight on his face.

As nonchalantly as if on the way to the checkout, Darren heaved the trolley out of the cold-room and down an aisle towards an EXIT sign.

'I hope they won't think I'm trying to avoid paying,' she said nervously.

'Don't worry. I'll vouch for you. If we're stopped I'll say you wanted to see the lorries off-loading, just to assure yourself that everything's fresh.'

The double doors swung open as he pushed against them and the air, though warmer than the freezing compartment, was colder than in the warehouse. The loading bay was vast and flooded with the orange glow of arc lights. The noisy roar of articulated lorries echoed under the high roof. Rear doors banged open, men shouted instructions and fork-lift trucks zoomed into place.

Darren seized Vivien's hand and led her behind a deserted ramp, the trolley still acting as a screen. Vivien felt exquisitely small against his height as she tipped up her face to meet his mouth. Sweet young breath invaded

her, a soft tongue performing a dance of desire with
hers. Her nipples tingled with wanting and she took one
of his hands and placed it at the opening of her coat.
Carrying on kissing her, he undid the buttons and
slipped inside, finding the ribbed hem of her fine, wool-
len jumper, before lifting it and homing in on her
breasts.

She reached out and caressed the inside of his demin-
covered thigh, then went higher and tugged at the
zipper. It yielded, and she felt the smooth head of his
cock poking through the slit in his underpants. Her hand
closed round it. He jerked and pumped with his hips.

'Wait,' she cautioned throatily and fumbled in her
pocket. Glancing down between their bodies, she saw
his long penis slanting upwards and started to roll a
condom over it. Darren moaned, hardly able to contain
himself as Vivien eased its tightness down the length of
his quivering cock. He was impatient now.

'No,' she said. 'Pleasure me first, like you were doing
at the freezer.'

'You want a finger-fuck?'

'To start with.'

While she continued to fondle his cock, he thrust a
knee between her knees and opened her. The French
knickers proved no hindrance, and his finger landed
unerringly on her clit. He rubbed it briskly. Vivien came
in sharp spasms. Fumbling and eager, he lifted her, and
she straddled him and locked her legs round his waist.
She gave a stifled yell as his cock slid past the delicate
satin gusset and plunged into her wet heat.

He came at once, sighing and shuddering. He was an
impetuous youth who had not learnt how to wait.

'What's going on?' A heavily built man appeared
suddenly round the corner of the trolley. 'What you up
to, Darren?'

'He's satisfying a customer,' Vivien said promptly,
while Darren stood looking sheepish, his hands over his
still-swollen cock.

'Is that so?' the man said, casting a lecherous glance over her. 'And are you satisfied, madam, or would you like some more?'

'You're Bill Owen?' she said, unabashed. This rule that all the employees displayed their name and position on their badges was more than just customer-friendly.

'I am. Supervisor,' he said, looming over Darren, who seemed to shrink in his presence. 'I reckon I can give you more than this whippersnapper.'

'Do you, Bill?' Vivien asked, taking up a stance, one hip thrust forward, the juices of her recently enjoyed orgasm wetting her pubes.

Bill was fifty if a day, overweight, and far from a picture of health. But Vivien was in the mood for anything. Heated up by the boy, after being filled and brought to climax by him, this new situation had enormous appeal, and the fear of being seen was almost as arousing as Spanish fly.

'Now, how about doing something for me?' Bill said. 'And you can have another go while she's sucking me, Darren. Go on, lad, get behind her. I want to watch you.'

He stood over Vivien as he spoke and, wordlessly, she sank down in front of him. He clawed at his jacket, opened it wide, and pulled open his belt, then thrust down his trousers and white underpants. Releasing his elongated cock, he aimed it at her face. She stretched her neck and let her lips encircle the helm, working up and down the stem with her fingers. His clothes lay in a constricting band around his ankles.

It did occur to her to wonder what the hell she was doing there, her knees on cold concrete, a stranger's prick in her mouth and another's worming its way between her buttocks. Then she gave herself up to the strange pleasure of it.

Eyes closed, concentrating on the feel, taste and smell of Bill's cock, she dipped her head, moving it forward, then back, sliding her lips down the straining column, feeling it stiffen and surge till it touched the membrane of her throat.

It was then that she knew they were being watched. Lifting her head, which made her temporarily lose her grip on Bill's dick, she saw a trucker and a West Indian forklift driver watching with obvious pleasure. Both men had instant appeal; the trucker's hairy arms were canvasses for the most amazing tattoos, and the West Indian was lithe. Walking over, he moved like a dancer, and his dreadlocks cascaded down from under his rasta hat.

'Can anyone join the party?' he asked with a wide smile, in a voice like rich syrup.

Both men were unbuttoned, and caressing their cocks. Vivien noted that the trucker's was smallish but stiff. The agile forklift driver's was coffee-coloured and turgid, and he stood close enough for her to see that the head gleamed with secretions.

Vivien smiled and closed her eyes again. She had died and gone to heaven. She applied herself enthusiastically to sucking Bill off and at the same time, felt Darren approaching his second orgasm among the folds of her silk underwear. Both her hands were occupied, too, each clasped round a warm, hard cock and, when her impromptu lovers came at almost the same moment, she heard a cheer and a round of applause from the interested audience of drivers who had gathered in the bay.

Much later, when she had paid for her goods and driven back to the hotel, leaving Reggie to the unpacking in the kitchen, she drifted up to her room, thinking, 'I'll need to take my coat to the cleaners. It's covered in come. I wonder if Marlene Dietrich ever had this problem.'

Chapter Six

'You're cheerful this morning, Jenny. What's happened? Have you won the Lottery?' Kim asked, sitting in the kitchen with a cup of tea in her hand.

'Better than that,' Jenny answered, glancing at her while unloading the dishwasher.

'Oh?' Kim hoped it wasn't something that would take Jenny away. She relied on her, and was worried about running the house without her. The only time she had been without staff was during term-time at college and it wasn't something she wished to repeat. She had grown up with servants in her father's house and couldn't imagine life without them.

'You'll never guess,' Jenny said, grinning from ear to ear. 'Liam's asked me to marry him.'

'Congratulations,' Kim exclaimed, then added anxiously, 'Does this mean you're going to leave us, or start a family, perhaps?'

'Oh, no. We're happy here. We don't plan to have babies for ages.'

'That's good. I'd be lost without you. So, when's the wedding?'

'Don't know yet,' Jenny replied, busy all the while, scouring the already whiter-than-white Belfast sink.

'Liam has yet to buy me an engagement ring.' She radiated happiness, and it was infectious. Kim almost stopped feeling bad about Jack, and what they'd done last night.

'Well, if you need time off,' Kim said slowly, twisting the platinum ring with its cluster of rubies and diamonds which Oliver had given her and which she always wore above her gold wedding band.

'Solid setting, not claw,' he had told the assistant in the jeweller's shop when they went to choose it. She had been awed by his superb mastery of every situation. When the man had gone to fetch a tray of expensive rings from the safe, Oliver had whispered in her ear, 'With solid setting you can wear it ad infinitum without losing the stones. I want it always on your hand, whatever you're doing, in the bath, on the beach, in the pool, in our bed.'

Kim was brought back to the present by Jenny's voice.

'I might need a day or so off. There's so much to think about.'

'I know. I can remember when I married Oliver. It was hectic.'

'But you must have had a big do,' Jenny put in.

'Oh, we did,' Kim answered, her mind filling up with confused memories of white lace and flowers, a church packed to capacity and her father there to give her away. She had loved, trusted and respected him then. Her mother's terminal illness had brought her parents even closer, or so Kim had imagined. But her mother hadn't lived to see her married.

Depression swept over her. How could he have been so two-faced? Behind the façade of proud father and grieving widower, he had secrets too damaging to his reputation ever to be brought to light.

'We'll have to keep it modest,' Jenny was saying. 'I've three younger sisters and, even though everybody chips in these days, it'll still cost my Dad. Of course, all my relatives will want to come and Liam's lot will be arriving from Ireland.'

Kim realised that she had learnt more about Jenny in the past few moments than during the whole time she had worked for her. Jenny had a life beyond Glen House. It made Kim ashamed to think how much she had taken her for granted.

'Your sisters can be bridesmaids,' she suggested.

'Oh, I don't know if we can run to a white wedding,' Jenny said.

Kim thought how radiant she looked in the grey light of the November morning. Always attractive, now her eyes were shining and her body seemed to bloom, lush and ripe and inviting under the jeans and jumper. She was a woman who had recently had sex with the man she loved and had selected to share her future.

It's true then, Kim thought. As the poets have always said, love lights you from within. Did I look like that after Oliver proposed? She ached to experience that euphoria again. How long does it last, that magical glow? Six months? A year? Until daily contact and familiarity dull it? But I love Oliver. I really do! she told herself.

'And Jack?' murmured the voice in her head, a sneering demon who showed no mercy.

'I don't love Jack. I hate him!' she answered.

'Your pussy doesn't,' it continued, lodged in a crevice of her brain.

'Are you all right, Mrs Buckley?' It was Jenny, not the demon speaking. Her face swam out of the darkness that misted Kim's sight.

'Yes, I'm fine. I was just thinking,' she said, pasting on a bright smile. 'You simply must have all the trimmings. Bridal white for you and morning suits for the men. How about having the reception here, in the Spring? We could put up a marquee on the lawn and get in musicians. A ceilidh band in Liam's honour, or a disco with a DJ, or whatever you wanted. It would be your day.'

'I'd love that, but I'll have to talk it over with him,'

Jenny answered eagerly, already sold on the idea. 'Maybe Barry would help with the food.'

'Nonsense. We'll hire caterers.' Anything to divert my mind from Jack, Kim thought frantically. Maybe he'll be gone by then, but no, the work won't be completed for ages. And he's buying a house. Then suddenly she remembered. The church; oh, God, I've promised to meet him there!

'Yes, it's all down to sex,' whispered the demon. 'You can't wait to have him thrusting into your snatch. Or up the arse, perhaps? You're still a virgin there.'

'But I doubt we could afford – ' Jenny went on.

'Don't worry about that,' Kim insisted. 'It'll be our wedding present. Oliver adores organising events. Please think about it, and give Liam my congratulations.'

'I will, and we'll get this sorted right away. Thanks again.' Jenny whisked away in search of him.

It wasn't yet eight o' clock, but Oliver had already left, dropping a kiss on Kim's head in passing and saying he'd be late home. He had to fly to Glasgow to see a prospective client.

She had mumbled something in protest as he swung out of the door, briefcase in hand. But it was useless. He had gone and she was left alone to face the day and Jack. In half an hour she must head for Palmer's Emporium. She had promised to help out and, apart from this, needed to talk to her level-headed friend.

'But I can't tell her,' she said, talking aloud. 'I can't say "I've done it, I've fucked another man." Not only that, he's a blood relative.'

Not that Elaine would be shocked. She was the most liberal-minded of people. But Kim knew she'd consider this an unwise move, to say the least. Adultery needed thinking through. If found out, Kim had so much to lose, and the scandal would be even greater if it came to light that she'd been doing it with her half-brother. And if we were unlucky enough to have a baby it might be born with two heads! Before allowing herself to become too panicky, she remembered she was on the pill.

She knew all the arguments, had gone over them a hundred times and didn't particularly relish hearing Elaine reiterating them. She wondered if she could ring in and plead a migraine, then decided not to. Jack was encouraging her to tell enough lies as it was.

She took the BMW, unable to stand the idea of being stranded in the city and having to use public transport after taking part in whatever weird scenario Jack had planned for them. It had been bad enough having to find her own way to the Byron's car park the night before, thoroughly disorientated as she was by the uncontrolled lust on the stairs.

She couldn't remember the drive home, and reached Glen House in a trance. Thankfully Oliver had not yet returned, and she'd never been more glad of anything. Had he opened the door for her, she'd have fallen at his feet, confessing everything and begging his forgiveness. Meeting no one in the hall, she had run upstairs, torn off her sex-tainted clothes and drawn a deep, hot and heavily perfumed bath. She hadn't been asleep when Oliver came in, though she pretended she was. He'd had a monumental hard-on, and a layer of ice had closed round her heart as she wondered if it had anything to do with Flyte. This unpleasant thought made it easier to feign sleep, and even went some way to justify what she had done with Jack.

Nothing justifies it, she thought miserably, as the wipers tick-tocked like metronomes. Damn the traffic! It ground to a halt and she shifted uncomfortably in the driver's seat, her tight, crushed-velvet pants cutting into her cleft. It was unbearably stuffy and she turned down the heater, then eased her arms out of her chenille jacket. Her breasts were unusually tender, the nipples chafed by her fine wool sweater. She slipped a tape into the deck, not caring which one. A soul singer intoned the sadness of lost love.

115

Oliver? Could she bear it if they parted? My heart would break, she thought. I'll tell Jack this afternoon, and say we must never meet again alone. What happened last night was a mistake, an aberration, complete madness.

She tried to ignore the slippery wetness at her crotch. It pulsed in time to the heavy thud of her heart as her imagination conjured up Jack's lean face and those fiercely hungry blue eyes. Casting a quick glance at the cars hemming her in, she slipped a hand between her legs. No one could see. The windows were too steamy and rain-washed. She opened her thighs and massaged her humid crotch.

Immediately, she was somersaulted back in time. The boat-house, and Jack's finger, not her own, applying that delicious pressure. Oliver had nearly caught them at it. Now, as then, she went hot and cold.

A car horn blared. Guiltily she removed her hand. Fumbling for the gears, she followed the slow-moving crocodile into town.

'Traffic bad this morning?' Elaine asked as Kim walked in and the brass doorbell clanged.

'Diabolical. There'd been an accident,' Kim said, dumping her shoulder bag on the couch. 'Any chance of a coffee?'

'Sarah, be a sweetie and brew some, will you?' Elaine carolled to her girlfriend, the waif-like woman with cropped hair and heavy eye make-up. Sarah uncoiled her spidery limbs and slid from the top of the counter.

She bared her teeth in a smile, and Kim caught a glimpse of the little bolt that passed through the end of her tongue. It never failed to make her shudder. The nose stud she could tolerate, the triple eyebrow piercing and rows of gold rings stuck in Sarah's lobes and along the outside rim of her ears were acceptable, but the bolt in her tongue was not. Did it turn Elaine on? she mused. When Sarah went down on her, did the metal rubbing against Elaine's clitoris bring her to a raging climax?

116

Kim found it hard to visualise. Lesbianism was an unknown territory to her.

'Jenny's getting married. She told me this morning,' Kim said. She was desperate to strike up a normal conversation.

'Who's the lucky man?' Elaine was studying her day-planner, hardly glancing at Sarah as she set down a steaming mug within easy reach.

'Liam,' Kim answered. 'They'll be staying on with us, apparently. They have no plans to move. I've offered to help her with the arrangements.'

'When is it?'

'Oh, not yet. Maybe in the Spring.'

'Then what are you doing for Christmas? Going away?'

'No. Oliver likes a traditional Christmas at home. Why?'

'Well, Sarah and I thought of going to India for a month. Goa, to be exact. We wouldn't leave till Christmas Eve, and the shop will be closed until the first week in January. Trade will be quiet then, though I'll have a few sale items on offer. Could you cope? I'd get someone else in to help you, of course.'

'All right,' Kim answered and could have kicked herself. Why can't I ever say no? I'm a bloody people-pleaser! she fumed, while adding, 'If it's OK with Oliver, that is.'

Elaine swept her into a perfumed embrace, exclaiming, 'Thank you, darling. I'll book the flight right away. I really need a break. Mrs Wilson's driving me nuts, to name but one awkward customer.'

Crushed against those pert, tip-tilted breasts, Kim found herself burning with curiosity. How would it be to lie in bed with Elaine, stark naked between her and Sarah, among silken, hairless limbs, soft breasts and taut nipples, with women's musk rising from between open thighs? As if picking up on her thoughts, Elaine held her off a little, looking at her with her shrewd, dark eyes.

117

'It's a pity you can't come with us,' she said. 'We could show you so much. Not only India, though it's an extraordinary country. Perhaps we could teach you about sex shared by women. One thing's for sure. I guarantee you'd never be satisfied with a man again.'

'I don't think so,' Kim replied stiffly, stepping back, annoyed because her cheeks were flaming, and that hot feeling was echoed in her loins. 'I like making love with men.'

'Have you ever tried the alternative?' Sarah chipped in, her gamin face alive with curiosity.

'No,' Kim said. 'You know, don't you Elaine? I'm boringly heterosexual.'

'The love between two women can be very deep, very intense, very sensual,' Elaine continued, and her hand came to rest on Sarah's tiny bottom which was barely covered by a tartan mini-skirt. 'It's so close. You'll never experience such passion, such desire, such oneness with a man.'

'Thanks, but no,' Kim stammered, trying to lighten the atmosphere. 'I like things as they are.'

'Do you?' Elaine subjected her to a searching stare. 'I sense there's something wrong. You're looking peaky.'

'I'm starting a cold. That's all,' Kim lied.

'Maybe you'd better go home and rest,' Sarah said, pulling a face. 'Can't have you spreading germs.'

'I was going to tell you that I can't stay this afternoon. There's something I have to do,' Kim said quickly.

'You're meeting Oliver?'

'No, as a matter of fact, I'm looking over a property with my brother.' Kim was astounded at the ease with which she said it.

To her relief, Elaine didn't cross-question her, simply saying, 'Right. I expect we can manage. Actually, I've given myself a day off from that monstrosity of a house in Surrey. It's looking much more respectable, but the wear and tear on the nerves! I'll enjoy a quiet time here with Sarah. We might even put up the CLOSED sign, and spend the afternoon in bed.'

And she folded Sarah in her arms, the younger girl snuggling up against her. Kim turned away, busying herself about the showroom, embarrassed and aroused to see them kissing.

This will suit me down to the ground, Jack thought, letting himself into the vestry through an outside door. He entered the main body of the church. It seemed to spring to life around him, the sound of his footsteps echoing through the interior.

'I can just see it,' he said aloud. 'The vestry will become a kitchen and I'll add a cloakroom, and turn the nave into a superb living-room. Terrific acoustics for stereo. Maybe I'll build a baronial hearth and put in mock logs and a gas-fire, with an antique basket. Don't want to spoil the outside line by adding a chimney.

'The chancel will be partitioned off and have sliding glass doors. Plenty of space for my drawing boards and computer,' he went on, his creative imagination working overtime. 'I'll make half of it into an office, then poach Lara from Oliver. She'd be a willing secretary, and I could give her one whenever I felt like it. That monstrosity of a staircase built by some cack-handed dork will have to go. I want something more impressive to link the lower storey to the upper. I'll construct a master bedroom with its own bathroom, and at least three smaller ones, and another shower, and still keep the exposed space that goes way up to the roof. A minstrels' gallery would look good there.'

He jingled the impressive bunch of large iron keys; he had talked the estate agent into letting him come alone. The rain had stopped, and watery sunshine, penetrating the arched, narrow, thirty-foot high windows, threw coloured patterns on the chevron floor tiles.

The stained glass was dazzling, filled with finely detailed pictures of angels and the apostles and certain saints, executed in the style of the Pre-Raphaelites. Jack stared up at one depicting the armour-clad martyr after whom the church had been named. The altar had stood before it until it was dismantled by the church authorities when the building was deconsecrated.

If I believed in such things, I'd put up one of my own, and dedicate it to Beelzebub, thought Jack. This would be a ideal venue for a Black Mass, he added, with wry humour. Maybe I will later, but just for now I'll buy a refectory table and this can be a dining area. I could use a couple of those pews for seating. Bloody lovely, they are! Get a load of that carving. This gets better and better!

His trained eye noted the fine, fluted columns, their capitals decorated with pagan symbols, and grotesques with leaves sprouting from their mouths, as well as the Green Man who had been adopted by the early Christians. The roof towered above, spanned by arches. The whole smacked of an age when this had been well-patronised, and the focal point of a wealthy parish. There was even a full-sized organ behind the choir-stall, with marvellously elaborate pipes and an exquisitely fashioned frame.

'I'll have it restored and learn to play,' Jack promised himself gleefully. 'It'll be like *The Phantom of the Opera*.' He flung out his arms in an expansive gesture, shouting, 'And now it's very nearly mine!'

And the echoes repeated, 'Mine, mine!'

The crypt proved to be everything he desired; dark, dank and dismal. He could see by the litter strewn around that it had recently sheltered vagrants. There were crumpled fish-and-chip papers, cigarette stubs, squashed beer cans, and a disgustingly filthy sleeping-bag. Judging by the smell that hit him as he reached the bottom of the steps, it had also been used as a urinal.

Jack shone his torch around, and the single beam landed on the rusted wrought-iron railings that had once guarded the resting places of the crypt's dead. The stone plinths and ledges for coffins were now empty.

He smiled. This was superb. It would provide valuable storage space, but he also had other uses in mind.

Back in the nave, he opened the half-door of the pulpit. With its canopy of dark oak, it was surmounted by a gilded eagle with unfurled wings. He took the steps two at a time, hands skimming over the seasoned wood once lovingly polished by a verger or the devoted ladies of the church committee. His imagination soared. Now he occupied the podium from which generations of vicars had looked down on their captive audience, a Bible opened on the lectern with its tarnished, brass rail.

'Brethren, we are gathered together to fight the battle against sin, lechery, wickedness and fornication. Praise be the Lord!' he declaimed in the tones of a hell-fire preacher.

'Jack! What are you doing?'

A solitary face swam out of the dimness below from among the rows and rows of empty pews.

'Kim. You're early. Were you so hot for me you couldn't wait?' he said from his exalted position. 'Don't you think I suit this? I might take it up, wielding power over the superstitious masses. I'd cut a dash in vestments. The women would sit there creaming their knickers.'

'You shouldn't mock such things,' Kim said reprovingly, glancing into the gloom nervously, seeking relief from the wood and stone and darkness, but there was none.

On arrival, she had realised she was early. She'd left the car at the back of the deserted square where weeds and couch grass sprang up between the cobbles. It had been like stepping back in time.

On reaching the gate leading into the churchyard, fear had almost stopped her from lifting the latch. The flagstoned path winding between the graves was cracked and pitted, and when she looked up at St Edwin's she saw how its walls were eroded, and crumbling in some parts. Wild plants sprouted from the guttering, and it wore an air of extreme melancholy.

Standing in the porch at the main door, she had listened carefully. She thought she could hear someone inside. Screwing up her fading courage, she had walked round to the back. The vestry door was unlocked. There was a smell of damp, and she had bowed her head before venturing into the church itself.

Walking up the aisle between the pews, her eyes fixed on the figure in the pulpit, she had experienced terror mixed with excitement. On an everyday level, she knew it was Jack, but in that other, nightmarish world of the imagination she thought it was the ghost of some long-dead parson.

She had been there before with Oliver and the agent, but it was different this afternoon. For one thing, her former visit had taken place in the middle of an August heatwave. Now it was winter and icy cold. She could feel the chill penetrating her suede boots and climbing her legs inside the velvet trousers. The shadows in the church deepened as the sun's weak rays came and went.

Jack was suddenly down from the pulpit and next to her, his hands on her arms. The chenille jacket formed no barrier against their heat; she might as well have been naked. He pressed her into his side and took her on a guided tour, explaining his plans as they went up the rickety stairs to the half-completed platform above.

It was perilous. There were gaps between the floorboards.

'Whoever did this should be shot!' Jack said angrily. 'I can't stand shoddy workmanship.'

'When will it be finished?' she asked, and she couldn't stop shivering, as if the cold had entered her blood, guts and spirit.

'Three months. I'll not let the builders hang about. I'll move in before that, just as soon as the central heating is connected and there's a crapper and somewhere to put a bed.'

'And a kitchen,' she said.

He shrugged. 'That's not important. I can eat out.'

He took her hand and wouldn't let go as he propelled her downstairs again, and from there to a doorway near the vestry.

'Where are you taking me?' she cried, suddenly scared.

'To the crypt,' he said, and the door opened with a loud creak like a pistol shot.

'No. Jack, please. I don't like creepy places. There may be spiders.'

'It's OK. I've already had a look. No moulding corpses or bones or skulls. Disappointing really.'

'All right, I'll take your word for it. Aren't you afraid of anything?'

'Not a lot. Come on.'

'I'd rather not,' she said, and she tugged at her hand ineffectually.

'But you must,' he said, his mouth set in a hard line. 'I told you last night, I'd never give you a choice again.'

More steps came under her reluctant feet. Jack obviously liked steps and dark recesses; she added this to the few things she knew about him. The air in the crypt was sour. The torch flickered on walls shiny with damp, on rubbish-filled corners, on a heap of charred wood under a sooty patch on the ceiling where someone had tried to get a fire going.

Jack led her through the wreckage to an open space in front of spear-headed spikes surrounding further darkness. A lop-sided gate hung on worn hinges. He took his lighter to half a dozen candle stubs stuck on the stone or jammed into bottles.

'Has someone lived here recently? How awful!' she said, the horror growing and taking hold of her.

'I guess they were drop-outs and scum,' he answered callously. 'They always leave a trail of filth behind them.'

'But that's dreadful. I thought there were schemes for the homeless.'

'There are, but not everyone wants to use them. You haven't a clue how the other half live, have you, Kim? You're so sheltered from the wicked world.' He backed her against the railings and hissed, 'Take off your clothes.'

'You can't be serious? I'll get pneumonia,' she said desperately. 'Anyhow, I came here to talk. We've just got to thrash this out. It's over, Jack. We must never, never repeat what happened last night.'

'Oh? Who says?'

'I say. It's wrong. That's what I came to tell you. I love Oliver. I was happy till you came along.'

'Bullshit! You were playing house, that's all,' Jack said, lugging her close to him, making her aware of the solid length of his cock pressed into her belly. 'This is what you really want. Me.'

'It's ridiculous. I don't want you.'

'Liar.' His voice grated, and his hand shot down to clasp her between the legs, lifting her, the pressure on her mound an unbearable mix of need and revulsion.

'Jack, put me down. Stop, please,' she moaned, all her good intentions melting under the passion he inspired. 'We can't. It's illegal. We'd go to prison if we were found out.'

'That's a narrow-minded view. This isn't the first time siblings have fucked one another. It's been going on forever,' he murmured, his mouth close to hers, his breath warming her icy lips. 'There've been some notorious ones. What about Cesare Borgia and Lucretia? They were the Pope's bastards. And the only woman Lord Byron ever really loved was his half-sister, Augusta. She gave birth to his daughter.'

'I'm only concerned about us. Those people are dead, dusty stories from history, but we're still alive. I know it's wrong.'

'I don't. But as you're obviously feeling so guilty, would it ease your conscience if you were punished?'

She was shocked by the amusement on his lips and the strange look that had taken over in his eyes. It was as if he mocked her very soul, daring her to rebel against all her certainties. She was an open book to him, whereas to her, he was still a stranger.

She could smell him. As on the hotel stairs, he wiped out the stench of dirt with his vital, earthy aroma. And all the desire she had been holding at bay as she tried to erase him from her thoughts came rushing back to invade her.

'Are you suggesting I do penance?' she said, hoping he wasn't serious, but then he unbuckled his belt and drew it through the loops at his waist. The narrow leather strip was like a black snake in his hand. Her skin prickled.

'What would make you feel better? A chastised bum?'

'No. Let me go. I've seen the church, and it's ideal for you. I really must get on. I'm meeting Oliver.'

'You're a lousy liar, Kim, and you're not going anywhere. I'm tired of your disobedience. Undress.'

He didn't touch her, but she was more conscious of him than if their bodies had been locked together. With her fingers on the buttons of her classy, knitted coat, she stared at him, thinking about the resolutions she had made over the past few hours, and finding none of them coming to her aid. One at a time, the buttons slipped through their holes, and she had to accept the abysmal truth that he had robbed her of her will.

She quaked with cold as the jacket came off. Even in her excitement, she remembered it was new and that she didn't want to drop it on the dirty floor. Jack stood with his legs apart, the belt taut between his hands, watching her as a tiger might watch its prey. She jumped when he moved, but it was only to take the coat from her and lay it over the shoulders of a stone angel with broken wings.

'The rest,' he said.

Heat flushed up from her groin to her face. With shaking fingers she gripped the bottom of her figure-hugging jersey and pulled it off over her head. She gasped as the cold bit her skin. Her nipples were iron-hard peaks.

'That, too,' Jack ordered, pointing at her lacy bra.

Kim stretched her arms round to unhook it. The cups remained in place for a moment, shielding her from his predatory gaze. He nodded imperiously, and she slid the straps over her shoulders, glaring at him defiantly as he held out his hand for both jumper and bra. Just for an instant, he put them to his face, and inhaled her perfume. Then they joined the jacket on the sorrowful angel.

I'm glad I wore trousers, she thought, then realised they wouldn't help. It would be awkward to remove them with any kind of grace. Why am I bothering about that? she wondered hysterically. He's going to do whatever he likes with me anyway.

She found an upended block of masonry, and sat on it, aware of its rough surface chilling her bottom. She worked her feet out of her boots. Knee-high socks came next, and her toes cringed at contact with the slimy floor.

'It's no use fighting me, Kim,' he said, staring at her intently. 'There's a bond between us that's impossible to break. You thought I was dangerous and had begun to doubt your own sanity. You came here determined to end our intimacy. But you can't do it. Look at you, about to take down your pants and expose your pussy in a squalid hole like this. It's a doss-house for druggies and winos. Can you smell the excrement? Did you ever, in your wackiest dreams, imagine that you'd be in such a place, about to offer yourself to someone like me?' He cracked the belt like a whip and brought it down across her thighs. 'Take them off,' he growled.

Petrified, her skin smarting, Kim got out of her trousers. The tip of the leather glided along her belly, just above her feathery mound. Without waiting for

126

more, she wriggled her panties down. He extended a hand and she gave him the warm silky triangle. It was stained with her juices. Her body seemed like a wanton thing that refused to behave.

He was close to her, and there was just his breathing and hers, and the rustle of clothes as he moved in to kiss her neck.

'Oh, Jack, Jack,' she whimpered. 'Don't make me do this. Why do you want to humiliate me?'

'I'm doing you a favour, bringing you to life,' he murmured, his voice vibrating down her spine.

The sweetness of desire rose in her as he caressed her skin gently, moving over her back, tracing the muscles and the curves, dipping down into the crease dividing her buttocks. Her legs parted of their own volition as a single finger found her anus and then her vulva. She relaxed against it, wanting more, but then she jerked as he pressed the belt to her labia, working it edgewise into her swollen folds. They parted, slick-wet, as he dragged the leather upwards until it rubbed over her clitoris.

'Oh, yes,' she sighed, unable to stop rolling her hips as the pleasure increased. A little more of the slippery feel of it over her bud, and she would come. She was caught up in the rhythm of it, reaching that precious plateau from which there was only one return, when he took the belt away. She gasped in disappointment, her bare feet numb with cold. The flickering candles threw his huge, menacing shadow on the wall. He smiled tauntingly as he prowled round her, touching her nipples with the belt's end, then trailing it down to her cleft, never lingering long enough to do anything except rouse her to frenzy.

Now the touch became more purposeful. He drew back, raised his arm, and let the belt fall with measured force across her breasts, belly and thighs. Her pussy spasmed. Her clit tingled. Pleasure became pain as the strap kissed her skin with a sting that left a mark.

'Don't! If you bruise me, Oliver will see!' She suddenly

sobbed, tears running down her face and dripping off her chin.

'Oh, dear, we can't have that, can we?' Jack sneered. 'Mustn't let holier-than-thou Oliver guess that his wife's a dirty little slut. Don't worry, Kim. I know exactly how far to go.'

'You're experienced, I suppose,' she snarled, raging to think of him treating other women to these cruel, exciting, intimate attentions.

'You could say that.' He was giving nothing away and it drove her crazy. 'You've had enough? You want me to stop?'

'Yes, yes –' she began, but her words lacked conviction.

He was behind her. 'Move,' he said.

'What? Where?'

She couldn't think coherently. The pink stripes were smarting, their heat throbbing in her sex. She missed it now he'd stopped belting her, and was aghast at such a reaction. No one had ever hit her before. Her lovers had never expressed the need for anything out of the ordinary. Oliver might dominate her with his intellect, but never physically. This was an entirely new dimension.

'Over there,' Jack said, and prodded her in the back.

Straight ahead were intricately fashioned iron bars, standing like tall, spiked guardians of the intense gloom beyond. Kim took two paces and stopped, but Jack pushed her closer till her cringing flesh was pressed into the unyielding metal. His hands were between her legs, spreading them wide, and she couldn't stop raising her bottom towards him, begging for his cock. He ignored this, roping her ankles.

Then he seized her wrists and pulled them above her head, binding the belt round them and looping it tightly to the bars. Her scrabbling fingers encountered the cold, rust-corroded iron. Her nipples rubbed across them. She moved her hips ever so slightly, and a carved lily touched her clit, making it ache. She ground her pubis harder against it, moaning at the intensity of the sensation.

It was harsh. It was horrible. It was erotically exciting.

Jack's hand was on the back of her neck under her hair, forcing her face against the bar. 'I'll bet the undertakers never saw anything like this when they laid the bodies to rest inside there,' he whispered. 'You, with bare tits and pussy, fucking an inanimate fence. Go on. Rub harder. Bring yourself off.'

'You're twisted. Mad, perverted sod! Untie me! Let me go!' she yelled, her voice sounding muffled in the close confines of the underground chamber.

'Tut, tut! That's no way to speak to your brother,' he scolded, gently but with a threatening undertone. 'If you don't shut up, I'll have to gag you.'

When he pinched her tender bottom flesh, she cried out again as pain shot through her. He was feeling her, his fingers toying with her inner lips. Oh, he did it so well. Rubbing along the slippery sides, tracing the stalk of her clit to where it was rooted deep inside her, then circling the head, teasing it.

She sobbed aloud, beside herself with wanting, and his finger rotated on the fat, little button. 'Ah,' she sighed, starting to ride the wave, sure she was about to come.

But suddenly he vanished. She couldn't catch any sound, movement or smell of him. Supposing he had decided to leave her there? No one would hear her if she screamed. No one would rescue her from this hellish place.

'Oliver,' she whispered, and his face and the loving concern in his amber eyes filled her mind. 'Oh, God. Oliver! Find me. Save me.'

There was no way of knowing how long she had been hanging there – it could have been minutes or an hour – and there was still no indication that Jack was anywhere around. Her cramped arm muscles seemed to shriek in protest. The rope ate into her ankles. Yet her arousal was building, second by second, and she moved her hips, stimulating herself on the metal flower, wondering if she could climax that way. It was warm now, and slippery with her juices. The cold and fear was of little consequence against the enormous well of lust that yawned within her.

Where was Jack? She wanted him inside her, filling her up. She was prepared to agree to any bargain, to sell her soul to him, to do whatever he chose, just to have the bounty of his cock lodged in her depths. Holding the rails tightly, she moved her hips again in a voluptuous movement and gave herself up to pleasure, working the lily against her pulsing spot. Her energies had become one-pointed, her thoughts fixed on her impending orgasm.

A movement behind her made her stiffen. Then, without warning, a biting pain stung her. Smack! The hand hit her full force on her rump, the white-heat of it roaring along her nerves. Her body bucked in anguish.

Before she had time to recover, he slapped her again, his hand cracking down on the crown of her bottom, making her buttocks shake. She thrashed and yelped, trying to escape the pain, but he went on smacking her for what seemed an eternity. A part of her welcomed the punishment. Jack was assuming the mantel of avenging angel. She wept against the metal railings as he lowered his aim and belaboured the backs of her thighs. A hot, carnal glow suffused her body and spread to her womb, while her clitoris itched and pulsed greedily.

Her awareness converged on all the sensations, on thighs that trembled, on a rump that clenched in anticipation of another blow, on an exposed delta that convulsed hungrily. The nature of her feelings underwent a subtle change. Nothing mattered any more except that they should go on indulging in this strange union. When the chastisement ended, as suddenly as it had begun, she felt utterly bereft.

Jack's slaps became lighter. Each one was a tiny smart that swiftly spread outwards in waves of pleasure. He slipped his hand under her and his probing fingers found her sex. She writhed on them as he plunged inside and moved them rhythmically up and down. His thumb pounded hard on her bud. She screamed. The floodgates opened and she dissolved in a tidal wave of ecstasy.

He let her spasm on his fingers, then slowly withdrew. He untied her, and massaged the life back into her arms and feet. His big hands stroked her punished buttocks then he pressed his erection into her from behind, driving in hard. He was so close that it took no more than a dozen strokes before he reached his release. She felt his heartbeat slowing against her back, and unwonted tenderness swept through her.

It was then, as she was coming down from the heights, feeling as if her body would never be the same or even belong to her again, that she became aware of a grating noise coming from the darkness on the other side of the railings.

'Jack,' she said urgently. 'There's something there.'

Filled with terror, she was sure it was an apparition, visualising a gibbering death's head grinning at her. It was even worse. There were real faces in front of her, staring through the bars.

As her eyes widened, she saw them more clearly; figures in threadbare coats and ragged scarves, an odd assortment of hats rammed down on their heads. Their smell, the acrid odour of dirt and sweat and unwashed flesh, infiltrated her nsotrils. Were they men or women? It was hard to tell. They stretched their arms towards her, and the candlelight gleamed on saliva-smeared lips in incredibly dirty faces.

They were leering at her and gibbering. Several of the men had their cocks exposed, rubbing them vigorously. One of the women whipped up her tattered skirt and stuck her bare bottom out, wagging it lewdly as she worked her hand into her hairy cleft. An acne-blotched young man, flaunting greasy rat-tails, was also offering his arse to anyone who might be interested.

131

Those at the forefront surged closer and Kim felt them fingering her between the bars, hands on her breasts, tugging at her nipples, nails clawing at her mound, dipping between her legs. She shot back against Jack with a shriek. He chuckled, while the crowd snarled and muttered and drew in on themselves, afraid of him.

Jack moved forward. 'Get out of here or I'll call the police.' he shouted. 'The party's over, folks, and you're trespassing. The church belongs to me.'

They slipped away like muddy water, disappearing from sight, and Kim struggled into her clothes. She was feeling nauseous, her hands trembling with cold. 'You knew they were there,' she said accusingly.

Jack lit a cigarette, his black clothing melding into the surrounding darkness, his face a pale wedge, eyes glittering. 'Not at first,' he said calmly. 'There must be an underground passage connecting with the outside. I'll have it secured with a strong door.'

'Why didn't you stop? How could you screw me with those horrible creatures looking at us?'

'I was too far along the line to care. It added a certain piquancy to the situation,' he answered with an unrepentant grin.

'You're not normal,' she shouted, angrily gathering up her belongings. 'There's something sick about you.'

'And you love it,' he countered, and slung his combat jacket over one shoulder.

'I don't. This is the last time, Jack. I swear it.'

'Don't look so dejected, sister,' he murmured, and blew out the candles. He shone the torch so that she could find her way up the stairs.

'I mean it,' she warned as they reached the top and stood in the rapidly darkening nave. 'Don't phone me again.'

'I shan't,' he answered, smiling down at her with that arrogance she found so infuriating. 'You'll be calling me.'

132

Chapter Seven

'*I*'ve got to stay here overnight, Kim. The deal's almost in the bag, but we've a few more ends to tidy up, and by the time we're through it'll be too late to leave. I'll be with you lunchtime tomorrow. Maybe we can spend the afternoon together. Sorry about this.'

Oliver's voice sounded tinny as Kim listened to the recorded phone message. Her first reaction was one of relief. She was glad he wouldn't be there until the next day, convinced she bore the imprint of Jack's hand on her flesh. The second reaction was one of distress. Never before had she been anything but disappointed if Oliver was delayed. Now guilt had made a traitor of her.

The lounge was comfortable, tastefully lit by wall-lights, and the table lamp – a slender woman holding an opalescent globe – was a sign of gracious living. It was comfort indeed.

Just for a moment, Kim was back in the crypt. Had she become one of those lost things who had nowhere else to sleep but in squalid hell-holes? With a start, she held her hands out in front of her, but they were pale and clean, the oval nails lacquered a deep peach. She didn't smell of dirt and disease, only of Jack's come, and her own juices. This was bad enough. She stood up and began to pace the carpet restlessly.

Should she ring Oliver? He would be expecting it. Normally, there'd be no question about her wanting to share the events of the day with him. But not tonight.

The evening yawned ahead. What should she do? Usually, she would have enjoyed her own company. She had the latest Discworld novel to read. There was one of her favourite soaps on the box, and the première of a film. But none of these appealed. It was that dead hour of six o'clock; too early for dinner, too late for tea.

Jenny popped her head round the door. 'I thought I heard you come in. I've had a word with Liam and he thinks a wedding here would be great. Thanks so much, Mrs Buckley.'

'That's settled, then. Something to look forward to. I haven't told Oliver yet. He's away tonight, but I'll phone him later. I'm sure he'll be as chuffed as I am.'

'If you're quite sure it'll be all right?' Jenny said uncertainly.

'Of course it will. Don't worry any more and don't bother about dinner. I'll have a snack in the conservatory.'

Damn all men! Kim thought gloomily, going up to her room, pulling off her clothes and pivoting round to examine her bottom in the mirror. It was most definitely red. What can I tell Oliver if it hasn't faded by tomorrow? She panicked. Yet heat crept through her body as her lustful pussy begged for caressing fingers. She remembered everything that had taken place in the crypt. She wanted to grip Jack's erection, sucking it inside her until he shot his seed.

What's happening to me? she thought, alarmed. I'm turning into some sort of sex-mad nympho! Her heart leapt into her mouth when the phone bleeped. Was it Jack?

'Hello,' she said, a crushing snub forming on the tip of her tongue.

'It's me. Polly.'

It was her neighbour, not Jack with his smooth voice that turned her to jelly. Awash with relief and disappointment she dragged on a dressing-gown and sat on the bed, but even this slight pressure from the mattress tantalised her lips.

'Hi, there,' she said encouragingly. Polly liked to talk, and the call might take some time.

'I was wondering if you and Oliver would care to pop round for drinks this evening. I've got rid of the kids. Mummy offered to have them for a couple of days, so I thought we'd invite a few people in.'

'Oliver isn't here. He's in Scotland on business.'

'Oh, well, you could come, couldn't you? It would stop you being lonely. I've asked Sandra to drop by and she suggested that I give Jack a call.'

'Jack?' For a second, Kim couldn't take this in.

'Your brother,' Polly continued cheerfully. 'Sandra's got quite a thing about him, and I thought: why not? He seemed awfully nice that one time I met him. Have you seen him lately?'

'This afternoon,' Kim answered grimly. Damn Polly and her well-meaning meddling.

'I rang him half an hour ago and he said he'd love to come. So that's fine, isn't it? Can we expect you?'

Too right you bloody can, if he's going to be there, leching over Sandra, Kim snarled inwardly. He's accepted on purpose just to annoy me.

To Polly, she said coolly, 'Thank you. Yes. What time?'

'Shall we say eight?'

Kim stamped down to the conservatory before she got changed. Completely off her food, she pushed the salad about on her plate, drank a glass of orange juice and stormed back upstairs again.

What to wear? There was no need to go over the top. Polly and Keith never stood on ceremony, but then there was Sandra. Kim didn't intend to be eclipsed by that

135

vapid bimbo; then again, she wouldn't attempt to ape her style of upper-class tart.

Common sense told her it would be far wiser to ring back and cancel, but she could no more do this than stop breathing. Jack and Sandra. Obscene images of the two of them together played in her brain, then rewound and played again.

I must get used to this, she told herself as she showered, then rummaged through the tallboy in search of lingerie. I'm bound to see him with girlfriends. It'll do me good. Make me get things into perspective. We have no future, Jack and I. We're not going anywhere.

But even as she gave herself a good talking to, her fingers were leafing through her wardrobe, searching for something – anything – that would stun him and make him see her, and her alone. Not an obviously vampish outfit, no basque. How about pure, white underwear and an extremely expensive, very modest dress?

She found just the thing. It looked simple but was cunningly cut, made of fine tobacco-brown wool, with a skirt that flowed over her hips and swirled out at the ankles. The waist was belted, and the tight bodice buttoned to where her breasts formed a deep vee. The sleeves were wrist-length, and the whole thing was redolent of class.

It was a fabulous dress, and one of Oliver's favourites. 'You look like a school-marm in it,' he had said. 'A very genteel, proper lady, but with hidden depths. There's nothing obvious about it, but damn, it's sexy!'

She put on her garter belt and slipped into the panties, watching herself in the mirror, seeing how her dark bush plumped up the fragile silk, and feathery fronds escaped each side of the crotch. It was impossible not to touch that inviting triangle and trail a finger into the shadow of the deep cleft. Her nipples crimped as she settled her breasts in the bra cups.

She, who not long ago had considered herself to be in control of her urges, now found every inch of her skin had its own particular itch, and had become extremely sensitive to the slightest friction, sending urgent messages to her clit.

'Get a grip!' she said firmly, and turned her taupe stockings inside out, then pulled them on and up her legs. After checking that the back suspenders were correctly positioned for straight seams, she slipped on a pair of medium-heeled shoes.

Once the dress was on, buttoned and belted with the utmost propriety, and that lascivious body concealed, she felt more in command. Make-up was essential as a mask with which she might cover her true identity. Oliver disapproved of all but the lightest of cosmetics, but Oliver wasn't there.

Sitting on a stool in front of the dressing-table mirror, she applied tinted foundation and a dusting of powder. Silver-grey shadow and black mascara emphasised the colour of her eyes. A dark pencil enhanced the curve of her brows. Rouge disguised her pallor and scarlet lipstick turned her mouth full and sulky.

Lifting a swathe of her heavy hair, she twisted it up and into a cascade of curls at her crown, keeping it anchored with grips and tortoiseshell combs, then finally, teasing out little tendrils at nape and cheeks.

Jesus Christ, I look almost grown-up! she decided, and didn't know whether to be pleased or sorry. Well into her twenties, she was still naive. It was high time she acted her age. Life's so complicated, she sighed. She did a twirl, checked that her seams were still straight, and touched herself between the legs. She was moist again. It seemed she was in an almost permanent state of arousal these days. If I were a man, I'd be walking around with an erection. However do they manage? she wondered.

It wasn't far to Polly's house, though the gardens of both establishments were spacious, both stretching down to the river bank. Kim threw on a chiripà, its Peruvian swirls in subdued greens and rusts complementing her dress, then headed for the garage and her car. She would have walked had Oliver been with her, but the way was dark and she wasn't feeling in the least brave.

On her arrival, Polly hugged her and kissed her on both cheeks. The large hallway was chaotic, with evidence of children everywhere.

'I just can't keep anything tidy, and the au pair's worse than useless in that department. It's my artistic streak, I suppose. There are always so many more worthwhile things to do with one's time. You must see my latest pots. They've just been fired and I'm rather pleased with them,' Polly said as she took Kim's wrap. 'I'll put this in my bedroom then it won't get snowed under.'

The lounge was huge, but looked small with the clutter. An extension had been added, but this too was filled with the accumulated hobbies, interests and hoarding instincts of two adults and three children.

'They're starting to invade my space,' Keith said ruefully, a stockbroker who rakishly sported a beard and long hair. He attended life-classes and went on painting courses whenever he could.

'Lay down some ground rules,' advised Jack from the depths of a generously cushioned settee. 'Don't have them messing with your PC, for a start.'

'You know so much about bringing up children, don't you, Jack?' Kim cut in sarcastically, sparks flying from the jealous ember inside her as she saw Sandra sitting with Jack, all long legs and deep cleavage. She was wearing a cross between a nightdress and an underslip; short, sleeveless, bare-backed and strappy, it put all her assets on provocative display.

'I've seen enough of kids to recognise intolerable behaviour. "Treat your dogs like children and your children like dogs," is no mean adage,' Jack said, shooting Kim an amused glance. 'Hello, sister. Fancy meeting you twice in one day. How sophisticated you're looking, unlike this afternoon.'

'One doesn't dress up to go scrambling about old churches,' she managed to answer pithily, despite the emotional carnage that the mere mention of that shameful episode evoked.

'Is that what you were doing? How come?' Polly asked, assembling plates of crackers, cheese, and pastry fingers covered in savoury spread, as well as dips, bread sticks, celery and sliced raw carrot.

'I'm buying St Edwin's-on-the-Marsh,' Jack said. In his drab olive army-issue chinos and T-shirt he looked like a rough trade model in some exclusive men's fashion magazine. 'I'm settling in London for a while. Kim's over the moon about it, aren't you?'

She chose to ignore this, and wished she could ignore him, longing for supernatural powers so that she could hurl him back to the black pit of Hades where he had undoubtedly been spawned.

'I think it's lovely that you're working with Oliver. I suppose you've not seen much of each other as you have been in America, Jack,' Polly murmured, big-eyed with wonder.

'That's right. Kim and I have a lot of catching up to do,' he answered, his arm stretched along the back of the couch, lightly touching Sandra's bare shoulders.

Kim couldn't look at them. She walked over to stand in front of the open fire, where the heat augmented that already scorching her loins and rump.

Polly's like a babe unborn, she thought acidly, accepting the long, cool Margarita she brought across. How can she be so impressed by him? He's a past master at pulling the wool over everyone's eyes, including that stupid Sandra. An illusionist. A trickster. And I'm sure I don't know the half of it yet.

'Isn't this nice?' Polly remarked with a contented sigh, sinking to the rug at Keith's feet before leaning back against his knees. Her bangles clinked as she moved.

She was wearing a retro plum and purple velvet smock dress. 'I'm quite pissed, you know,' she confessed, arching her throat and smiling up at her husband, her hand stroking his knee and sliding along his thigh.

Whoops! thought Kim. Even she's coming under the insidious influence of Jack's sensuality. Sex oozes through his pores. I hope she's remembered to take the pill tonight, or there'll be another little sprog for the House of Ashe in nine months' time. I don't think I could stand that; we'd have to move.

Leather-covered stools were fixtures each end of the brass and wooden fender. Kim sank down on one of them, glass in hand, the melting ice numbing her fingers, the potent cocktail infusing itself through her blood. She crossed her knees, her skirt sweeping the floor, and hugged her arms round herself and stared into the fire. Either this, or she would be glaring at Jack, watching his every movement, probably going in for the attack. She regretted coming but was excited by his presence. Fretful, nervous, she didn't know how she felt, or what she wanted to do about it.

'Canapés, anyone?' Polly asked behind her. 'Jack, be a lamb and take some to Kim, will you?'

He was there. She could feel his warmth, and smell his hair. She sat on her hands to prevent them from touching him. He set the plate on the broad fender top and murmured, 'I've been wanting to fuck your arse all evening. Have you ever been rimmed?'

'No. What's that?'

'Having your bum-hole licked.'

'Hush. Someone may hear you,' she warned, instantly aware of that tiny rosebud, feeling it pucker as if his tongue was already on it.

'Polly's talking too much to notice, and trying to get into her old man's trousers.'

'Well then, Sandra.'

'Sod Sandra. Can't we go back to your place? They tell me Oliver's away. I want to do it to you in his bed.'

'That's a dreadful thing to suggest,' she reproved primly, nipples swelling under the hypnotic effect of his honeyed voice.

His hand was on her nape, fingers stroking that erogenous spot where her neck joined her spine. She shivered, the yearning in her womb making her juices flow. She hated it, hated him with his assumption that she would fall in with his every desire.

'Arrange it,' he said, casually appraising her.

'No.'

The look in his eyes became intense. 'We'll see about that.'

'What are you going to do?' she asked, tortured by anxiety. It was terrible to be at the mercy of someone else's whims.

He swung round to the others, smiling broadly and announcing, 'Kim's just invited us across to use the pool.'

'Lovely,' Polly answered vaguely. She stood up, then collapsed on Keith's lap. 'Bring the booze, darling,' she giggled. 'We'll go for a midnight dip. Wait for me while I run and get my swimsuit.'

Keith untangled himself and said, grinning, 'You won't be running anywhere. I'll fetch it.'

'And yours, and towels, and warm sweaters for after,' she reminded, ticking off the items on her fingers solemnly as if she were sober and her children were around.

'I don't have a swimsuit,' Sandra said, unfolding her coltish legs and rising. Her short skirt was crumpled, and her stocking tops and satin gusset flashed as she yanked it down.

'I dare you to go without,' Jack said. 'I don't mind swimming bollock-naked.'

'I'll bet you don't,' she said, rolling up her eyes and smirking.

Kim only just prevented herself from hitting her. Two Margaritas had done little to improve her control. Jack, you swine, she fumed inside. How could you do this to me?

He and Sandra piled into her car, but Keith suggested that he and Polly walk; fresh air might clear Polly's head. Kim slammed the gears into reverse and shot out of the drive, careless of approaching traffic. Time had passed by quickly, and it was late, almost twelve o'clock. She really had had too much to drink to be on the road. She slowed down and took it steadily. There were no other cars on this quiet backwater. The midnight hour, when witches and warlocks roam abroad, to cast their spells and work their mischief. It seemed that she had their leader in the passenger seat beside her.

Sandra was drooping in the back, but Jack had his hand between Kim's legs, stroking tenderly up her thighs until he touched the short, kinky hair where they met. He buried his middle digit in her crack and teased her to further wetness. Her panties didn't stop him. He simply pushed them aside, massaging her clit with the greatest skill. All she could do was get to Glen House without delay, before she spilled over into climax. She was poised on the perilous edge as the electronic gates swung open to let her pass.

'I've arranged with Mum that we'll drive over to see them on Sunday,' Jenny said, kneeling between Liam's parted thighs. He sprawled in the armchair, idly watching the pictures flickering on the television screen, the sound turned down.

'I suppose I can't get out of it. Time to meet the folks now I'm going to make an honest woman of you,' he said playfully, relaxing like a big tomcat under the ministrations of her nimble fingers.

Jenny slid her hand over his leg and brushed against the swelling behind his fly. She never tired of watching the bump as his dick uncoiled and pushed against the worn demin, needing to escape its restriction. Such immediate response was flattering proof of his desire.

Aroused now, Liam sat up and seized her pliant body, dragging her close till her breasts pressed into the heat of his groin. Leaning down, he kissed her hard, his tongue forcing its way between her lips and into her mouth. Though usually gentle, he sometimes displayed an untamed quality that excited her, making her think of the rough Atlantic that pounded the Galway coast of his native land.

Stretched taut, the narrow gusset of her tanga all but disappeared into her folds, spreading them apart. Liam fumbled with the front of her blouse, opening it and exposing her bare breasts. He flicked her nipples, one by one. She ground her belly to the throbbing bulge at his fork, rubbing up and down.

'Oh, Jenny, you get me going every time,' he groaned.

As an answer, she gripped him round the waist, tugging his T-shirt out of his jeans, then attacking the hardened male nipples, feeling them stiffen under her fingers.

He hauled her across his lap. She was astride him, her thighs wide apart, blouse falling open, breasts bobbing gently, the tips like raspberries. He pressed his face to her warm flesh and started to lick her, beginning on the outside curve of her right breast and working inwards to the nipple. Jenny heaved upwards, thrusting it into his mouth, feeling she would die if he didn't give it a thorough sucking.

'Undo me. Get my cock out,' he begged, and his words, delivered in that lyrical brogue, were like arrows piercing her sex.

It was there in her hand, long and meaty, and she giggled as she whispered, '"A thing of beauty is a joy forever".'

'What are you on about?' he growled, hanging on to her breasts with both hands.

'Your prick,' she said. 'Take no notice of me. Just a sec. Let go of my tits.'

She eased up a little, arms braced on those of the

143

chair, then slowly lowered herself, the thong pushed to one side by his clubbed glans poking at her vulva like a pig rooting for truffles. The wet lower mouth parted, and closed on the ridge of retracted foreskin, the first three inches of shaft. Neck bent, she watched it move into her body until it was lost from sight, and her russet bush mingled with his inky one.

Jenny wriggled, impaled on his cock. It was pleasure crossed with pain. He clenched his buttocks and raised his hips under her, lifting her higher. She was in charge. It was she who set the pace of his strokes. There wasn't enough friction on her clit; the base of his cock missed it by a mile. She dipped a hand down and found the slippery node, massaging it firmly and, at the same time, rubbing his stem as she rode it.

Sweat trickled between her breasts. Spicy, feral odours rose from where their bodies joined. Liam's face was contorted in ecstasy, eyes tight shut. Jenny lost it then, hearing a voice babbling obscene phrases and garbled love-words. It was her. She jerked on his penetration and drove harder, clutching at her slippery wet lips, pinching her clit. She cringed, spasmed and shook. Her thighs felt like jelly where she had gripped him so hard.

He took over, turning her so that she lay beneath him. He was on his knees between her legs, galloping furiously towards his own release. He gasped, then slumped down, face buried in her neck, the weight of his body pressing her into the cushions. The room righted itself and Jenny thrust her fingers into his curls and ran a hand over his sweat-soaked T-shirt, loving him, cradling him, happy.

My man, she thought smugly, remembering the bride magazines scattered over the floor. On Sunday they'd be having tea with her family. Her sisters would be green with envy when they saw him.

Suddenly headlights arced through the windows. Jenny struggled out from under him. 'Kim's back,' she cried.

144

'That's OK,' he mumbled sleepily. 'She won't need us. She'll be off to bed.'

On her feet, adjusting her tanga and lacy hold-ups, Jenny peered through the window. 'She's not alone.'

'Who's with her?' He came and stood behind her, his drooping cock, in contact with her hind-quarters, starting to revive, his hands coming round to capture her breasts.

'I can't quite see? Mr and Mrs Ashe, perhaps,' she said and pushed him away. 'Don't, Liam. She's bound to want something.'

'Aye, I guess so. I'll go and see. You get off to bed. I want to find you there all warm and wet and horny, waiting for me. That was just an appetiser.'

She shook her head. 'We'll wait together. She may order sandwiches or something.'

'There's sausage rolls and vol-au-vents in the freezer.'

'That will do.'

She buttoned her blouse, smoothed down her skirt, fished around under the couch for her shoes and swung into action. She was used to adapting herself to situations. The Buckleys led a fairly quiet, routine existence, with the occasional party thrown in, but even these were never unruly. Jenny hadn't yet had to clean up vomit or dispose of used condoms or stumble across drunken forms copulating on the carpet. The Buckleys' guests were circumspect, and so were they.

There were no rows or slanging matches, no slamming of doors or smashing china or pounding up and down stairs. They seemed ideally happy and Jenny was glad for them and hoped it would stay that way. So much easier to contend with than employers who were always at each other's throats or teetering on the brink of divorce.

This left her and Liam free to carry on their own love affair with all those additional little perks only possible in a well-regulated household. The surreptitious use of the master's bed, for example, if he and his wife were

145

away, and the freedom to frolic in the pool, or round the pool, or anywhere they could indulge in their own form of water sports.

The glass-roofed area was as humid as a greenhouse. Moisture beaded the thick, shiny leaves of jungly bushes. A large, prickly opuntia was in flower. The pool itself was kidney-shaped, lined with lapis-lazuli tiles, and bordered with round rattan tables and sun loungers.

When Kim came out of the cubicle where she'd changed into her costume, the first person she saw was Jack, standing on the far side.

A bolt of desire riveted her to the spot. She met his eyes across the rippling, blue water. He smiled and lifted an eyebrow. She tingled at his warm, sexual appraisal as he looked her over. His impudent gaze flicked over her breasts which were outlined by form-hugging floral lycra. He examined the high-cut sides that exposed her hip-bones, then lingered on the pointed triangle at the juncture of her thighs.

He was totally naked. The light reflecting upwards from below the water threw every muscle into relief. Though they had shared the greatest intimacy, she had never before seen him unclothed. He was at home with his body, never losing that confidence he assumed when fully clothed.

And he has every reason to be proud, she thought grudgingly. He was broad-shouldered and narrow waisted, with a muscular torso and flat belly, taut flanks and long, strong legs. With his fair hair and smooth muscles, he could have posed for a statue of Adonis. He possessed an enviable all-over tan, and his skin gleamed, each sinew, curve and plane sharply defined. But it was his cock that attracted her attention. It was large even when relaxed, curving from its nest of brownish curls, his balls swinging loosely in their sac beneath it.

To see it flaccid was another first for Kim. On every other occasion it had been at full power, ready to ravage

146

her mouth or pussy. Even flaccid, it still maintained its virile quality, as if about to thicken and rise at any given second.

She wasn't the only one to be impressed. 'Gosh, you're fighting fit, Jack,' Polly exclaimed, floating on her back, wearing a skimpy, pink bikini. 'I wish I was as trim. I'm not fat, too skinny if anything, but three pregnancies have taken their toll on my figure. It needs toning.'

'Join a karate class,' he advised. 'I never miss a session if I can help it.'

Kim walked to the pool's edge, sat down and dabbled her feet in the water. Keith was swimming resolutely up and down. Compared to Jack he was positively portly but, like Jack, he had opted for nudity. As he executed a porpoise roll, his body appeared pale and bloated, his floating cock infinitesimal, his sagging balls buoyed up by the water.

Sandra swayed along the side, her flaxen hair hanging down and hiding her breasts. She had kept on her panties.

'Drop 'em!' Jack shouted coarsely.

'Leave her alone, poor girl,' Polly chided coyly. 'And why aren't you in the water? Too scared?'

Jack gave a saturnine smile and raised his arms above his head. Every muscle stretched. Kim caught her breath, wanting to run her hands over such perfection, to hold it, grasp it, lock it away and lose the key, keep it to herself for ever. He dived, cleaving through the water with hardly a ripple. The pool was no more than eight feet at the deep end, and he surfaced at once, and struck out to the shallow part where Kim sat lost in a wet dream in which he featured large.

Sandra descended the steps, giving little shrieks as the water lapped her breasts. 'Oh, Kim! It's cold!' she complained. 'Can't you up the temperature?'

'Always whingeing,' Jack mocked, and fastened his hand round Kim's ankle. 'That's the trouble with women. Even you did your share this afternoon.'

147

She tugged at her foot but he refused to release her. Sandra splashed towards them, reaching out to support herself on Jack's shoulders and rub against the length of his back. Jack took no notice of her, his attention focused on Kim who struggled but was unable to get a hold on the slippery tiles. He jerked, and she was in his arms under the water. The chill shock turned to heat as she felt his cock stirring, growing hard against her stomach.

Sandra, not to be outdone, wrapped one of her legs round his and ground her crotch against it, her hands groping his erection. 'Oh. Is that for me?' she asked, giving it a squeeze.

Staring down into Kim's eyes, he didn't answer. She placed her hands on his chest, forming a wedge between them, distancing herself. But his cock followed her, powered by his hips as he refused to let her go. Sandra gave up and trod water, her face expressing bewildered anger.

'Jack – ' she began again.

'Fuck off!' he grunted.

'No, it's all right. I'm going to swim,' Kim declared, and succeeded in escaping him, wriggling like a slippery mermaid. She struck out, half blinded by her hair, tossing it back off her face. Jack and Sandra were arguing. She hoped it wasn't about her. He took too many risks, and it terrified her. Polly and Keith hadn't noticed anything. They were boisterous and noisy, playing now they'd shucked off parental responsibility for a while. Their ducking and splashing quietened down, and Kim saw that they were embracing. Keith's hands were between Polly's legs and she held his penis. It had grown now into a sizeable rod, shining and red. Kim looked away. A glance back showed her that Jack had left Sandra and was pursuing her.

There was no escape, and she felt him grasp her and pull her to him, his cock slipping between her buttocks. Through the thin fabric it felt long and hard, pressing persistently against her anus.

Not here. Not now. Not like this, she wanted to scream.

Then it left her anus, and its length glided between her legs until the head was against her clit. The swimsuit was tight and the gusset had ridden up, almost as if her genitals were bare. She bottomed the pool and stood very still, her body responding to the hard promise of his shaft, and felt her loins grow heavy and her nipples tighten. He, too, was still; his only movement was the thickening of his cock.

'God!' Sandra cried behind them. 'You randy sod, Jack. She's your sister, for fuck's sake!'

'I'm showing her a meditation technique. It works well in water,' he replied blandly. 'What did you think I was doing? Shafting her?'

The irony in his voice confused her. 'No. How silly. Just for a moment there, I thought, imagined – '

'Don't worry about it. Your two brain cells will clash together and won't be able to cope,' he said with such blistering scorn that Kim pitied her.

She pulled away from the temptation of him, muttering, 'I'm cold. I need coffee,' and stumbled towards the steps. It took real effort to haul herself out. Jack sapped her energy; he was a sexual vampire who throve on the life-force of others.

She huddled into her towelling robe, buzzed Jenny in the kitchen and ordered hot drinks, then wound another towel, turbanwise, round her dripping hair. She refused to look at Jack, but could feel his eyes boring into her.

Jenny came in with the tray. Someone was with her.

'Oliver!' Kim exclaimed and rushed towards him. In an instant she was being held, soothed, comforted, though he couldn't have known how much she wanted that.

'I managed to make a late flight,' he said, when able to free his lips from hers. There was a quizzical look in his eyes as he took in the scene. 'And I find I've arrived home in the middle of a Roman orgy.'

149

'It's my fault,' Polly explained. 'I take all the blame. It started out at our place but sort of wound up here.'

'That's all right. You're welcome to use the pool,' Oliver said, and only Kim was aware of the fractional pause as he added, 'You, too, Jack. Any time you're down this way.'

Does he know? He can't possibly! Kim conjectured, her thoughts barrelling around frantically.

'Maybe I'll do just that,' Jack replied unconcernedly, leaving the water and knotting a towel round his hips before occupying one of the loungers.

As if by mutual consent, the others followed him, Keith trying to brazen out his nudity and not quite succeeding. He went to get dressed and so did Polly, but Sandra draped herself in a wrap and sat beside Jack, tossing her head to shower him with drops from her long, straight hair. Her attitude towards him was decidedly proprietorial. She must have a skin like a rhinoceros, Kim thought angrily.

Jenny poured coffee, and Oliver rid himself of his grey business suit jacket and sank into a cane chair with a sigh. Kim stared at him anxiously. He looked tired. There were fresh lines each side of his mouth. He worked so hard, driven by ambition and the need to prove himself to be top of his field.

'We'll go now, and leave you in peace,' said Polly, replacing her cup on the table. 'Ready, Keith? Are you coming with us, Sandra?'

'I'll see she gets home all right,' Jack said and stood up, the towel slipping below his navel where a scribble of hair joined that furring his lower belly. He shot Kim a glance. She turned her head away.

He's going to spend the night with her, she thought drearily, and the pain was as sharp as a butcher's knife. She hated herself for being so hurt, but the more she tried, the more unbearable the pain became.

'I'm hyped up,' Oliver said, stirring restlessly. 'I think

I'll listen to some music for a while before I come to bed, Kim.'

'All right. Don't sit up too long,' she answered, lifting her face for his kiss as he leant over her. He nodded to the rest and departed, his jacket slung over one shoulder.

Jack slapped Sandra across her towel-covered rump and said, 'Get your clothes on, woman. If you're not ready in five minutes, I'm out of here.'

Now they were alone, Kim was filled with deadly fear; for her well-being, for her future, for her security.

She stood up, faced Jack and hissed, 'That's it. I meant what I said earlier. This isn't fair on him.'

'Oliver? Do you think I give a shit?'

'Then what about me? Do you care that my marriage could be ruined?' It was hard to keep her voice down when there was so much anger raging inside her. She wanted to punch and kick him into seeing sense.

'I've told you. I'm doing it for you, to get you out of a situation which isn't right for you.'

'How noble,' she jeered.

He took hold of her belt and, using it like a rein, pulled her closer. 'You're a mass of contradictions. I can help you sort them.'

'I don't need your help and I don't need you.'

A smile touched his mouth. 'That's fine. Once you've learnt to love yourself and accept every one of your fantasies, even the dirtiest, then you might realise what love means.'

'I know what it means. It's what Jenny and Liam have. It's more than crude sex, more than a series of meaningless moments of lust. I want happy endings, and to know that the man whose bed I share will be there the next night and the next, stretching into forever,' she said, her voice low and hurried.

He inserted a finger into the wrapover of her robe and said, 'But you already have that, don't you? Then why aren't you blissfully happy?'

'I was. Until you came.'

He touched her ribcage, and the tip of one of her nipples, murmuring, 'You weren't. Not really. I think you were bored out of your skull.'

Kim gave him a hard push and freed herself. 'Just leave me alone!' she shouted. 'Don't phone. Don't call me.'

He chuckled wickedly. 'I shan't, but you'll call me. I give you a month.'

'Go to hell!' she shouted, and fled as if the Gabriel Hounds were after her.

Oliver slipped off his shoes, pulled off his socks and padded across the study to the CD player. He had gone beyond tiredness and knew that he now faced the hour of the wolf, the soul's midnight, when insomnia rules and all one's fears rise up to haunt you, each with a face more hideous than the last.

He selected the disc, poured himself a large whisky, took up position in his favourite armchair and pressed the remote button. The opening bars of Elgar's *Cello Concerto in E* seduced his ear. He almost purred. He thought about the soloist, Jacqueline du Pré, and her tragic, early demise, thought about music as a whole, the chords strung together by a master craftsman to move the listener to tears or laughter, passion or anger, even patriotism.

How did it work? It was a mystery and, for a while, Oliver sank himself into it with almost sexual relish. But, as the whisky went down, so his hold on rationality dissipated and he experienced the feelings that had swept over him when, on arrival, he had stood in the conservatory watching the swimmers without them being aware.

It had amused him to see Polly and Keith going for it, acting like two lovesick teenagers, but this had quickly been eclipsed when his eyes switched to Jack and Kim. The expression on his wife's face as she stared up at her brother had puzzled him, as well as the fact that they were standing as close as lovers, blanking out Sandra. Disturbed, though without knowing why, Oliver had waited until Kim left the pool. Her reaction to him had been that of a child rescued from a violent thunderstorm.

The music welled into a long, lingering, heart-rending cello passage that tore at his very being, and tears stung the back of his eyelids. There had been more recent recordings of the concerto, but to his mind, Jacqueline du Pré's interpretation was sublime.

Kim. If only he could share his passion for music with her. He had long ago accepted that this was not to be. She let him indulge himself, never questioned his right to spend money on CDs or concerts or opera. It left her unmoved. In the same way, her musical choices passed over him without impact, apart from the occasional meeting ground of ballet pieces.

Marriage is a question of compromise, he told himself. And if she enjoys Jack's company and they have the same interests, then who am I to deny her that?

I only wish I could get close to my brothers, he thought. We've always been rivals, and the truth is, I don't like them much. You can choose your friends but not your relatives. It isn't written in stone that you must get on with them.

His father was a successful industrialist and it was rather like a fairy story. Once upon a time a king had three sons and on his death he left them his fortune in equal measure. The three princes quarrelled, refusing to believe that their father had loved them equally. Each took his share and made of it what he could. One became a famous surgeon, and one an adventurer, squandering his fortune on seeking lost treasures in the depths of the Brazilian rain-forests. But the third and youngest son decided he would become even more prosperous than the king.

There should be a rider to this, Oliver decided, topping up his glass before settling back to listen to the concerto's finale: the youngest son succeeded, becoming

153

pre-eminent in his chosen profession and, in the fullness of time, married a fair princess.

And how have I handled my marriage? he questioned himself, slipping gently into the morass of whisky-induced introspection. Maybe I shouldn't work so hard? Perhaps we should think about having a baby? I'll make more time for Kim. We could go on a long holiday, somewhere she's always wanted to visit.

The CD finished, but Oliver didn't move, slumped in his chair, glass in hand, seeing over and over again Kim's face as she looked at Jack.

Jenny slipped out of her clothes and snuggled under the feather-filled duvet. Liam turned to hold her tightly, his hands running up and down her back in long, soothing strokes. The impromptu swimming party had added to their workload, and it was now two o'clock in the morning.

She lay there, appreciating the massage, thanking her lucky stars for this simple, uncomplicated relationship. She believed in romance, absorbed novels about it, watched sentimental movies, had an unshakeable faith in marriage and the power of love that brought two people together. There wasn't a cynical bone in her body.

But something was bothering her. She rolled on her back and drew her knees up, tenting the covers. 'What's the matter?' Liam asked, folding his arms under his head and watching her in the glow of the bedside lamp.

'I dunno,' she answered slowly. 'It was after they'd all gone, apart from Mr Loring. I was just going to go in and clear away the cups when I saw them standing together, talking.'

'Who?'

'Mrs Buckley and him.'

'So?'

'It looked like they were arguing.'

'And?'

'It was odd, but if I hadn't known better, I'd have

154

thought she's been carrying on with him. There was something in her body language.'

'Don't be daft. He's her brother.'

'Exactly,' said Jenny without much conviction, then switched off the light, dived down under the duvet and mouthed his cock.

Chapter Eight

A month, Jack had said. Possibly the longest month Kim had ever known.

A hectic, busy month, with Christmas in the middle of it, and Elaine's departure for India and Kim taking charge of Palmer's Emporium. There was so much to do, so much to think about, in fact too much to waste time worrying because she hadn't seen hide nor hair of him.

Now Glen House had been restored to order. The towering fir tree that had dominated the entrance hall was stripped of tinsel and shining baubles and dragged into the garden for burning. The withering, dehydrated holly had gone the same way, and the ivy and mistletoe.

'The Festive Season is so bloody stressful one needs another holiday to get over it,' Oliver said one January morning. 'What d'you say, Kim? Shall we up and off somewhere?'

They were sitting in bed, drinking tea, reading the morning post and avoiding getting up. She had guessed this question was bound to come up again soon. He had already broached the subject before the hectic activity of card-writing and present-buying and the choosing of people to be invited for Christmas dinner or the New Year's Eve celebration. In fact, looking back, she realised that he had first mentioned a holiday the day after that disastrous swimming party.

There had been an expensive card of the business variety from Jack, addressed to both of them. That was all they had heard from him. She had drawn a blank with Polly, apart from gossip concerning Sandra's upset because Jack seemed to have dropped her.

And not only her; me as well, Kim had thought, then she had been extremely sensible about it, telling herself it was all for the best.

With his knack of reading her mind, Oliver now said, 'Funny, we haven't heard from your brother lately. He's been in and out of the office, of course, and Transglobe are over the moon about his work, but he seems to have gone to ground, almost vanished from the social scene. Though he's stolen my secretary, the bugger. Lara's decamped to work for him.'

'He has his own premises?' An image of toffee-haired Lara, with the generous tits and Cupid's-bow mouth, shimmied across her mind.

'I hear through the grapevine that the church is coming on apace. He's already moved in and set himself up.'

'Really?' she said carelessly, every vestige of her hard-won serenity going down the tube as she wondered if Lara liked dank vaults and being tied to rusty railings and flogged.

'I'm surprised he hasn't told you,' Oliver remarked. He squinted at a bill and grumbled, 'Bloody hell, if you own a telephone company these days it's a licence to print money.' Then he gave her a slanting glance, and added, 'You two seemed thick as thieves when he first turned up. Have you fallen out?'

'Not exactly,' she replied, swinging her legs over the mattress edge and standing up. 'It was never that important. I found him a drag, to tell the truth.'

We're supposed to be so close, Oliver and me, she thought, walking naked to the bathroom. Yet I can lie and he appears to believe me. But does he really? I'm not so sure. He's too canny by half. Help! I'd hate to have been having a real affair. There's so much subterfuge and lying.

Then what, may I ask, were you doing with Jack if it wasn't an affair? queried her inner demon, stern as an inquisitor. Playing tiddlywinks, perhaps, or taking an earnest stroll round the National Gallery? Maybe even doing charity work among the poor, the disgustingly lecherous poor of St Edwin's? Now Lara's wearing your Salvation Army hat. I'll bet the tramps get off on her luscious bum and big, bouncy jugs.

'I shan't phone you, Kim, but you'll call me. I give you a month,' she heard Jack saying again, his voice over-riding the demon's. He was so powerful, like the ruler of the netherworld hordes.

'Glance through these travel brochures when you've a minute,' Oliver called from the bedroom. 'I don't mind where we go as long as it's somewhere warm.'

'I'll try. I haven't much time. Elaine's shop –'

'There you are, you see. She's gone on holiday and saddled you with it. Totally without conscience, that woman.' He sounded impatient and a tad resentful.

She didn't bother to take up the gauntlet. It was all right for Oliver to manipulate her, organising her life, having her fall in with every single plan he made, but she must not attempt it. How unreasonable men are, she concluded, staring at her face in the mirror over the pedestal washbasin and thinking how strange it was that she could appear to be absolutely normal with so much churning inside her.

'OK. I'll study the brochures during my lunch break,' she agreed, then toilette complete, stuffed them in her handbag.

Inside the shop, she stooped to pick up the mail from the coconut mat set in its brass-edged well. It was mostly junk; lottery offers, firms touting for trade, promises of big cash prizes. But there were a couple of official-looking brown ones with plastic windows which probably contained bills. Elaine had given her *carte blanche* to open all correspondence, settle outstanding accounts and bank the takings daily. Kate, one of Sarah's cronies who came in part-time, was trustworthy but spent more time changing the colour of her nails than contributing to sales.

Then, at the bottom of the heap, Kim noticed a large, manila envelope. She picked it up. It was addressed to her. No clue from the writing. The label was printed and it had been delivered by hand.

A late Christmas present? Maybe a calendar. But from whom?

Her heart started to pound with slow, heavy beats. Her fingers tingled as she turned the thing over and over, searching for an answer. Carrying it and the rest of the letters, she walked to the back of the showroom. Elaine's mail went on the top of the desk, next to the computer, to be dealt with later. Kim sat on the operator's chair, swivelling back and forth as she held the package.

It was almost half past nine, and opening time, but still she sat there, mesmerised, staring at it. Then she grabbed Elaine's paper-knife and slit the flap. She drew out the contents, and read the print-out. 'Enjoy. J.'

It was as if he was taunting her. She could feel his presence, her heart jumping, her clit thrumming. How did he know where she worked? She hadn't told him. Had Oliver mentioned it?

With shaking fingers, she opened the neatly wrapped folder. And there they lay, impossible to dispute: photographs of herself in stark black and white, but as no one else had ever seen her. Half a dozen pictures, taken from behind, her profile hidden by her hair. That was a small consolation. There was no denying it was her in the abandoned crypt, suspended from the railings, wrists bound over her head, legs tethered wide apart, her pussy, her arse, the sides of her breasts, on display. He had even used a zoom-lens to get in close, a silvery trickle of juice highlighted as it glistened on her pink and vulnerable sex.

Kim's mind was appalled, but her body was on fire. How little it took to make her rampant for him again. Someone was knocking at the door and she guiltily thrust the envelope and its incriminating contents into her bag, jettisoning Oliver's travel brochures to make room. Opening a drawer, she crammed the bag inside and slammed it shut.

'Coming,' she called to the customer outside. He was stamping his feet and blowing on his fingers. She let him in, burbling cheerily, 'Sorry to keep you waiting. Yes, it is bitterly cold, isn't it, but I suppose we must expect it at this time of year.'

She was working with the surface of her mind only; the rest was a teeming quagmire of fear, horror, indignation at Jack's nerve, and overwhelming, knicker-wetting lust. She was kept busy throughout the morning, and it was gone one o'clock before she could lock the door. Though she could have used the help of the part-timer, Kate, no matter how inefficient, she thanked her lucky stars that she wasn't in that day.

She threw the bolt to make doubly sure of privacy, and was at the desk within seconds. She spread the photos out and studied them, obsessed with the pictures. Each one was evidence of her submission. She was so hot that her hand went down to her crotch without her realising what she was doing. She rubbed the hard nodule now swelling at the top of her cleft, her finger moving swiftly over the slippery lingerie satin. This wasn't enough. With a gasp, she seized the elasticated waistband and pulled her knickers down, sitting low on her spine in the chair, thighs fallen apart. And, as she masturbated, she couldn't stop looking at the photos.

She wished that she could see him, his hand punishing her bottom, his cock ravishing her helplessness. He should have fixed up an automatic camera or had a buddy press the button. She had no snapshot of him of any kind, yet his face was imprinted on her memory, the sound of his voice etched on her eardrums, the feel of his hands branded into her flesh.

She imagined him there, standing in front of her, looking down and watching her with his sinister smile and icy-blue eyes. They would bore into her, penetrating her pussy, as he urged her on, saying, 'That's it, Kim. Rub yourself harder. What about your arsehole? Wet it. Push your fingers into it. That's right. Do it.'

She moaned, obeying his imaginary command, dipping a finger into her copious wetness and smearing it over her anus. 'I can't,' she whimpered, the tight ring refusing to yield.

'Do it,' the phantom Jack repeated.

Suddenly, the muscles relaxed. Now she wriggled her finger in, mastering the strange sensation and controlling the urge to reject it. These were new sensations. But it was to her clit that she returned, stimulating it and losing herself in the orgasmic waves that buffeted her. She could feel it coming, rising from the tips of her toes to her groin.

'Jack! Jack!' she cried aloud, the inescapable rush leaving her gasping and shaking.

Head back against the chair, she lay sprawled like a rag-doll, too exhausted to move, the spasms gradually relinquishing their grasp. With a sigh, she opened her eyes, surprised to find he wasn't there. His image had been so real. She stared at the photos. Now, lust sated, she viewed them with disgust. How many more copies did Jack own? Had he destroyed the negatives? Where and how did he get such things processed? Not by post, that was for sure.

The word 'blackmail' sounded in her ears, a doom-filled drumroll.

He couldn't! He wouldn't! He would!

She reached for the phone. His mobile number was engraved on her heart.

He answered almost at once, saying coolly, 'Hi, Kim.'

The low timbre of his voice vibrated through her. If she felt weak before, it was nothing compared to how she felt now. 'How did you know it was me?' she succeeded in mumbling.

'Let me guess,' he teased. 'When you got into work this morning you found an envelope containing artistic – though some might call them pornographic – photos. Right?'

'Jack. Listen to me. Are these the only copies?' She held the receiver to her ear and could see her future crumbling before her eyes as she waited for his reply.

'No,' he answered.

'Will you let me have them, and the negs?'

'Not sure if I can. I'm a sentimentalist under this macho exterior, and want to have some pictures of my only sister.'

'I can give you others, a dozen if you want, but please, please give those to me or burn them.'

'Don't fret. No one knows about them, apart from Vivien.'

'You showed them to your mother?'

'When I went to Bristol for Christmas. Never fear, she's very broad-minded.'

'You went home?' Was there no end to the complexities of this man?

'Sure. We had a great time. There's loads of clubs, gay or straight. Viv fancies herself as a fag hag, and she also enjoys clubbing and picking up men. She has a very healthy sexual appetite.'

'Trust you to have a mother like that.'

'Calm down,' he cautioned. 'Dear me, what a state you're in. What did you do when you saw the photos?'

'I hid them till lunch.'

'And then?'

'I looked at them.'

'While you masturbated. Am I right?'

God, he's a mind-reader, a psychic in disguise, she thought. Oliver's a novice compared to him. Jack has become a part of me, knowing my every thought and deed. I can't keep anything from him, she fumed. She replied, 'I don't have to discuss it with you.'

'Spoil-sport,' he chided. 'Not over the phone, maybe, but when you meet me after work.'

'You must be crazy. Oliver will be expecting me to be home when he gets back.'

'Oliver will be unavoidably detained.'

'How do you know that?'

'I've been with him this morning, in his office. He had a phone call and arranged a business meeting for half past six. And Flyte rang, too, wanting his advice on something or other. Just an excuse, I expect. He's calling in on her afterwards.'

'How do I know you haven't made it all up?'

'Check your recorded messages when you get back. I was there when he rang you. He cursed like fury because he didn't have your work number.'

'I gave it to him,' she said, trying to be sensible. Oliver was going to meet Flyte. She hated the woman. And Jack wanted to see her, she dared not disobey. He had the negatives.

And above all and through all was her aching, persistent hunger for his body and, more damning still, the longing to feel the weight of his hand on her cringeing buttocks.

'I want you to follow my instructions,' Jack continued.

'I haven't said I'll be there.'

'You will. Now listen up and listen good. You'll take off your clothes before you leave, but keep on your stockings, suspender belt and shoes. Are you wearing high heels?'

'For work? You must be joking. I'm wearing comfortable moccasins.'

'Borrow some from Elaine.'

'I don't know if we're the same size.'

'Try them on. I know she's a dyke, but no doubt she owns kinky footwear.'

163

'How do you know about her? What are you, some sort of master spy?'

'I keep my ear to the ground. It's astonishing what the jungle drums pick up,' he conceded pleasantly. 'Right, you'll wear your coat to cover your pussy. You have brought a coat with you?'

'Yes.'

'Long?'

'Yes. Jesus, you know so much about me I'm surprised you have to ask.'

'Don't be pert! I detect a note of rebellion. That will have to be punished.'

'Jack, stop these silly games,' she pleaded, but though the ripples of orgasm had faded, she longed to clench her inner muscles round his cock.

He ignored her protestations, issuing further instructions. 'Go out dressed like that and drive your car to the Transglobe site. I'll meet you there.'

'But I thought – The church –'

'Don't argue. Just do it.'

'I won't,' she said, tempted to put the phone down.

'You're not hearing me,' he replied calmly, as if nothing she had said moved him. 'If you want me to be reasonable about the negatives, you'll do as I say. I'm sure Oliver would find them interesting.'

'All right, but I'm coming fully dressed.' Yet even as she spoke she could feel her resolution crumbling.

'All you need is your coat.'

'Naked underneath?' she said, shivering at the thought of herself going out into the street like that.

'Correct,' he answered, and she could feel herself wilting under the resonance of his voice.

'But I can't. Why the building site? What are you going to do?'

'Be there at six o'clock,' he said, and the phone clicked off, leaving her with the buzzing emptiness of a dialling tone. She replaced the receiver on its cradle.

Silence filled the showroom and, as Kim shuffled the

photos into their envelope, she realised that he had succeeded in getting his way again. Nothing had changed in four weeks. She sighed quietly, admitting that her desire for him had in no way abated.

Jack put down the mobile and resumed moving his cock in Lara. She was on her stomach across his desk, arse lifted to the ceiling, thighs angled so her feet in those absurdly high wedges rested on the floor. He had been screwing her when Kim phoned.

Pleased to observe that Lara obeyed his orders to the letter, arriving for work every day without panties, he had tormented her for ages by ignoring her signals, until she was practically screaming for it. He had made her languid with desire, a rich, oceanic aroma seeping from her hot and naked avenue. He was amused by the way in which she angled to touch him with her shoulder, or breast, or her thigh, while performing simple movements like leaning over to hand him a letter to sign. And every day he had left her unfulfilled, and imagined her rushing back to her flat and playing with herself, all the while pretending it was him.

That morning, however, fired by the knowledge that Kim would be receiving the package, he had judged matters so accurately that she rang just after he'd entered Lara's succulent portal, but just before he climaxed.

'Don't answer it. Let it ring,' Lara had implored, her honey-coloured hair tousled, her cheek pressed to the glass top, her bum wriggling against his shaft, almost precipitating his crisis. He had slapped her hard to make her lie still, and spoken into the phone.

Lara fidgeted throughout the conversation, sliding her hand under her mound and massaging her clit, then trying to reach his cock base. A sharp pinch made her quieten.

Now she said, 'Who was that? It sounded as if you were talking to Oliver Buckley's wife.'

'What if I was? She's my sister.'

'Funny sort of conversation to have with your sister,' she mumbled.

'Keep your nose out of my business,' he snapped, and gave an extra hard thrust that made her squeal.

He pulled out and flipped her over on her back. Her legs scissored round his waist as he positioned himself at her brownish-pink, juicy entrance. He teased her with the tip of his cock, circling her pussy until she moaned and pushed up against him. Then he thrust in hard and slid out slowly, increasing her torture. He savoured every stroke, his mind filled up with Kim. He wanted to laugh out loud, picturing her shocked face when she first saw the photographs.

The tension was building in his balls and, concerned only with his own pleasure, he lay still until the throbbing in his cock died down. Lara moaned in protest, her vaginal muscles contracting. He pushed his hands up under her sweater and played with her nipples. She moaned again, louder this time, and this added to his mirth as he wondered if the workmen on the scaffolding round the church roof would hear her. They were a coarse bunch, and he'd already seen how they gloated on Lara whenever she minced up the path. He toyed with the idea of offering her to them as a sort of bonus to complete the job quickly.

They weren't as fast as the Transglobe gang, but had, nonetheless, performed a small miracle, enabling him to set up heating and water, with his office *in situ*, and his bedroom almost ready. Vivien was coming to inspect it soon and he'd have a dinner party.

'Don't dismiss the workmen until I've looked them over,' she had said at Christmas.

'I won't. It'd be more than my life was worth,' he'd promised.

'Go on, Jack, please,' Lara was urging frantically.

'Ask me nicely,' he ordered, though his breathing was laboured as she arched her back and thrust under him.

'Fuck me, fuck me, please, Jack, fuck me,' she crooned.

That sobbing entreaty was like the sweetest of music. She lifted her legs higher, resting her ankles on his shoulders, every part of her open and eager.

He grunted in reply, and drove his cock in and out like a piston, surrendering to the force. With his eyes fixed on the stained-glass window that fronted his desk, he allowed his mind to sink into the colours, just as his body was sinking into Lara's.

She was whimpering softly, her nails digging into him under his shirt, and he could feel the fire blazing down his spine, gathering in his groin, his orgasm ready to burst.

'Oh, God, I can't –' Lara cried, and her hand shot down to her mound, her fingers finding the centre of her pleasure. She worked on it, grinding her hips in a circle.

Jack was helpless against the giant hand that seemed to lift him and toss him high. His semen shot into the condom in heavy spurts, his orgasm wringing out the last remaining drops.

Almost at once, he stood up, drawing his penis from Lara and unrolling its latex covering. Dispassionately, he watched her as, unsatisfied, she continued to rub herself until her back arched again and she shuddered. Her hand slowed its frantic pace, cupping her mound gently.

Jack zipped up his jeans, and said, 'Make me a coffee and then get on with that letter to Japan.'

'If you get the commission there, can I come?' Lara ventured, jumping down from the desk and righting her disordered clothes.

'I shouldn't think so,' he answered, already at his drawing-board where the new building for a Tokyo conglomerate was already taking shape under his pencil, nearly ready to be transferred to the computer. 'There'll be lots of meek little geisha girls around.'

But he wasn't thinking about a diminutive Madame Butterfly. Kim occupied his mind, and the idea of seeing her that evening flooded him with excitement, his cock stirring again in his pants. This reaction was not entirely physical. It pained him to admit it, even to himself. He had missed her.

The rush hour was over, but London was still busy. Kim found her way to Aldermar Street, driving round to the back of the high, gaunt, unfinished building. It resembled a bomb-site more than a new travel centre. She could hardly believe that it was where world travellers, and even tourists to the moon, could pay their money and take their pick.

It was one of Oliver's brain-children and he was deep in cahoots with Transglobe's directors and, it seemed, with her brother Jack.

'I stand to make a lot of money out of it, darling,' he had said to her at the onset. 'Bear with me if I'm delayed sometimes, and can't spend as much time with you as I'd like.'

Time divided between myself and Flyte, she thought angrily, as she got out of the car in the deserted area behind the building. She scanned the darkness for Jack. The wind whistled up her legs and stippled her naked flesh. It had felt odd to be bare as she drove, the silk lining of her coat sliding under her bottom, the lubrication of arousal making a tiny damp patch on it.

She wasn't used to the footwear. Elaine's black leather boots were banded with silver and had four-inch stiletto heels. They were a nightmare to drive in. She had found them in the wardrobe, remembering what Elaine had said about them.

'I only wear them on high days and holidays, or when I've just finished a relationship and do the club circuit, on the pull. Borrow them whenever you like.'

At the time, Kim had laughed and shaken her head, the idea too far-fetched to be taken seriously. But now she was balancing on those outrageous stilts in the middle of a wind-whipped building site, her nipples stiff with cold, her insides quaking as she waited for a man who wasn't her husband. She leant against the car bonnet, ready to dive back inside if danger threatened.

She almost skidded into action, pulse racing, when a figure detached itself from the gloom.

'Kim,' Jack said, and it was as if they had never been apart, perhaps carrying on this morning's conversation, or the one by the pool.

Horrible though it was, she couldn't deny an affinity with him. If only we could see each other as supportive siblings, she thought sadly. It would be good for us both.

'Jack, you're here,' she said, keeping her voice low.

'I am.'

He came closer and lifted her coat. Batwing-sleeved and swing-backed, it was so easy to wear, so easy for a man to plunder, especially a man determined to find out what she had on under it. She stood absolutely still, absorbing the sensation of his fingers circling the soft, leather top of her right boot then walking up her thigh, scratching over the stockings, finding the suspender clip and stroking across her bush.

'Well done,' he whispered. 'You're learning.' And he kissed her, his lips tasting of the cold. His middle finger entered her. 'No. Keep your legs together,' he ordered. 'It makes your quim tighter. That's it. Clench those muscles.'

His measured strokes imitated intercourse. First his finger, then his whole hand, was wet with the essence he milked from her. She wanted his hand on her clit: it was now sticking out from her pubis, and begging the blessing of his touch there.

He left her aching with desire, and sniffed his fingers. 'Lovely,' he said. 'Though alike in many ways, every woman's pussy smells different. As for men's arseholes? That's something else.'

'You don't go with men, do you?' she whispered, horror-struck, yet not entirely surprised, beginning to believe that Jack would screw anything that breathed.

'Variety is the spice of life. I'm lucky to swing both ways. Many people do, of course, but stay in the closet.'

He slung an arm round her neck and guided her towards the massive, dark hulk made up of steel and concrete. The basic structure of the lower floor was already completed. That giant area which would soon be floor-to-ceiling windows was mostly covered in acres of tarpaulin or boarded up. Jack took a key to the padlock that sealed a makeshift door.

'I squared it with security,' he said, nodding to where lights gleamed in a Portakabin across the lot. 'They're on duty twenty-four hours a day with their Alsations.'

The gaunt, concrete wasteland that would one day be the complex's nerve centre seemed to stretch for miles. Bare electric light bulbs hung on cables suspended from the endless universe of the ceiling. Kim felt dwarfed and insignificant, but Jack, whose creation this was, strode confidently over to a lift and drew back the gate.

Fences. Bars. She crossed the threshold and stood inside, an animal in a cage, her trainer was with her.

He shut the gate with a metallic clash. They began to rise. She didn't feel safe: the elevator was open-sided save for the bars, reminding her of photos she'd seen of coal miners coming up out of the Stygian darkness of the pits. She would have appreciated Jack holding her steady, but he had positioned himself on the opposite side. The lift clanked and rumbled on its way skywards.

'This is a makeshift for the workmen,' he said. He wore a black bomber jacket, black T-shirt, and leather trousers, and his face looked surprisingly haggard in the unrelenting glare of the bare bulb overhead. 'I've designed a series of elevators like glass lozenges. They'll glide as smooth as silk, up and away, high over the plants in the foyer. I thought something formal, gracious and peaceful. A trickle fountain, bonsai trees, a Zen garden. This will also appeal to Transglobe's oriental clients. What do you think?'

He was actually asking her opinion!

'Sounds fine,' she said.

'I wanted you to see the scale of it,' he added. 'We should be wearing hard hats, of course. Security will bawl us out if they catch us, but it would have spoilt your hair.'

He cared about this? She couldn't understand his motivation. 'How far are we going?' she asked, dragging her coat further together over her nudity.

'To heaven, to the stars. As far as you want,' he said, his face expressionless.

She could feel the power radiating from him. He was tall and strong, but more than that, he had a reservoir of energy which he could tap at will. A smidgen of it had given birth to this imposing structure.

Up and up they went, the lift creaking and juddering. Kim could see blackness dropping away below them in the gaps between the flooring, and her stomach heaved.

'How many storeys, for God's sake?' she gasped, clinging to the fencing for dear life.

'As many as it takes to get to the sky,' he replied cryptically.

Then, when she thought she couldn't take any more – she was never very good with heights – he stalled the lift, but didn't open the gate. Instead, he pressed her against the chain-linked side and lifted her till she was astride his hips. She had not seen him unzip, but his cock was there, bare and huge, pushing up into her flesh. He used her as he might have used a blow-up doll, his eyes hooded, mouth set, pumping her up and down. Her pleasure was of no consequence.

Sweat sheened her skin and pain jabbed through her as each downward pull rammed her cervix against his cock-head. Then he paused, and she was shaken by the heavy thudding of his heart. He held himself still within her, preventing the eruption of his orgasm, then slowly withdrew and set her on her feet.

The gate clashed as he slid it back and, arm round her again, he led her through the top floor towards a canvas-covered aperture in an outer wall. It was freezing up there, the awnings straining against the hawsers in the strong wind. The lights bobbed on their power cables, and Kim screamed as he pulled back a section of the covering and she found herself standing on a narrow ledge.

She clung to him, and could feel laughter shaking him. 'Look at London,' he shouted joyously. 'It's a map spread out below you. Look at the river, like a silver snake. There's the dome of St Paul's and the Post Office Tower. It twinkles like an alien spaceship. Look down, Kim. One careless step would launch you into eternity.'

'Don't!' she gasped, pulling back.

'Don't? You're saying that to me?' he said, without a change in tone. 'I can see that you'll have to be chastised again soon.'

Her skin crawled with remembered pain and ecstasy. She would welcome his hand if he would stop tormenting her, keeping her dangling, never knowing whether or not her craving was to be satisfied.

Back inside, she trembled with relief, no longer forced to tread the edge of the abyss.

Jack pushed her back against a concrete pillar and opened her coat, spreading it wide. Her nipples were so hard they felt sore. He bent his head and tongued them, nipping and nibbling until she moaned, her hands going to his head, her fingers tracing over the short, spiky hair.

He went lower, lapping down her ribs, before his tongue forked into her navel. She could feel the rhythm of his breath tickling her skin. He went down till he licked the outer rim of her sex. He drew her lips apart, exposing her clit. He was on his haunches between her thighs, making the damp fronds of her bush even wetter, rubbing the swollen folds each side of her little organ, then drawing it into his mouth, flicking his tongue over the tip.

Kim went rigid, her arms stretched like a crucified criminal, her head thrust back against the concrete column. She had imagined him licking her so often in her fantasies. The reality of it made her legs unsteady, and she gripped the stone harder, all the heat of her most terrible desires now surfacing. He strummed on her bud wickedly, sending shocks all through her. His thumb revolved on it now, and he pushed his tongue further into her folds. It felt large and muscular as it executed circles just inside her, then thrust in hard, as far as it would go.

He explored every crevice, rousing her lust, and a hot, heavy feeling in her belly. She put her hands in his hair and pulled him tight against her. His fingers speeded up, his thumb flicked faster, and she came in a sudden rush of heat, an explosion of pleasure so intense that she blacked out for a moment.

He took her down gently, gently, his hand lingering on her mound. Then he was on his feet, and she assumed the submissive pose, lifting her face to his cock.

'Kiss it,' he said.

The smell of him was pungent. She reached between his legs and fondled his balls. His erection pressed against her lips and she took it in, her jaw tightening round the meaty stem, and the more she worked it, the more she could feel his excitement building. His hand was on her head, and she heard him stifle a groan.

Her hand played with his shaft while she sucked his helm and foreskin. His hips bucked and he came quickly, spurting into her mouth. She swallowed his strong-tasting come, and wiped the residue from her lips on the back of her hand.

She didn't remember much about the ride back down in the lift. Jack took her to her car and, as she sat in the driver's seat, she wound down the window and stared up at him. He leant over and kissed her. She could taste herself on his lips.

'When shall I see you again?' she asked, beyond pride now, her resolutions falling about her.

'When I want you,' he replied, and the night swallowed him up as if he had never been there.

Oliver was in the study, playing solitaire on the computer. Music welled from the stereo, two flat speakers attached to the wall. Kim had heard enough opera by now to recognise the plush, tenor voice of Placido Domingo.

'Black Jack on Red Queen,' she said, looking at the screen over her husband's shoulder.

'I know,' he snapped tetchily, and clicked the mouse. The Jack of Spades flew across to join the Queen of Hearts. 'It's late. Where have you been?'

'At the shop. Stock-taking.'

'I found the number and rang it, but there was no reply.' Click. The Ten of Diamonds settled cosily over the black Jack.

'I popped out for a take-away. It must have been then.'

The nimble lies sprang to her tongue with the same ease that she'd dressed in the back of the car, hidden Elaine's boots and concealed the photos. Was it true that women were born with a degree in duplicity? She hadn't believed this until now.

'Ah, yes. I see,' Oliver answered without looking at her.

It made her uneasy. She was certain that the odour of sex hung about her like a miasma and that he would smell it. Unsure of what to do and how to make a convincing exit and dive for the shower, she said, 'I'm pretty whacked. The shop's been ultra-busy today. I think I'll go on to bed.'

'You do that,' he said, his eyes on the cards.

Still she hung around, while Domingo's magnificent voice declaimed the anguish of Othello, tortured by jealousy.

'Don't be long, will you, Oliver?' she asked, inside hoping she'd be fast asleep before he came up.

But it wasn't technically infidelity, she tried to tell herself. Jack didn't put it in me. Well he did, but only that one time in the lift, and then he didn't finish. Where does heavy petting end and adultery begin?

You're splitting hairs! mocked her demon.

'I'll finish this game, maybe have another,' Oliver said indifferently, and went on playing solitaire.

Chapter Nine

V ivien paid the driver and got out of the cab, saying
uncertainly, 'Are you sure this is right?'

'Yes. That's St Edwin's. Somebody's spent a zonking
amount of money on it by the looks of things.' An
ebullient Cockney, he'd been chatting her up all the way.

'My son bought it,' she said, gave him a smile and
accepted his homage. She was confident that she looked
fit in her full, leaf-green skirt, loose, matching jacket,
calf-high boots and a Hermes scarf. The outfit was
expensive and stylish. The driver grinned, saluted and
drove off.

Though her wardrobes were overflowing, she had
bought these clothes especially for her visit to London,
and had her hair touched up and styled into a smooth,
ear-length cut. She'd refused Jack's offer to meet her at
Paddington. Experience had taught her that you never
knew who you might meet travelling, or where such
encounters might lead. She cherished fond memories of
men she'd fucked on trains or ferries. She'd practically
invented the Mile High Club.

Reggie had insisted on driving her to Bristol's Temple
Mead station, fussing as he located her reserved seat and
settled her and her luggage into the first-class carriage.

It was cleaner than the common-or-garden variety, with linen antimacassars on the headrests and smelling of air freshener.

'Don't you worry about a thing,' Reggie had insisted, his heavily jowled face reminding her of a St Bernard dog. All he needed was the brandy cask round the neck. 'I'll make sure the hotel runs like clockwork. Just enjoy yourself, but spare a thought sometimes for those who care about you.'

Amidst the noise of slamming doors, the thrum of the diesel engine, and the general bustle that heralded departure, Vivien had regretted – as often before – that this faithful friend didn't float her boat. She wasn't getting any younger and, while those brief, sexual athletics at the Cash and Carry or various other lust-inspired venues offered instant gratification, there was a niggling doubt in her mind these days. Maybe she should opt for security and become Mrs Reginald Arkwright, though without relinquishing any of her business assets. The Rockburn Hotel was hers alone, and she had willed it to Jack.

Reggie had stood at the compartment door, looking at her with those soulful, devoted eyes. He was as bald as an egg and had very little going for him to her mind, though female friends had said he was still attractive. Fine if you liked the square, corpulent type and didn't hanker after lean, young men with tight bums and skin like velvet.

But needing to be absolutely sure of her power over him, she had beckoned and, when he leant down, kissed him on the lips. 'I'll phone you when I get there,' she had promised, and reaching out, had palmed the fullness in his crotch. There was one thing in his favour: he was extremely well endowed, as she had cause to know.

Mid-afternoon, and the day was drawing to a close. She stood at the lychgate of St Edwin's. There was a bench where a bier could be rested. Churches had never been Vivien's strong point; she always felt distinctly uncomfortable in and around them. I must have been a heretic in a former life, she thought, perhaps condemned by priests and burned at the stake. A shiver ran down her spine. 'Someone's walking over my grave,' she said to herself.

She stood her lightweight flight case on end and dragged it by the handle. The castors trundled over the paving stones as she went under the little arched roof and came out on the path. Leading from the south wall of the church was an area still owned by the council and used for burials. On the east side was a patch of ground littered with builders' rubble. There stood a battered caravan where they could brew-up and champ their way through their lunch. But according to the drawings Jack had shown her, one day it would be transformed into a lawn and garden, bordered by tombstones propped up against a mossy wall.

The church changed shape as she approached it. From a distance it was a fine edifice that dominated the residential square, its spire pointing to the sky like an accusatory finger. Scaffolding was still in place, but as she got nearer, the church became a series of separate angles and spaces, some warm, some cold, some in perpetual gloom. She could see where decaying buttresses had been shored up, ivy clinging tenaciously to some surfaces.

'Good grief, Jack, what have you landed yourself with? A bloody white elephant!' she said aloud, and wondered about the state of her bank balance once he had finished paying for the extensive repairs.

He had his own money, naturally. It was a substantial amount of money for one so young. But she had laid her savings on the line as security on a loan, should he need it. It very much looked as if he would.

There was a singular lack of activity, then she remembered that it was Saturday and the workmen had probably knocked off. This was disappointing, for Jack had whetted her appetite by describing their attributes in graphic detail. Now she'd have to wait until Monday morning.

The sound of which she had been aware as soon as she left the taxi became louder: sonorous chords. Jack had talked about having the organ restored, but she hadn't taken him seriously. It seemed she had been wrong. And who was playing it? Not him, surely? Although he had reached Grade Eight on the piano, the church organ was hardly his style.

Vivien had to admit there were many things she didn't know about her son. He was full of surprises, not the least of which appeared to be his fixation with Kim. He wouldn't admit for a moment that it was a fixation, but Vivien knew better, and her coral lips curved into a pensive smile as she recalled that he had invited the Buckleys to dinner. This promised sport indeed.

She reached the porch with its old, stone coffer, and pressed a hand against the postern set in one of the double doors. It opened, creaking. She hesitated, and the music swelled deafeningly.

Stepping inside, she passed a heavily carved wooden screen, half expecting the usual layout of nave and altar and pulpit. She paused at the sight of the huge room where logs flamed in an open grate under a stone hood. Light blazed through the high windows, kaleidoscopic where it fell on the Persian rugs strewn over the tessellated paving. She craned up at the perfect proportions of its arches, its great, grey pillars and groined roof. Half of the space had been floored over to provide a second storey, finished off with a little gallery. The warm air was fragrant with paint and varnish, linseed oil and turpentine, the sharp odour of sawdust and freshly cut wood, yet there lingered the unmistakable odour of dusty hassocks and oppressive piety.

The furniture was gargantuan, but was swallowed up in the vastness of the living room. There were four luxurious chesterfields, several sideboards and court cupboards, deep armchairs, a forty-inch TV screen and a hi-fi system. The altar had been replaced by an ancient refectory table. It had church pews down its length and a thronelike chair, black with age, at the head; Jack's, presumably. He'd certainly been busy at the auction sales and in antique shops. Vivien admired his taste but flinched at the cost.

Now she could see the source of the music. Organ pipes glinted and banks of ivory keys gleamed. The light from the music-rest also shone on stops and pedals and on to a high seat occupied by a man whose hands spanned the octaves and brought forth those wondrous, shattering chords.

Leaving her luggage, she walked towards the dark, absorbed figure, but though her heels made a sharp clack on the tiles, he went on playing. She mounted the steps until she was standing at his side, wondering how to make her presence felt without giving him a heart attack. She need not have worried, meeting a pair of sparkling dark eyes reflected in a mirror in which the organist had once viewed the choir-master. He lifted his hands from the keys and the music ceased abruptly, lingered for a moment among the rafters, followed by profound silence.

'I didn't mean to disturb you,' Vivien exclaimed, lying through her teeth. He was a male and, as such, had no business being absorbed in anything but herself.

He smiled over a flash of white teeth, his olive skin and blue-black, curling hair suggesting Mediterranean origins. 'That's OK,' he said. His accent was fascinating. 'I've nearly finished testing for Jack. This is a very fine instrument. It has the Foundation, String and Orchestral tone, and softer mutations, too. I've been overhauling and tuning it. It suffered from neglect, mice and fluctuating conditions, mostly cold and damp. Organs don't like this, you know. The hand-bellows system had been modernised and it's powered by electricity, but it's old – mid-eighteenth century – and the maker's name is well known.'

'How fascinating,' Vivien cooed, feasting her eyes on his classical profile. Such a handsome, thirty-something musician; educated, too, so different to the customary bits of trade she usually brought home. 'You're not English, are you?'

'No, Italian. I come from Milan,' he said and swivelled on the organ stool, turning towards her. 'My name is Davide, Davide Ettore.'

'I'm Vivien Loring.' She hesitated then decided to come clean. He could like it or lump it. 'Jack's mother.'

He leapt to his feet, capturing her hand and lifting it to his lips. 'Madama Loring! I don't believe it. You look so young, more like Jack's sister than his mama. He has talked so much about you.'

'You're a friend of his?'

'Yes. He asked me to look at this so fine instrument. I travel all over the country carrying out repairs. I had ambitions as a concert pianist but it wasn't to be, so I've settled for this job. At least I'm in daily contact with music.'

'Do you ever come to Bristol?' Vivien asked, her thighs tingling and her breasts aching to feel those long, strong hands on them.

He smiled again, as if guessing her desires. 'Yes, sometimes. It depends.'

'I run a hotel there. You'd be a most welcome guest,' she murmured and swayed towards him, losing her balance in that confined space. He caught her effortlessly, and her breasts pressed against his short, zip-fronted jacket.

'I'd be delighted,' he answered. 'A fine hotel and a beautiful owner. What more could a man ask?'

He's shooting me a very smooth line, she thought, but who cares?

'Jack may be in at any moment,' she whispered, her hands resting on his shoulders, her pelvis jerking helplessly, seeking contact with his cock.

'Not yet. He told me half after six.'

'Then we shouldn't waste time. Where can we go?' Vivien said. This opportunity was too tempting to miss.

His hand caressed the side of her cheek, and his eyes were tender. 'We have time, *cara.*'

His mouth hovered above hers, and his dark hair fell over his brow. He reminded her of foreign adventures and hot starry nights and gondoliers singing passionately on Venetian canals. When Vivien wasn't being a hard-boiled cynic, she was an incurable romantic. This lovely man was such an unexpected treat, just when she had begun to think that all she had to look forward to was Reggie. He made her feel youthful and bubbling over with sex.

His tongue probed between her lips and he groaned deep in his throat as he tasted her and she, unsure of herself, trembled like a girl in the hands of a much older man. He was a master of the art of kissing, his tongue magical, delicately sipping or thrusting strongly, never for a moment letting the kiss become dull or routine. She could feel the gusset of her French knickers getting wet and sticky. She wished they were in her bed together, that opulent couch where she had known divine pleasures. Davide would appreciate it; he was a voluptuary, like herself.

'Here,' he said and led her through a door. 'This is where the choir used to change into their robes.'

Jack had turned it into a cloakroom. She saw sand and spice, strong colours for the walls and carpet and narrow, pointed windows, darkening now. Davide clicked on the spotlights, using the dimmer switch, then pressed Vivien back against the washbasin. She could smell sandalwood soap and pine disinfectant, and him. His clothing, his choice of aftershave showed him to be a fastidious person who appreciated the best life could offer.

She clenched her hands round his backside, loving the feel of a taut arse covered in tight jeans, her fingernails scratching over the surface. Inside her was a litany, a catalogue of her wants: fill me, fuck me, drive your cock into me.

Her hands were at his neck where his hair grew long. She pulled his face down to hers, her mouth like a voracious sea anemone absorbing his tongue. This would do for the moment until she could lip his balls and suck his cock. That bulge behind his fly was her goal, and she unzipped him. He was naked underneath and she pushed her hand inside, feeling the hot, damp ripeness of his testicles, and the hard length of his shaft.

She wanted him, wanted other men to take her, too, and saw the lorry drivers in the loading bay, yearned to be their whore and have them pump into her, one after another, recalling that glorious moment when her hands and every orifice had been full of cock.

The cloakroom seemed to be crowded, not just with her and Davide, but with the ghosts of the choristers who had once donned their vestments there. Mature men who'd sung bass or baritone or tenor, trying to be respectable but plagued by impure desires, and alto youths whose balls had only just descended. They would have been testosterone rampant, their thoughts dominated by night-time manipulation under the bedclothes and visions of women's breasts and that unknown area between their legs.

Vivien wanted them, each and every one, while Davide sighed into her mouth and pushed up her skirt, coasted along her thigh and lifted her knickers aside. He stroked her from cunt to anus and back again, then paused just below her pubic bush to find her clit. She moved her hand over his cock in time to the exquisite rhythm. Her nipples rubbed against her bra, and she opened her sweater and darted her fingers from one to the other. The nylon lace caused a delirious friction, the sensation echoing that in her clitoris.

She came, her orgasm culminating in one huge wave of glorious pleasure.

'That's it. Come for me,' he whispered, his accent more marked. 'Ah, what a woman!'

He lifted her, her back supported by the basin, and she hooked her legs round him. The clubbed head of his cock slid effortlessly into her. He thrust hard and Vivien cried out, her muscles clenching as he drove faster and faster. Eyes closed, she was in her fantasy world, swamped by men's hard muscles and lean, hairy bellies. Huge pricks, opening her wide, pounded into her, making her shake from head to toe.

'Do it to me. Do it,' she grated harshly, feeling Davide tremble, and his final surge as he spent himself.

She lowered her legs to the floor but kept her arms around his neck. His eyes were shut, his breathing harsh, the heavy beating of his heart vibrating through her. Her skirt remained hitched up and she rejoiced to find that he was still half hard. Give him a few moments and they'd be at it again.

Then the door opened and Jack sauntered in, remarking, 'There you are, I see you haven't wasted any time in introducing yourself to Davide.'

There was no answer to that, and Vivian didn't bother to move as Jack strolled to the cinnamon-hued lavatory, lifted the lid and unzipped. He stood with his feet apart and released a stream of urine into the porcelain bowl.

'So you're James's daughter.'

Kim stared into the eyes of the speaker, a handsome, well-preserved woman who Jack had just introduced as his mother. She had known she must go through with this ordeal when Oliver told her that Jack had asked them to dinner to meet Vivien Loring. She had not expected it to be so painful.

Jack might have warned me, she thought. He could have rung me up and told me he was expecting her, or even asked me if I minded meeting the woman who had slept with my father. But no: he would have thought it funny to spring it on me when I had no chance of

184

refusing. It would have appealed to his warped sense of humour.

'I don't want anything to do with her, Oliver,' she had said, trying to avoid the evil hour. 'I would have thought you'd understand that. I loathe and despise the wretched woman. Why should I make small talk with her over dinner? She probably made my mother very unhappy.'

'You can't be sure of that,' he had replied calmly. 'Your mother didn't know, did she? And if she suspected him of infidelity, then I guess she knew there was more than one. Better to lay the ghost to rest. You may find she's a very nice person, as much taken in by your father as everyone else.'

It was too risky to argue. She was doing her best to pretend that she was indifferent to Jack and annoyed by his claims to kinship. Best to bite the bullet and go along with it.

But it was torment to stand in the warm, softly illumined reception room of St Edwin's and to be greeted by this confident, smiling woman who looked much younger than her years.

Kim couldn't refrain from saying, 'Yes, I'm his daughter and you're the mother of his illegitimate son.'

There was a moment's hush, while Oliver's hand tightened on her arm, Jack chuckled and Vivien didn't even blink. Then she said, 'You're like James, my dear. He had dark hair and the same colour eyes. I'm so pleased to see you at last. I think we should let bygones be bygones, don't you?'

'Why? You think I should forgive you? You want to be told that everything's all right? Play happy families, perhaps? I don't want to know you, Mrs Loring.' Kim had never spoken so rudely to anyone before. Her face was flushed and her breasts shook as she breathed fast.

And she was remembering that the woman had seen the photos of her and discussed them with Jack, even approved of what they were doing together, encouraging incest. As she stood there in her elegant evening attire, smiling serenely, she must be thinking: Jack's tied Kim up and screwed her. Bully for him. Three cheers for my selfish, sexy son. I don't give a damn.

It was like some nightmarish surreal scene where nothing was the right way up. Kim couldn't look at Jack, but his powerful presence overwhelmed her, reducing her to nothing. She retreated, saying no more, and Oliver came to her rescue, carrying on a meaningless conversation with Vivien.

Though he could prepare food with the same flair that he applied to any other task, Jack preferred to leave mundane matters to others. In the same way that he had stolen Lara from Oliver, so he'd lured Andy away from the Byron Hotel to be his housekeeper. But though using them both ruthlessly, to him they were members of staff and, as such, weren't invited to the dinner party he held on the night of his mother's arrival. Andy was there, of course, serving a menu compiled by Jack, which he had spent the day working on.

Now Jack looked round the refectory table with satisfaction. His vision and foresight had been rewarded. The value of the church had doubled in the short time he'd owned it. It was his first real home, and he revelled in its grandeur.

He felt like a sultan in his palace, concubines on either side of him, his mother smiling approvingly at him down the candlelit board, and his catamite bringing in one superbly cooked dish after another. The only skeleton at the feast was Oliver.

It stuck in Jack's craw to be polite to him. All he wanted to do was shout, 'I've fucked your wife,' and wipe the superior smile from his face. Self-satisfied prat, he thought angrily. In revenge, he placed a hand on Kim's knee under the table and stroked it suggestively. The place settings had been planned with her availability in mind. She was on his right and Sandra on his left. It amused him to see them glowering at each other, though pretending to be friendly.

'More wine?' he asked down the table's length to where Oliver sat.

'Not for me, thank you,' Oliver replied, looking up from where he was in conversation with one of Jack's other guests, Ralph Barnes, a middle-aged entrepreneur whom he had invited with purely mercenary intentions.

Ralph Barnes was accompanied by his mistress, not his wife, and Jack had succeeded in enmeshing him, hinting at untold delights on offer if you knew where to go. He had found out that Ralph was more than a little interested in the kinkier aspects of sex. Jack had taken one look at his companion, Imogene Carlyle, and recognised in this leggy brunette a gold-digger who was after Ralph's money. That makes two of us, he had thought.

'But, Oliver, you can't remain sober. Being tipsy is in the nature of a house-warming,' Jack protested. 'I intend to break open bottles of champagne.'

'Sorry. Another time. I'm afraid we can't make a late night of it. I'm off to Brussels in the morning.'

Excellent, Jack thought, smiling and toasting Vivien. You can leave your wife in her brother's care. We'll look after her, won't we, Viv? He admired the sophistication of his mother's simple, black dress and devoré jacket. She certainly knew how to dress for an occasion. And he applauded the way in which she had made a captive of Davide. She was leaning on one elbow, her other hand out of sight under the table, no doubt playing with his crotch. The Italian leant forward, taking fruit from the pyramid that had appeared along with an elaborate pudding of steamed apricots in brandy sauce topped with ice cream. He placed a grape between Vivien's teeth. She popped it and licked his fingers clean.

No one can hold a candle to my mother when she's playing the seductress, Jack thought. I wonder what she makes of Oliver and Kim. We'll have a long talk later.

The way she handled herself when they met was pretty to watch. Kim acted like an idiot and nearly gave the game away. She should take lessons in diplomacy from Vivien.

'I love champagne,' Sandra vouchsafed, touching Jack's hand as if to remind him that she was there.

'I expect you do. No doubt Nanny put it in your feeding bottle,' he answered tersely, then turned away.

'Why did you invite her?' Kim hissed, her eyes on Flyte, who Jack had deliberately seated between her escort, Jason, and Oliver. 'It's bad enough your mother being here.'

Kim was picking at her dessert. He'd noticed that she'd eaten little throughout dinner. He sensed her agitation and smiled secretly. He moved his fingers on her knee ever so slightly, feeling a shiver course through her.

'Why not invite her?' he asked innocently. 'I met her at your place. I even gave her an orgasm while we were dancing. It seemed politic to include her, and I want to talk to Jason about clothes. Did you know he's her slave?'

'I didn't, and I'm not sure what you're driving at. But you know I can't stand Flyte,' Kim went on. 'And your mother is a hard-faced, calculating bitch!'

'Tch, tch, that not a pleasant way to speak of mater,' he scolded. 'You're jealous of Flyte, and maybe justifiably so. Oliver does seem to be at her beck and call.'

She looked at him from under her lashes, obviously confused and uncertain. She must be in a total spin, sitting at table with her husband and her lover/brother, Jack mused. Poor Kim.

'"The ceremony of innocence is drowned," as the poet Yeats so brilliantly put it,' he said, speaking low.

'And what's that supposed to mean?'

'Never mind.'

He gave her a hungry smile and she started as his cool hand explored her hot flesh. He fondled her thigh, listening as Oliver said, 'I never thought the church would be near completion, and in so short a time. A fine job, Jack.'

'Hasn't he done well?' Vivien cooed. 'I gather that you told him about it, and Kim helped him decide.'

'That's true, Mrs Loring,' Oliver replied levelly.

Jack wondered what he made of her. Did he think her vulgar? Was he brooding inwardly on James Millard's adulterous relationship with her? Oliver was a cool customer, watchful, calm, never giving anything away. If he considered it odd that Jack had arranged this meeting between Vivien and Kim, then he didn't betray it by the flicker of an eyelid.

The thought of bringing Kim to climax with her husband watching, though unaware, was so exciting that Jack's pre-come juice made a damp patch on his silk boxer shorts. He liked that feeling, liked the contact between his fingers and her skin. Her shivers and half-hearted attempts to close her legs made his cock twitch and it stiffened even more.

She was clutching her glass as if it was a lifeline. The tips of his fingers brushed against the thin strip of silk covering her mound, and teased the crisp pubic hairs. He paused and withdrew his hand when Andy stood at his elbow, ready to pour coffee. Jack nodded, the fragrance of roasted Turkish beans seducing his nostrils, mingling with that of Kim's juice on his fingers. He sipped the coffee and it was like dark, sweet nectar, so strong that the buzz shot straight to the back of his cranium. He'd be awake for hours.

Kim was fiddling with her spoon, stirring it round and round the tiny china cup. He knew she wanted him to continue fingering her and she was in a state bordering on panic. To have such power over her was as much a hit as the caffeine injection.

Flyte was discussing art with Ralph; Oliver was talking about music with Davide; Vivien had entered into a lively argument with Jason concerning the length of

189

skirts, and Imogene was engaged in horse-talk with Sandra.

Only Andy, standing to attention with a snowy-white napkin over one arm, caught Jack's eye and smiled as he saw him drop his hand into Kim's lap again. Jack winked, knowing that he knew about the affair, and had seen them on the stairs at the Byron. Though women didn't excite Andy, seeing a strong male like himself shafting one of them made him horny as hell. If she wouldn't oblige him later, then Andy certainly would.

Jack traced arabesques over Kim's sex and came to rest on her clit, feeling it harden. Control over another person's reactions was a powerful aphrodisiac, and this was a double dose, for he was arousing Andy, too. He could feel his finger settling into Kim's slippery groove, the tip rubbing her so firmly that she gasped.

'Oliver wants me to demonstrate the sound quality of the organ,' Davide announced. The others murmured in agreement.

'Right. When everyone's had enough to eat and drink, you can give us a recital,' Jack said, and felt Kim throb under his touch and knew she had reached her crisis.

'That wasn't so very terrible, was it?' Oliver asked, snuggling down into bed beside Kim.

'It was dreadful. The worst possible scenario!' she cried, startling even herself with her vehemence.

'Mother Loring could have been much worse,' he offered, nuzzling her ear, his hands sliding over her shoulders and breasts. 'Not too much of a gargoyle; quite an attractive woman, I thought.'

'Did you? Of course, she's old, but then so is Flyte. You seem to have a liking for mature women.'

'Meow! Who's rubbed your fur up the wrong way?'

'No one. Her. Jack. Life.'

'And me?'

'Oh, no. Never you. You're so good to me, Oliver,' she

190

said, flooded with shame when she thought of the orgasm she'd had at the dinner table, and how Jack's devilishly clever fingers had brought her to ecstasy. Oliver didn't deserve such shabby treatment.

She curled against him, arms wrapped round his body. He gave her a worried look, saying, 'What's wrong?'

'Nothing's wrong,' she said, smiling and touching his hair, longing desperately to regain what they had once had, when her desires and emotions were simple and straightforward.

She wanted to make love with Oliver, whipping up her passion by thinking of those early days of marriage when his hands were new on her skin and his every touch was electric. The courtship had been brief and he hadn't had sex with her before the marriage. The wedding night had been something special.

Wanting to relive those times and make everything right, she grabbed at him and they rolled together across the mattress, tangling in the valance sheet. Oliver lay over her, his weight on his elbows as he looked down into her face, stroking her hair back from her temples and chuckling as he said, 'It must be my new aftershave that's turning you on.'

'No, Oliver,' she answered sincerely, looking him straight in the eyes. 'It's because I love you.'

'You funny thing,' he said, and there was a shadow hovering over his response. 'Do you really, truly love me? Not as some kind of father-figure, but for myself?'

'You know I do.'

Now she was feeling uncomfortable, a chill piercing her heart, that upsurge of genuine love tinged with guilt. Don't think about Jack! she said to herself. It's only Oliver who matters.

'That's all right, then,' he said, and slid to one side so that he could move his hands all over her body, her breasts, nipples, concave belly, pointed hip bones, and the dark seduction of her cleft.

She treasured the feel of his lips, rejoiced in the clean, honest rightness of it. He was adding to her, not diminishing. She clutched at his cock as he pulled apart her lips to play with her clit. So reliable, those lean fingers, skilfully bringing her to the peak. She turned into him, arms coiled round his neck, her face buried in the light fur of his chest. And she came, sweetly, easily, running her hands through his brown hair and drawing his lips to hers, sighing her orgasm into his mouth.

He spread her wide open under him and penetrated her, his hands clasped with hers above her head. His cock was lodged deeply and she raised her hips so that his final thrusts shot out his come with full force.

After Oliver slipped out of her, he kept an arm round her neck as they settled back among the pillows, and said, 'Come to Brussels with me.'

'I can't. I've promised Jenny to go wedding-dress hunting tomorrow.'

'Ah, the wedding. So I suppose we shan't be able to take a holiday until it's over. When exactly is it?'

'May. There isn't much time to get everything ready.'

'OK, darling. I'll be gone two days, three at the most,' he said, hand coming over her shoulder and idly cradling her breast. 'Can you survive without me, lost in a jungle of bride shops?'

'I can try,' she said with a smile.

Oliver folded both of his arms round her then, as if she needed protecting, and Kim felt his lips on the back of her neck and smelt their mingled odours. She wriggled her buttocks into his groin, his limp cock undulating as he breathed in sleep. Did he have everything figured out? she wondered, feeling like a rudderless boat that had found a haven in the storm. Did he, too, have doubts, or, having chosen his path, did he adhere to it confidently?

She drifted in and out of dreams between then and morning, clinging on to the thought: I won't see Jack again. I'll positively refuse to return his calls.

What I have with Oliver is more important to me than anything.

It was there when she got into work the next day after a morning shopping with Jenny; a cardboard box tied up with string. Her name was scribbled across it.

'Where did this come from?' she asked.

'Your brother dropped it in early and introduced himself. You're right about him. He could charm the birds right down out of the trees,' Elaine answered, darkly tanned and glowing from her sojourn by the Indian Ocean. 'Aren't you going to open it?'

Wanting to, yet afraid, all her good resolutions melting at the very mention of Jack, she carried it into the back room. Elaine drifted behind her, jingling faintly, tiny bells on her pendant earrings, arms banded by thin silver bangles, completely enamoured by artefacts she'd bought in Goa's street markets

Kim wished she wasn't there, wanting to be alone when she examined Jack's present. It was almost bound to have a sexual connotation. Too shy to ask her to leave, she fumbled with the knot, then lifted the lid.

'Gosh. Sexy,' Elaine exclaimed, leaning over her shoulder. 'What's going on?'

'A fancy dress party,' Kim replied off the top of her head.

'Looks more suitable for a fetish club, if you ask me,' Elaine said slowly, lifting out a black, leather basque and a skirt no bigger than a lampshade. 'And look. He's even included a riding crop.'

Kim could feel herself going bright red as she glanced from the whip to Jack's note that said, 'I'll pick you up at seven. Wear these and tease your hair out. We're talking sluttery here.'

'What's the theme?' Elaine asked, reading it, too. 'Vicars and tarts?'

'I guess so,' Kim answered miserably, ashamed of the

193

heat that fired through her pussy, the leather gear and the crop inspiring lewd images.

'You're not telling me the whole story, are you?'

'It's nobody's business but mine,' Kim replied huffily, even as she took up the basque and held it against her. It was wasp-waisted with underwired cups that would support her breasts without covering the nipples. Gilt suspenders dangled from it and Jack had included a pair of slit-crotch panties, lacy hold-ups and high-heeled black shoes.

'I'm your friend, remember? If you're in some sort of trouble then maybe I can help. And Jack looks like trouble with a capital T. Never seen such a bad, bad boy. Makes me glad I'm a lesbian,' Elaine said, shooting her a shrewd glance.

'I don't want to talk about it.'

The phone beeped and Elaine answered, then held it out to Kim. 'For you.'

'Have you tried on the clothes?' Jack said abruptly.

'No, and I shan't.'

'You will, and you'll be ready when I call for you.'

'No, Jack, I definitely decided last night. It's over. I want to be with Oliver.'

'Bollocks! Be ready when I come.'

'But, Jack –'

It was too late. He had hung up on her.

'And you're trying to tell me there's nothing going on?' Elaine scoffed. 'Jesus Christ, you look terrible. What's wrong?'

'Nothing I can't handle,' Kim replied stubbornly. To put what was happening into words would be to give it a credibility she was trying to deny.

'OK. Have it your way, but I'll be around if you need me,' Elaine said. 'Come back here if you don't want to go to Glen House. That is, if you decide not to spend the night with you brother.'

'Why should I want to do that?' Kim snapped, thinking unhappily, guilt makes bad-tempered fiends of us all.

'Only you know the answer. Come on, let's see you in your outfit. He judged your size well. It's almost as if he'd studied your measurements intimately.'

'I'm average, aren't I? And I'll dress up later on. We've a business to run.'

Elaine grinned. 'Don't remind me. Does Oliver know you're gadding off?'

'He's in Belgium chasing a deal. Anyway, he's not my keeper. I can do what I want,' Kim retorted, but was aware that her defiance fooled no one.

Time did a double shuffle that day, rushing ahead, yet dragging. When Elaine locked the door at half past five, Kim showered and then, towel-wrapped, gazed at the articles spread on the bed. They were as brash as a display in a sex-shop window. Kim had never seriously considered dressing in such enticing underwear, but now wondered if Oliver might like it. Were Flyte's voluptuous curves encased in elastic and boning beneath her fashionable outfits? And Jack's mother's?

She was covered in droplets from the shower, but drenched between the legs. Her hand moved to her breasts under the towel and her nipples stiffened. Her throat tightened and a pulse fluttered in her belly.

'Try them on. Let me be your dresser,' said Elaine, coming into the bedroom.

Not long ago Kim would have refused, alarmed by this suggestion coming from a woman who loved women. But Jack had somehow tapped her wellspring of desire and she no longer minded Elaine seeing her naked. Soft hands released the towel from around her and removed it. In the long mirror she could see Elaine standing behind her, a tender expression in her dark eyes. Kim wanted to feel her fingers on her breasts and feel them caressing her sensitive sex. Wantonness had overcome hesitation or shame.

Elaine smiled and said, 'Something has changed you. Or is it someone?'

As she spoke, she picked up the basque and placed it round Kim's body, easing her breasts into the half-cups, easing the lower section over her waist and upper belly. When she was satisfied that it fitted properly, she started to lace it at the back.

Kim gasped as her breath was forced from her by the strength of Elaine's pull. Before her eyes, her waist became smaller and smaller till it was almost doll size. Her breasts bulged in contrast, shamelessly provocative. Her pubis was framed by the long suspenders. Elaine knelt and pulled the lacy hold-ups up Kim's legs. Her face was so close to Kim's mound that Kim could feel the whisper of her breath on the sensitive hairs.

Elaine paused, waiting for her reaction. Kim lifted her hands and played with her nipples, pleasure shooting down to her clit. Elaine kissed her thighs between the hold-ups and her vagina, moving with a delicacy Kim had never experienced with a man. Elaine gave her time to assimilate each sensation, fingers following lips until finally she alighted on the dark triangle that hid Kim's delta.

Kim wanted to say, 'Don't stop,' but was still too shy. Yet her body spoke for her, the muscles in her buttocks responding, easing her pubis forward. As delicately as if she was parting flower petals, Elaine trailed her middle finger along Kim's inner lips, teasing them open.

Kim sighed, head up, eyes closed, wanting to see or hear nothing, lost in exquisitely pleasurable sensations.

She dreamed, her own hands becoming those of slave-girls in some eastern seraglio where she was the head concubine. And Elaine was her favourite, kneeling at her feet and lapping at her clit. She could feel her holding the outer lips apart, giving her free access to the hard nub of flesh, and she moaned louder, then gave an un-dulating cry of extreme excitement as her orgasm broke.

Standing there on shaking legs, she opened her eyes

and the bedroom righted itself. Elaine stood up, supporting her with her arm and making no comment at all, as if this was the most natural thing in the world.

'Shoes and panties next,' she said. 'After which we'll do your make-up and hair. You want it tarty? This should be fun.'

Jack arrived dead on seven, and his eyes widened as he saw Kim. 'I knew you could do it,' he exclaimed, grinning.

'Elaine helped,' Kim said.

'Fine. Then let's away. You shall go to the ball, Cinderella, but first you need this or we shan't get very far on the street.'

With a flourish he shook out superbly matched jaguar pelts that had been fashioned into a loose-fitting coat with a wide collar.

'Are those for real?' Kim asked, eyeing the garment with distaste.

'Oh, don't be so fussy,' he chided impatiently. 'It's old, made in the thirties. No recent spotted puss-cat has been killed, so you can wear it with a clear conscience. You won't be stoned by the animal liberation movement.'

Kim looked across at Elaine helplessly. She would have much preferred to stay in her company that night. Yet Jack's mastery made her shiver. He had done things to her that had existed only in vague fantasies. Just to be in the same room with him turned her weak.

'Don't forget. If you need somewhere to stay,' Elaine reminded her, and Kim could see that she didn't much care for Jack.

'There's no need to worry about her. She'll be with me,' he answered coldly.

Elaine subjected him to a steady, calculating stare and said, 'That's exactly why I'm worried.'

He held out the coat and Kim huddled into it, only her calves and the high, patent-leather shoes showing.

But the shop mirror threw back an image of a harpy. The wildly tousled hair and heavy make-up, combined with the fur coat, hinted at dark alleyways and pick-up joints and sex sold for money.

Kim was afraid. What were Jack's intentions? Was he planning some further humiliation for her?

Chapter Ten

'*E*laine's had you, hasn't she?' Jack said, yanking at the car door before pushing Kim in.

'Yes, just now,' she answered pithily, putting as much insolence into it as she dared. 'You shouldn't have sent such sexy stuff to the shop.'

'I wanted her to do it. All part of my plans for you, sister. But you should've waited till I gave permission. I intended watching you with a woman.'

He threw himself into the driver's seat. She looked at his face in profile and sensed his rage, and triumphed. So, even he had an Achilles heel. Jealous of a lesbian? Afraid that Kim might prefer her love-making to his?

'Was it your first time?' he asked bluntly.

'Yes.'

'And did you suck her off?'

'No. She brought me to climax, asking nothing for herself.'

He turned the ignition key and the Jaguar purred. In the red glow from the dashboard she could see his strong, sinewy hands on the wheel and recalled their punishing force. He turned into a main street, the car weaving effortlessly through the traffic.

'I didn't say you could let her touch you,' he said coldly, his eyes on the road. 'This deserves a beating.'

She didn't really hear his words, only the angry tone. He was enraged because she had followed her own instincts.

'You can't do that. Oliver will see if I'm marked.'

'He's away.'

'He'll be home in a couple of days.'

'I don't think so,' he remarked, lighting a cigarette as they paused at a junction. 'He told me he might go on to Paris, depending on the outcome in Brussels.'

'He didn't say that to me,' she said sharply, hackles up. What right had Oliver to confide in him and not her?

'It's only a maybe. He'll probably phone you. You know business is his life's blood. Anyhow, he thinks you're all involved in Jenny's wedding. That's fine by me. I can screw you legless in his bed.'

'I shan't let you. You have no say over what I do,' she retorted icily. 'You're not my husband, and even if you were, it wouldn't give you the right to order me about. We're not living in the Dark Ages.'

Jack chuckled wickedly, irresistibly attractive, his tight jeans tucked into the tops of burgundy boots, his leather jacket over his shoulders, his spiky hair touched with green from the traffic lights. The car eased forward and Kim's skin prickled as she wondered where he was taking her.

'Ha!' he mocked, and his slanting glance was glacial-cold. 'And when have you ever defied Oliver? He pulls your strings like a puppet-master.'

'That's not true. I respect him and trust his judgement. He wouldn't treat me this way, ordering me about, sending me tasteless clothes –'

'Encouraging you to let a dyke tongue-fuck you,' he reminded her acidly and stretched out an arm, his hand clamping her knee, one nail catching in the hold-ups. 'No, Kim. You've not yet learnt the meaning of sub-

200

mission. You're a very lucky girl. But I'm here to teach you. And don't forget, I have the negs of those compromising photos. Never mind about Oliver seeing them, I know newspaper editors who'd kill for the rights.'

Imogene Carlyle was no stranger to Flyte, though Flyte had been rather surprised to see her with Ralph Barnes at Jack's dinner party.

She and Imogene had trawled the scene, not together, but coming across one another often enough. The in-crowd were a small, select group and one often saw the same people at the same clubs or parties. Even the addition of masks and outrageous costumes didn't necessarily provide perfect disguises.

When Imogene had invited her to her penthouse suite at a prestigious address in Knightsbridge, Flyte had accepted, her curiosity honed. Would Ralph be there, and if so, was it possible to interest him in the Harlequin Gallery? There was always room for another backer.

She found the address easily enough, and drove her car through the gates and into a parking area designated to the apartments, then, after showing identification to the porter, entered the impressive foyer. An elevator bore her smoothly upwards. She stepped out and saw an open door across the corridor, and the main reception room occupied by a dozen couples and several singles.

'Hello, Flyte,' Imogene carolled, coming towards her.

A shocking-pink lurex bodice jacked up her breasts, and an azure tutu brushed the tops of her gold-mesh stockings. The stiff muslin dipped and lifted as she teetered along on shiny, turquoise ankle boots, displaying her long thighs and giving glimpses of her fork with its neatly trimmed bush.

'I nearly died when I saw you at Jack's. I didn't know you knew him,' she went on. 'He's the new kid on the block. Did you know, the word is that he's shagging his sister.'

'What!'

Just for a moment Flyte's hard-won cool slipped. A lot of things slotted into place. She had sensed for a while that there was something troubling Oliver. He always turned up at her door when he needed reassurance, and this had been happening with increasing frequency.

'That's the gossip,' Imogene answered gaily. 'They'll be arriving soon.'

'Don't tell them I'm here,' Flyte said quickly. 'I'm her husband's friend and I want to see what's going on.'

'All right, darling. Anything you say.'

Flyte's thoughts buzzed in her brain like angry hornets. Surely Oliver can't suspect, can he? He'd have said something by now. What game is Kim playing? A highly charged one, if the story is true. Fucking her half brother? But then she thought: wouldn't you? He's a fallen angel, a devilishly sexy beast.

She wandered towards the bar, nodding to the guests. She wore a black, leather waistcoat and tight trousers laced at the sides, ornamented with buckles and chains, and zips in all the right places. She had not yet discarded her cloak. The other women's costumes were varied, each giving rein to flights of fancy. Birds trailed magnificent plumage, ponies pranced in harness and feathered top-pieces, flaunting flowing manes, with tails rooted deep in their backsides. There was a predominance of leather, open crotches and nipple slits. The men dressed casually in contrast to the provocative attire of the women.

Flyte smothered a yawn. Go to one funky gathering and you've seen the lot, she thought. Yet even so, a dark skein of lust started to tug at her loins. She could feel the handle of her switch burning into the palm of her glove. Who would it sting tonight? Or might she end up submitting to a master, hung up and dripping sweat while she experienced the fury of the birch and the inexorable beat of desire?

She handed her cloak to an attendant dressed in a

severe, navy-blue uniform with holes cut in the skirt to show her backside. The dimpled, white flesh bore a ladder of crimson marks. Flyte smiled and perched herself on a stool at the bar, one heel hitched on the rail, the other leg on show in the thigh-high PVC boot. The bartender was worth a second glance. He must have been hired for the night by Imogene. The bar itself was a part of the decor. Grey, white and black predominated, the huge space made larger still by high, uncluttered walls, a smoothly tiled floor and a minimum of furniture. The interior had been planned along art deco lines.

Within minutes of her ordering a cocktail, Ralph appeared. He looked out of place there, wearing a dinner jacket and bow tie. 'I'm glad you came,' he said to Flyte, his beefy features dotted with little beads of sweat. 'Imogene throws great parties. It's an eye-opener for me. What a girl!' Then he hesitated, running a finger between his collar and bloated red neck. There was obviously something on his mind.

'What's the matter, Ralph?' Flyte asked with a downwards glance at his fly, her tongue tracing circles round the rim of her glass.

'It's a bit forward of me, but do you think I could lick your boots?' he asked, smiling nervously.

The night was getting off to a good start. 'I don't know about that,' she replied. 'What's it worth?' She eyed him inquisitively, stroking the switch in her lap.

'Anything you want,' he stuttered. As he followed the path of her fingers, sweat began trickling down his brow.

Flyte pretended to think about it, then said slowly, 'Will you come to my next exhibition of contemporary art? I'd like you to put some money into the venture.'

'Yes, yes. I'd be honoured,' Ralph agreed eagerly, and fell to his knees.

'That's not the way to address me. Have you no manners?' she said sternly, the birch slap-slapping against her calf.

'I'm sorry. Forgive me. What shall I call you?'

'Goddess,' Flyte answered imperiously.

'Yes. Goddess. Nothing less, of course.'

'You may proceed, until I tell you stop,' she said, with the regality of an empress.

He cradled her foot and, after signalling the barman to pour another drink, she sat there unmoved as he lowered his face and began slurping at the shining plastic and running his tongue over the mock spur.

Flyte considered him dispassionately. He had a bald spot at the crown of his head. She knew him to be the head of many a successful organisation, a tycoon with the power of hiring or firing, yet here he was at her feet, adoring her and highly aroused by this act of servitude. His hand was clasped round the considerable bulge in his evening trousers and he was rubbing himself as he polished her boot with his saliva. Flyte began to find it boring. She needed excitement; her nipples were chafed by the restricting waistcoat, and the hard stool pressed against her damp furrow.

She cast a predatory glance around, seeking her first prey of the night. Imogene's guests were relaxing and the atmosphere was charged. Flyte could smell alcohol and perfume, the oceanic scent of aroused women, the musky odour of horny men, the sweet fragrance of joss-sticks and joints. A large video screen occupied part of one wall and people lounged on chrome and leather couches, watching the image of a nude girl in bondage.

Forgetting the grovelling Ralph, Flyte focused on the screen, and that warm, lubricious feeling increasing between her legs. The porn actress was blonde and big-breasted, her master a muscular hunk in a leather jockstrap. The blonde was suspended on a crosspiece, her wrists tightly roped, her legs bound at the ankles and forced open by a wooden strut fixed between her knees. The master gave the contraption a twirl.

Now she faced the camera, tears streaming down her face and into her ringleted hair. Her master trailed the whip up her cleft, then took one breast in his hand and fastened a metal clamp on the nipple. The girl screamed. He stood back, admiring the crimson blush spreading from her areola. He gave it a pull, then did the same to the other.

Her agonised cries reverberated through the speakers. Or were they cries of pleasure? Flyte thought they were a mixture of both, her own nipples burning with the memory of such exquisite torment. The sight was arousing, and she couldn't help slipping a hand down and touching herself.

The master spun the cross again. The pale body rotated, presenting the narrow, hunched shoulders, the slim waist, her rounded buttocks and plump thighs waiting to receive the lash. His muscles bunched. The whip hissed viciously and landed with a crack. The blonde yelped. He palmed her mound and rubbed her clit. She squirmed her hips, fighting the pain, fighting her bonds, desperate for relief.

Flyte splayed her legs, wishing it was real, not a film. She longed to touch the girl, lay stripes on that inviting flesh, tweak the nipple clamps and explore her sex, just as the master was doing.

The spectators were responding, too, the room filling up with carnal heat. Flyte writhed on her leather-covered finger, and orgasm shot up through her. She was aware that Ralph was grunting, his tongue swiping frantically over her foot. His trousers were unbuttoned. His short, stubby prick protruded from under the curve of his belly and he was working it hard. It wept. He gave a final jerk and came into his fist.

Flyte hardly noticed. The movie, and the panting man crouched at her feet, were suddenly of no importance. Jack and Kim had just walked in.

Kim was relieved to find that the costumes of the other women made her own seem modest in comparison.

205

'Lovely coat,' Imogene said, smoothing the pelts sensuously. 'So barbaric, darling. Your idea, Jack?'

He smiled and poked a finger into the top of her corset, making her nipples stand. 'It suits Kim, don't you think? She's a wild cat under that domesticated, tabby exterior.'

'And needs a night on the tiles?'

'You could say that, though I'd rather call it training.'

The apartment was lit by a multitude of spots set in the ceiling, and by the huge screen where a girl was being flogged then penetrated by a man with the physique of a body-builder and a ten-inch cock. Kim couldn't stop staring as it reappeared from the girl's wet hole, the camera angle emphasising its thick shaft and circumcised head. How could anyone take a thing that size inside them?

'He's famous for it in the porn-film industry,' Imogene observed. 'Gets paid thousands of dollars a poke. I'd love to meet him. He can park it in my pussy any time.'

'You're just a trollop,' Jack teased, watching the salacious antics on the screen, his hand in the groove of Kim's bottom as he murmured. 'Would you like it up the bum, sweetheart? All that steamy meat buried in your arsehole.'

A waiter brought a tray of drinks. Kim took one to give her hands something to do. She was acutely nervous as she followed Imogene and Jack through the apartment. She'd never seen a film like that, or witnessed live couples abandoning themselves to sex. They were fornicating all over, in the reception room, in the bedrooms, in the hallway, on the stairs. The Jacuzzi seemed a favourite, where water sloshed and bubbled over a tangle of naked limbs: male, female, it didn't make any difference.

The plush surroundings had acquired the ambience of a whorehouse. Bowls of condoms of every shape and colour jostled for place on the buffet tables with the caviar, the smoked salmon, the game pie, garlic bread,

fresh pineapples and champagne. Tall, glamorous trans-
sexuals vied for attention, often ousting those who had
been born women. Gay men took their pleasures as
fancy dictated, and Kim blushed to see a naked man on
hands and knees, his mouth fastened round the cock of
an older participant, while a third, tattooed, moustached
and crop-headed, plugged the young man's rectum with
a generously proportioned prick.

'It takes all sorts,' Jack commented.

'And you've done that?' she returned, striving to
appear unfazed.

His eyes were pools of ancient, perverted wisdom.
'Yes.' he said. 'But tonight is your night, Kim. Your
initiation, if you like. I'll be with you every step of the
way.'

'What do you mean?'

'Come with us,' Imogene put in, her cool fingers on
Kim's arm. 'Welcome to the heart of my kingdom.'

A door opened before her and she was inside a large
room; at least she assumed it to be large. The corners
and ceiling were drenched in shadow. Various devices
loomed out of the gloom: a whipping-post like the one
she had just seen in the movie; a contraption like a
vaulting horse; a wooden bench with holes sawn in
strategic spots; racks of canes, whips and paddles. Some
of the objects were in use.

She registered this before a blindfold went over her
eyes. She was petrified. 'Is that you, Jack?' she ventured,
her voice shaky.

'Trust me,' he murmured, his breath caressing her ear,
his tongue working round the lobe.

His hand was on her bottom, guiding her forward
with fingers that probed her, skirt lifting, the lace-edged
slit in her panties parting. Someone slipped a collar
around her throat. Though smooth, it felt as if it would
cut her to the bone. She felt the pull of a leash, jerking
her onwards, and Jack's penetrating fingers wriggling
inside her. It was hard to walk with him part-lifting her

like this, but the collar was choking her. She stumbled, arms stretched in front of her but meeting nothing, hearing voices, murmurs, muffled laughter. Sight was denied her, but her other senses were razor sharp.

She was pulled to a standstill.

Where was Jack? She couldn't hear or smell him.

She'd never felt more alone.

The hand on the leash didn't let go. Cold steel touched her skin, and her skirt dropped away. The blade sliced the narrow ties each side of her panties. Now her lower body was bare.

Hands were on her breasts, lifting them from the basque, fondling, arousing. Despite herself, her body flooded with desire. Warm breath was on her thighs and a mouth sucking at her pussy, a woman's mouth. She thought she could smell Imogene's perfume. She wanted to reach down and touch her hair but her hands were seized, and metal snapped round each wrist. This wasn't Jack's touch, but the hands of strangers, several of them, making free with her, touching her in every intimate sexual place.

Then she heard Jack speaking from somewhere behind her.

'You're their plaything to treat as they like. You won't know who it is bringing you agony or pleasure. It may be me, or a stranger. Endure and learn.'

She was slapped hard on the pubis and breasts, then shoved into other hands that bound her tightly.

'Let me go. What are you doing?' Kim cried as she was lowered on to a padded surface, then rolled over.

Her basque was stripped off, the air suddenly drying the sweat on her back. The wrist cuffs were fastened in such a way that her arms were spread open, and her ankles, too. She was vividly reminded of her spread-eagled position in the crypt, and the hollowness inside her began to fill up with the slow burn of lust.

She whimpered into the dark, disorientated, the scarf

pressing against her eyelids. 'I want to see,' she shouted. 'Take this thing off.'

Pain answered her, the white-hot scalding pain of a leather thong landing on her rump. She bucked. The cuffs tore at her wrists and bruised her ankles. The lash landed again, placed expertly so that it didn't cross the first stripe. Kim braced herself for the next, accepted it, rode it, screamed under it, then felt fingers sliding in and out of her pussy and heard the soft, slippery sound they made. She began to absorb the pain, overwhelmed by a different torrent of feeling.

Now a cane rapped on her skin, adding to the pain already inflicted by the whip. No one tried to gag her passionate wails of agony and longing. There was the woman – only one – and cocks pushing into her mouth and ramming at her pussy and clit. She was terrified of further violation to come, shrieking when someone inserted a huge object into her anus, pushing on it inexorably. Not a man's prick, surely? It didn't feel human. Its warm sleek surface gave off the odour of rubber.

She bore down in an attempt to eject it, then her muscles softened, and it shot into the forbidden depths. It smarted and throbbed as it started to vibrate, the rhythm pounding into her clit. A cock discharged into her mouth, another spewed warm rain over her back, and the dildo made her lose all sense of reality. Nothing mattered but this tempest of sensation.

No one was beating her now, and gradually she became aware that the strangers went away once they had taken their pleasure. She hung somewhere between dreams and reality, accepting the ebb and flow of movement, the scalding pain of her welts adding to the fire of her thwarted desire. Now there was only one person; a large hand cupping her breasts, fingers rubbing her clit. The dildo had been replaced by something equally thick and long and wet, but undeniably human.

It stretched her, forced its way into her, her anal ring

embracing it as it plunged and bucked in that tight hole. It was horrible and wonderful, a sensation of being ripped apart that made her groan and come. She cried and thrashed and felt her assailant pour out his tribute, his finger slowing on her clitoris until it was no more than a light caress.

Jack opened his eyes, his hips still jerking with the compelling drive of orgasm. Kim was stretched out under him. He saw the beautiful spectacle of her helpless, whipped and writhing body, then looked straight up into Flyte's face.

'Ah, you,' he said.

She glanced down at Kim, put a finger to her lips, then whispered, 'You rotten sod. I'll speak to you later.'

What would she do, Jack thought, Oliver's devoted mistress? Run to him with tales of his wife's misdemeanours? The immortal words of Rhett Butler floated in his brain as he allowed himself a smile. 'Frankly, my dear, I don't give a damn.'

'Where are your keepers tonight?' Jack asked Kim, going from room to room, picking up ornaments, fingering damasks, assessing the value of the contents in a greedy, mercenary manner that made her wish she'd been strong enough to close the door on him at the end of the evening.

'Who are you talking about?' she said, passing a hand over her eyes wearily.

'Jenny and the inestimable Liam. I expect Oliver instructs them to look after you, doesn't he? And report in if you have visitors?'

'No, he doesn't, and they're in Ireland, visiting his relatives.'

'Good girl,' Jack said, balancing a delicate jade figurine on the palm of one hand. 'So we're alone here?'

'Yes,' she answered, wishing it wasn't so.

She had known that when the blindfold was removed

and she opened her eyes, it was Jack's face she would
see. They had been alone in the torture chamber, and he
had smiled at her, well pleased, and anointed her sore
body with soothing balm. Then he had found her shoes
and her bag and wrapped her in the fur coat and taken
her out to the car, and back to Glen House.

Too upset, sore and confused to argue, she had now
betrayed Oliver, unlocked the door of his fortress and
invited his enemy in.

Jack was going through Oliver's possessions, sitting in
his chair, helping himself to his whisky. It was as if a
thief had stolen in, ready to ransack the place.

'You can't stay here,' she began, kicking off those
impossible shoes. She wanted to discard the coat, too,
but this wasn't feasible, not until she could reach her
own clothes, and they were in the bedroom.

'Darling Kim,' he mused, turning the tot in his hand
and squinting at the prisms in the cut crystal. 'What
more will it take to convince you it's useless to defy
me?'

'I want you to go. Now.'

'Come here,' he said, and put the glass down.

Her mind screamed no, but her bare feet moved over
the carpet towards him. He reached up and unfastened
the furs. His hands cruised over her breasts, circling a
bruise here and an abrasion there. She bit down on her
lip, wanting to withdraw, but longing to remain under
that subtle caress. He pulled her between his thighs,
kissing the taut flesh at her waist, the concavity of her
navel, the sharp line of hair that led to her mound.

'That's enough, Jack,' she pleaded.

'I haven't even started yet,' he said, looking at her
with his sinister smile. 'Do you realise you haven't
shown me the upstairs? I'm intensely interested in old
houses, and this is a fine example of Edwardian architec-
ture. You're not doing your duty as a hostess, Mrs
Buckley.'

He stood up, held her under the fur, kissed her mouth until she was breathless, then led her up the curving central staircase and, still kissing her, along the corridor to the bedroom. There he slid the coat away and stood her before the mirror. She saw the marks on her torso and, turning, saw others on her buttocks, the purple bruises and thin scarlet lines.

'How am I to hide these from Oliver?' she said on a sob.

'Don't sleep with him,' Jack counselled, moving behind her.

'I can't not. He'll think it strange. We've always slept together.'

'I don't know. Say you're on your period.'

'That won't make any difference.'

'Well then, say you've got 'flu and don't want him to catch it. That seems a wifely thing to do.'

'Oh, Jack, Jack! What have you done to me?' she cried, her skin shivering in anticipation as his hands glided over it.

She saw his louche smile in the mirror, watched him touch her body. His fingers were soft on the blemishes, tender on the red stripes. Was it him who had laid them on her? She knew that even when they had faded she would still be aware of them. As she gave in to the strange desire to have him punish her more, they burned even hotter.

Turning in his arms, she looked back over her shoulder so that she could watch him touching her weals. He watched as well, running a finger along the deep divide of her buttocks, across her anus and then her pussy, searching out all the sensations they contained. Twisting his wrist, he slid his middle digit up her crack and tickled the underside of her clit.

'Leave him,' he whispered, and she rubbed against that tantalising pressure.

'I can't,' she said, her voice strangled in her throat as desire took her over.

'You've your own money, haven't you? Our father left you a packet.'

'I know. It isn't that. Ah, go on, Jack, please!'

He slowed the pace, and she hung there on the crest, disappointed, baffled, wanting to hit him.

'When I can get away from the Transglobe project, I'm travelling to Japan. Come with me.'

She pressed against him, ground her thighs together, frantically seeking orgasmic release. It didn't happen.

Japan. She so much wanted to say yes, to put thousands of miles between her and her guilt, not to have to own up to Oliver, kidding herself that she was free, like Jack, needing only him. Exotic cities, new sounds, new sights, a new life. And Jack there all the time, with his strange and fascinating ways of loving. Her master, her brother. She couldn't bear to think about that.

'I can't just up and go.'

'Why not? You have a passport.'

'There's Jenny's wedding. I've promised her. I can't let her down.' But inside her another creature was saying, 'None of this matters. Rub me, Jack. Take me to bed.'

'My schedule's flexible. We can leave the minute it's over.'

'What about Oliver?'

'Forget him. He's a dead issue right now. This is for real. This lovely bed, this splendid room, you and me and our future together.'

'We have no future,' she said, clinging desperately to sanity.

'You're wrong. It's the only one for us. I know it. You know it.'

'We can never marry.'

'That doesn't matter. Marriage is a worn-out institution anyway.'

'Not to me. I like being married.'

'Then you'll have to unlike it, won't you?'

213

The fear of Jack invading her bed faded as Kim felt his chest pressing against her back, his cock against her buttocks and his face buried in her hair. It seemed only right and natural. He sighed and rolled her over, the puffy duvet coming with her. She felt his solid thigh part her legs and her pussy yearned, opening for him. His hand was on her mound, his finger palpating her clit.

The phone shrilled. Kim reached for it on the bedside table. Jack continued to massage her. She glanced at the silver carriage clock. It was two o'clock.

'Darling? I've caught up with you at last,' Oliver said. 'I rang you earlier.'

'I've only just got in. I haven't checked my messages,' she lied, trying to restrain Jack's finger. He slowed, but didn't stop, rolling her little bud in a delicious motion.

'Where have you been?' Oliver sounded anxious and her conscience smote her.

'I went out for a meal with Elaine and Sarah.'

'Somewhere nice? Good food?'

'Javanese. I can't remember the name of the restaurant.'

'Are you on your own there?'

'Yes. I've given Jenny and Liam time off so he can take her to Dublin to meet the clan. I'm in bed. You woke me up.'

'I rang to tell you that I'm going to Paris instead of coming straight home.'

Beside her, Jack pulled an I-told-you-so face.

'Oh, that's a shame, Oliver,' she said.

How can you do this? she wondered. How can you lie to your husband while another man is playing with your pussy so wonderfully that you're on the brink of coming?

'So it'll be the weekend before I see you.' His voice became sweet. 'The main reason I rang was to hear your voice. Are you all right? You sound a little strained.' He sounded so familiar and so concerned that the fire in her

214

clit died down a little, and she found she could tolerate Jack's persistent fingering.

'There's a bug going round. I think I may have picked it up, a sort of 'flu virus,' she answered, while Jack's lips moved over her face and she felt the length of his penis entering her. She throbbed on it, her muscles gripping fiercely.

'Take a couple of aspirins, stay indoors and send for the doctor if it gets any worse,' Oliver advised worriedly. 'I'll get home as soon as I can.'

'I'm all right. Really. No need to bother.'

'But I do bother. I love you, Kim, and look, I think we need to do some talking when I get back.'

Fear stabbed her. 'Oh? Why?' she asked sharply.

'I'm spending too much time working. I don't want us to drift apart. I thought, maybe, you'd like to think about having a baby.'

This was embarrassing. How could she even contemplate such a thing with Jack's cock buried to the hilt in her centre?

'We're happy as we are, aren't we? We don't want to get like Polly and Keith, bogged down with bratlings.'

'Maybe not. We'll see. Let's at least talk, darling.'

'All right. Whatever you think best, Oliver,' she said, while Jack chuckled in her ear and whispered, 'Beware. He wants to lumber you with rug-rats.'

Oliver rang off reluctantly, and Kim blew out her cheeks in alarm. 'God. That was awful. I felt terrible,' she exclaimed.

'It'll get easier,' Jack assured her, moving his cock in her body.

'Oh, so you'd know about it, would you? You're used to lying and cheating?'

'Shut up!' he snarled and pulled her up and over him, controlling her round the waist, moving her up and down on his groin like a rubber toy.

She blanked out the vision of Oliver alone in his Brussels hotel, concentrating on the feel of Jack at her entrance. She still hadn't come and it was driving her wild. She wriggled against his stem, seeking friction on her clit.

'Just stay like that,' she begged, and could feel it coming, each contraction heralding another, bigger one.

She used her fingers, too, opening herself so that she could slide her bud over his solid, fleshy bough. Orgasm tore through her, and he thrust himself into her and propelled her flat on to her back, sitting astride her hips. His cock sank deeper till it was pressed against her spasming cervix. He stared down into her face, his eyes glowing, then drew his erection slowly in and out.

'Now tell me you don't want to be with me,' he said harshly, and slapped her across the breasts.

'I don't know what I want. Why can't I have both of you?'

'*Ménage à trois*? Impossible. Oliver would never agree to it. You want me more than him, don't you? You want this.' He rammed into her hard.

She felt his cock thicken in her, and that final spasm as he came, and knew a moment's tenderness of such poignancy that tears sprang into her eyes.

Why can't I love them both? she mourned. Why are there conventions that say it's against the law? It wouldn't have been like this had we lived in far-off times.

'It's not fair,' she complained, as they lay in each other's arms.

'Who told you life was going to be?' he murmured, kissing her ear and the side of her neck. 'You have to make a choice, Kim. Oliver or me.'

216

Chapter Eleven

'*T*hank you for finding Davide for me, Jack,' Vivien said when she phoned him. 'He's gorgeous. He's moved in. I think I'm in love.'

'Steady on, Viv. What about Reggie?'

'What about him? Reggie knows which side his bread is buttered. He won't give me any hassle. Anyway, I'll be e-mailing you soon, not phoning. Davide's teaching me to use the computer, and you know how I couldn't get the hang of it. He's an absolute whiz-kid.'

'You'll have to be careful what you put on paper,' Jack warned, relaxing on his bed, wearing only his dressing-gown, a pillow stuffed behind his head, a cigarette between his fingers. He had bathed, shaved, and was about to get ready to go clubbing with Andy.

'I know that,' she said quickly. 'And speaking of which, how's it going with Kim? Have you succeeded in breaking up the happy home yet?'

'I'm on the way. Let's say it's nothing like as idyllic as it was.'

'I could see the rot setting in when I was there,' she replied thoughtfully. 'You have such a way with you, Jack. She doesn't stand a chance. Oliver seems a decent enough bloke, and I almost felt sorry for Kim.'

'She's tougher than she looks,' he replied, his mouth setting. 'She can't quite make up her mind to leave him.'

'Maybe you should stop,' his mother advised.

'I thought nothing would please you more than to see her destroyed,' he said, his emotions on a seesaw.

'That's what I wanted, in the beginning. But lately, I don't know, I've been thinking that life's too short for stupid vendettas.'

'This has nothing to do with Davide's dick, I suppose?' he said nastily.

'It might have,' she answered with alacrity. 'I'm happy, Jack, for the first time in years. I don't want to give anyone grief.'

'That's all very well for you, but what about me?' he shouted, sitting up and grinding his cigarette stub into the brass ashtray. 'I'm in it too deep to pull out now.'

'How so? Are you in love with her?'

'Don't be daft! I never fall in love,' he declared forcefully. 'Love isn't part of my plans.'

'It wasn't mine either, but it's happened. Do you want my advice?'

'No, but I've a feeling you're going to give it me anyway.'

'Lay off Kim. Go travelling until you've got over her, then keep it cool, act like her brother, forget you ever screwed her. It's not worth it.'

'My God, you've done a complete turnaround, haven't you?' Jack was seriously angry, not only with his mother, but with himself for getting carried away by his feelings for Kim. He wanted to possess her utterly, with a long-term commitment, nothing temporary or casual. It shocked and terrified him.

'It's never too late to change,' Vivien said complacently.

'It's too late for me. You did a bloody good job, Viv. You taught me how to hate.'

'I'm fed up with hearing about our minds being warped by our parents,' she returned smartly. 'They get the blame for everything these days. Dysfunctional families and all that crap. Surely we must take responsibility for our actions somewhere along the line?'

'That's Davide talking, not you,' Jack opined. 'You're not the philosophic type.'

'How do you know what I am? Have you ever tried to find out?'

This had the makings of a full-scale row and Jack couldn't be bothered.

'I'm glad you're happy, Viv, even if it's only short-term. I can see you're cock-struck,' he said crisply. 'Don't worry about me. Stay tuned. I'll let you know what's going on.' He replaced the phone on the table, faintly amused as always by this piece of art nouveau kitsch: a naked female kneeling on a seaweed rock. You dialled under her rock, listened in her flowing hair and spoke into her pussy.

It was then that he heard someone outside. Before he had time to rise, Flyte came in, saying, 'You really should be careful to lock the vestry door, Jack. This place is stuffed to the gunnels with desirable *objet d'art*. No, don't get up. We need a heart-to-heart.'

'About what?' he asked suspiciously. This red-headed woman was just too dominating. She reminded him of his mother, and he was trying to forget her and the disturbing conversation they'd just had. Davide was obviously stepping into his shoes, and he didn't like it.

'You know what about,' Flyte said calmly, and took off her jacket. Beneath it she wore a grey, tailored skirt and dove-coloured silk blouse. Her nipples lifted the material in two stark points. Her superb legs were also covered in grey silk. Stockings or tights? Jack wondered, and his cock stirred.

He settled down to enjoy a bout of verbal fencing. 'Do I? I'm sure there are many subjects you and I could profit by discussing.'

'No doubt, but I'm here to talk about you and Kim.'

'I don't see why.' He knew what she was getting at, of

course. He had seen her at Imogene's, even though Kim, still blindfolded, had not.

The first hint of unease nibbled at his mind. She was – or had been – Oliver's mistress. Did she care what happened to his wife?

Flyte approached the bed, and Jack applauded her panache. She certainly was an impressive woman. 'I suggest you be frank with me,' she said, and slowly drew off the Givency scarf that softened the severity of her blouse. 'You've been teaching her, haven't you? Introducing her to all manner of wacky things. I saw her being whipped and fucked by all and sundry. I saw you buggering her. I want to know why. What have you got against Oliver? Do you take special delight in something as taboo as incest?'

'Why are you so keen to know?' he said, countering her attack. 'I'd have thought you'd be glad. You want Oliver back, don't you?'

'No, I don't. Maybe I did at one time, but he loves Kim and he'd be devastated if they broke up. I don't want to be left with the pieces, thank you very much. A man on the rebound is of no earthly use to me.'

'So? Why this visit?' he asked, watching her through narrowed eyes.

'It's in the nature of a warning,' she replied softly, and rucked up her skirt while Jack stared, hypnotised.

Stocking tops, lacy hold-ups banding her thighs, then a triangle of fascinating foxy hair. She lifted one leg and rested her foot on the bed, the chestnut floss parting over her deep slit. Jack could feel the heat crawling down his spine and into his groin. His balls hardened, his cock swelled, and Flyte knelt above him, her female aroma seducing his senses.

'I want you to stop plaguing Kim,' she continued.

'Does she want that? Have you asked her?'

Flyte lowered herself across him in one fluid, lyrical movement. 'We've not discussed it. She doesn't know that I know, and I've not said anything to Oliver, yet.'

'And you won't?'

'I make no promises.'

Jack was enthralled, absorbed by the need to push his cock into her, to feel her tight muscles clamping round him, to ram and ram inside her until he spent himself.

She placed her legs either side of his body and mounted him. She spread the robe and her hands drifted down his muscular torso. Jack bucked, wanting her fingers to tweak his nipples. He groaned when her long, blue nails flicked over one of them, groaned and became more erect, his penis nudging against her inner thigh, seeking her pussy. She moved agilely, preventing contact.

Reaching for her bag, she took out a tube, unscrewed the cap and, fingers at her crotch, anointed her clitoris. Jack heard her gasp and guessed at the rush of heat suffusing her delicate skin as the concoction sank in. No doubt it was a sexual stimulant, perhaps a cocaine mix, purchased through dubious channels. He wasn't unfamiliar with such things, and was willing to try anything to promote heightened sensation.

He wondered if she'd smear some on his cock, his balls clenching at the thought of the overwhelming orgasm it would cause. Even the touch of her fingers would be enough. Maybe he'd come just by fantasising about it.

She gave a feline smile of victory and let her weight settle on his stomach, her juices and the salve wetting the light coating of hair there. 'Nothing to say, Jack? No excuses?' she murmured, and her hand teased his nipples again.

'I never excuse myself. I do what I want, when I want,' he said through gritted teeth. Did she intend to screw him or not? he wondered, and knew that one caress on his purplish helm would trigger his release.

He looked down and so did she, her smile deepening as she saw the jism pearling his slit. 'Always ready, are you, Jack? Ready to service anything, man, woman or dog, eh? I'll bet sheep are glad you're not a shepherd. You pride yourself on your virility, take what you want and leave the rest. No consideration, no humanity. You're totally controlled by your dick.'

'I'm not. I never lose control,' he muttered.

'Then that's even worse. You do it coldly and deliberately. Time to make amends, Jack,' she said and, before he knew it, had wound the scarf round his right wrist and tethered it to the bedpost. 'No,' she ordered as he started to struggle. She slapped him smartly across the face, and sat on him hard. She fixed the belt from his robe round the other arm and fastened it securely.

'Bitch!' he snarled, heaving and kicking, but she merely rose, searched through the tallboy and came back with two neckties and a leather belt.

This was brought down with force across the tops of his thighs, catching his balls and striking the underside of his cock. 'You won't ask me to stop,' she observed coolly. 'I know you're going to enjoy this. I've been comparing notes with Imogene.' She bound his ankles with the ties, and slipped a noose round each footpost of the brass bedstead, then belted him again and again.

'Bitch! Bitch!' he repeated, furious at finding himself in this predicament, yet with sullen fires smouldering inside him. She was right. He was no stranger to pain, his intimate knowledge of its subtleties enabling him to mete it out so expertly. His thighs smarted, his balls stung, and his cock tilted back towards his belly, throbbing urgently.

Again Flyte rummaged in her bag, and this time she produced a vibrator. Switching it on, she applied it to her cleft, then, when it was thoroughly wetted, skimmed it over Jack's body. It tickled. It stimulated. When she held it to his nipple he couldn't restrain a bark. Her eyes were shining as she stared into his face.

'Had enough yet?' she asked huskily. 'This is how you like your victims, isn't it? Helpless under your control?'

She opened her mouth and licked the buzzing dildo, dribbled saliva over it, then passed it between his legs, round his scrotum and suddenly rammed it into his anus.

Jack clenched his muscles instinctively as the plastic prick dilated his arse with a terrifying force. This wasn't the first time by any means. He'd been initiated into anal sex by the head boy at school, and developed a taste for it, though usually preferring to play the dominant role. Flyte had worked him into such a state of arousal that he knew the vibration and pressure on his prostate would shortly precipitate a climax.

He ground his teeth together in an effort to prevent it from coming. Flyte pushed and the dildo dilated him even further. He could feel his ring clamping round it, feel the wetness of his cock as it wept tears of need. Not yet, he insisted. Not yet!

Leaving the dildo in place, Flyte straddled him, lowering herself to his chest while his cock strove to reach her slippery avenue.

'Flyte! For Christ's sake, sit on it!' he rasped.

'Not yet,' she chided. 'Maybe not at all.'

She moved higher, a trail of juice wetting his chest hair. Now she poised over his face and, he, looking up, could see her glistening pubic bush, her swollen lips and her large, flushed clitoris. It came closer, out of focus, and the air was filled with her strong, female smell. He closed his eyes and stuck out his tongue, forking round that demanding, fleshy bud.

She sighed, arched, plunged down again, grinding her clit against his lips. He was smothered in her wet heat, his mouth filling up with sex juice laced with the aphrodisiac, feeling her thighs clamping round his head as her whole body shuddered and convulsed.

No sooner had she come, than she withdrew from him entirely. She stood up and calmly righted her dishevelled clothing. She seemed preoccupied with this, and a surge of anger welled up in him.

'You're not going?' he shouted.

'I am,' she said, and shrugged on her jacket.

'What about me?' he demanded, feeling a fool.

'You? Don't worry. I've instructed Andy to come up in an hour and release you. He'll give you a wank.'

Her hand hovered over him and she leant down to examine his genitals. He felt her lift and weigh his balls and run feather-light fingers up his shaft, then rub the helm, but not enough to relieve him. She switched off the vibrator and slowly eased it from his rectum.

'You're a prize bitch, aren't you?' he snarled, but with reluctant admiration.

'You better believe it,' she answered, walking to the door. 'Finish with Kim, or next time I visit you I just might leave the vibrator on inside you when I go. Think about it, Jack. Andy won't be up for an hour. Could you stand it?'

Oliver was down by the river. Kim wandered out to find him. The garden was recovering from winter, crocuses unfolding, clumps of daffodils and narcissi making a brave show under the trees on the lawn. Birds were engaged in the frenetic activity of nest-building, and there was that definite zing in the air. It was the right season to be married, make a fresh start, start a new life. Kim had been caught up in Jenny's excitement, the wedding only a few weeks away.

Kim looked across at her husband. He was unaware of her, staring at the swiftly flowing water. The Thames was high. It had been a wet winter. A strange winter, she mused. Nothing had been the same since Halloween.

She was almost afraid to approach Oliver. The openness between them no longer existed. He seemed preoccupied lately, and she feared the reason. Yet, when they came together, there had never been such passion, not even in their early days. Jack had opened her eyes, stripped her of her inhibitions, and turned her into a sensual woman. Yet even this was hazardous. Sometimes in the middle of love-making, she would catch Oliver looking at her, questions in his eyes. And she would wonder guiltily if he knew she was thinking about Jack, that her brother was on her mind when she went to sleep and as soon as she woke up.

Now Oliver turned, saw her and waved. 'You've finished early, darling,' he shouted. 'I'm going over the place, seeing what needs doing. I'll have to have a word with Liam about it. The boat-house could do with a lick of paint. Summer's just round the corner. Can you feel it? We'll be able to spend lazy days on the river, just like *Wind In The Willows*.'

'That will be lovely,' she agreed and, reaching him, slipped her arm through his.

A thin ray of sunshine slanted across his eyes, turning them to gold, and he faced her squarely. She was embarrassed by his scrutiny as he asked, 'Are you better now? That was a debilitating bout of 'flu. You mustn't work too hard with Elaine. You know, we never did have that talk when I came back from Europe.'

'There's no need, Oliver. I'm perfectly content.'

'Not broody? I did wonder.'

'Not in the least. And we will go away after the wedding.'

'Let's do that. Bill and Joyce want us to visit them in Florida.'

Oh, God, she thought, not the chunky, affable Bill and his strident American wife who wanted to talk about her self-awareness therapy group all the time. On their last trip to London, she had tried to persuade Kim into going along to an English one with her.

If I had, perhaps I wouldn't be in this quandary, Kim thought. Had I had more confidence in myself, then Jack wouldn't have been able to blow my life apart.

She knew she must seize any opportunity to physically distance herself from him, and provide a concrete reason why she shouldn't accompany him to Tokyo. Every time she passed the Transglobe building her heart sank as she realised that it was nearing completion. She wouldn't be able to put Jack off much longer. And she wasn't sure if she wanted to. Whenever she was with him, logic vanished, and she couldn't justify her reluctance to burn her boats.

Oliver ran a gentle finger down the side of her cheek and along her jawline, and said, 'We need to be together, Kim, without interruption from friends or staff, or relatives.'

'Relatives? What are you saying?' She went stiff under his caress, feeling herself blushing.

'Your brother. He does seem to demand a lot of your time,' Oliver answered, so cool that her guilty fears subsided.

'Not for much longer,' she said.

'Oh yes, the Tokyo commission.'

'He's very enthusiastic about it, as he is about a lot of things,' she replied, trying to sound as if she took no more than a passing interest.

'You've become quite close, it seems.'

'Maybe. I do find him irritating sometimes.'

'You're lucky. I'm constantly irritated by my brothers,' he said, and she was conscious that his reserved smile didn't quite reach his eyes. 'But then, I expect that's because of early sibling rivalry. You hardly know Jack, do you?'

She could find no answer to that and remained silent as Oliver put an arm round her shoulders and they went back towards the house. The great Spanish chestnut was showing signs of leaf-break. The grass was spongy under Kim's feet after its first cut of the year. I can't leave all this, neither can I leave this lovely, caring man, she thought despairingly. But oh, Jack, you light my fire, make me blaze, take me on a rocket to the moon.

'So, all the invitations have gone out,' Jenny said, busy with her wedding preparations.

'And the suggestion list regarding presents? We don't

226

want to be given half a dozen toasters when we'd rather have the money,' Liam reminded.

'All taken care of, though it does seem a cheek,' she said, as he beckoned and she went across to perch on his knee. 'Most people know we're in service and not setting up a home of our own yet. Liam, I can't believe it's really happening. Me, a bride, wearing virgin white.'

He hugged her, then his fingers slid under her coppery hair, stroking her neck. She arched against him, her thrusting breasts seeking his touch, while he said, 'I can't wait to see your dress.'

'Not until we're in church. You know the rules: you have to stay away the night before. You'll be off on your stag do, and Mrs Buckley has organised a hen party for the girls. We're going to a club with male strippers.'

'Are you indeed? I don't know if I approve. You might fancy one of them more than me. Supposing he's bigger?' he said, and took one of her hands. She watched hungrily as he placed it on the front of his jeans. She ran down his zipper and explored inside the gap.

'Bigger than that?' she asked, smiling and giving his cock a squeeze. 'I don't think so.'

'Flattery will get you everywhere,' he growled, and the look in his eyes made her toes curl.

'It's not flattery. It's God's honest truth,' she murmured, a blend of desire and happiness flowing through her whole system as he reached under her skirt and met smooth, bare flesh. Going higher, he found her damp panty gusset and parted her lips which were so inadequately covered by the thin, white cotton.

'We've not had much time lately for jig-a-jig,' he complained, his finger alighting on her tingling clit.

'Only every night,' she reminded him breathlessly, wriggling her hips against that seductive motion.

'Not in the day, though, not at odd times and in unusual places. You've either been with Mrs Buckley, planning or shopping, or we've been visiting our folks.'

'Never mind, Liam, we'll soon be on our own. Think of the honeymoon. Wasn't it kind of the Buckleys to give us a trip to Venice, as well as paying for most of the reception?'

'It was,' he said, but she could see that his brain was no longer functioning properly, as if the blood that fuelled it was now channelled into his groin.

Men were decidedly handicapped, she thought; they were never able to concentrate on more than one thing at a time, and when they had a hard-on, nothing mattered but that they get rid of it somewhere. This was why they couldn't remain faithful. Hand it to them on a plate, and they'd be unable to refuse.

'You'd better not play away, Liam,' she warned, gripping his cock hard. 'If you ever get tempted, then tie a knot in it. Should I find out you've been shagging someone else, I'll chop it off.'

'What, me shag another woman? Never. I swear it,' he declared, but his attention was not on her words, only on her pussy.

She twined her fingers with his at her wet pussy and joined in the rhythm, but even as her heart pounded, and she knew she was not far off crisis point, she voiced something that had been troubling her recently.

'We may have our own home sooner than you think. I'm not sure about the Buckleys any more.'

Liam's eyes had become unfocused, but now they sharpened. 'Oh? What's brought this on?'

'She's different. I can't quite put my finger on it, but I'm sure it's got something to do with her brother. I told you before that I didn't trust him. Well, last time Mr B was away, I think he stayed here.'

'Do we have to talk about this now?' Liam pleaded, and turned his attention to her breasts, pushing up her crop-top with his free hand and exposing them, the rosy tips peeking through white, cotton lace.

'It's been on my mind. I can't tell anyone but you,' she answered, closing her eyes and straining towards his hand. The delicious feeling as he rolled a finger over her nipples fanned right down to her womb.

'He stayed in one of the guest rooms, I expect,' Liam suggested, as he watched her nipples stiffen.

'I checked when we got back from Ireland. I'm sure none of them had been used.'

Liam was impatient, wanting to get on with the important things of life, like fucking. 'Then on the settee, on the floor, on the pool table. I don't know. Perhaps he went home.'

'I don't think so. I've a bad feeling about this, Liam. She'd been using the washing machine, doing her own sheets, duvet cover and pillow cases. She always leaves that to me. What was she afraid I might find? Come stains?'

'I don't care, Jenny. It's not our concern,' he cried and pushed her from his lap and down to the carpet, then knelt over her. 'All I know is that I want to fuck you, hard. To hell with Mrs Buckley and her brother. Get your knickers off.'

'I don't know what to do,' Kim moaned, sitting at Elaine's stripped-pine dining table. She had accepted her invitation to stay on and eat with her and Sarah; anything rather than go home.

She'd had too much wine. Soon she would have to ring Oliver and tell him that it would be wiser not to drive. He'd offer to fetch her, but she didn't want that. She knew that she only had to get in touch with Jack and he'd be at the shop like a bolt from a crossbow. She didn't want that either.

Elaine looked at her in the soft light of scented candles and said, 'Why don't you talk about it? I know you've been troubled for months.'

'Oh, dear,' Kim answered, sinking her head in her hands. 'It's such a mess. I wish I'd never started it. I knew it would lead to this, but he just wouldn't leave it.'

229

'Who? Are you having an affair?' Sarah's eyes brightened. There was nothing she liked more than hearing about clandestine relationships, as long as they didn't pose any threat to her and Elaine.

'Worse than that,' Kim said, raising her head and looking at them, both so easy with one another. She decided to come clean, the secret too heavy a burden to carry alone any more. 'It's Jack.'

'Your brother? I thought as much,' Elaine commented, and lifted the bottle of red wine, pouring more into Kim's glass. 'I could tell by the way he looked at you, and that get-up he sent. Hardly a normal brotherly thing. Where did you go that night?'

'To a party where I was blindfolded and whipped and fucked by strangers, but ended up with Jack's cock up my bottom. I was so bruised I had to pretend to Oliver that I was ill to avoid sleeping with him. And even after a week, I made sure I undressed in the dark.'

'But you enjoyed it? Got pleasure from masochism?'

'He's tied me up and slapped me before. He likes to humiliate me and I must admit that it makes me hot.'

'And he's been shafting you for ages, has he?'

'It started shortly after we met. I tried not to, and told him it was wrong, but I can't refuse him. He has this hold over me. He's dangerous and exciting, too beautiful and wicked to resist. He wants me to leave Oliver and go away with him. Part of me wants to agree, but the other, better part –'

'Tells you not to risk it,' Elaine put in. 'Apart from the fact that you're breaking the law – and who says that really matters – do you still love Oliver?'

'Of course I do!' Kim pushed back her chair and paced the floor agitatedly. 'He's my husband and I do love him, truly and deeply, but Jack, ah, Jack's something else entirely.'

'The alpha male, the bad, cruel anti-hero most women fall for, knowing they shouldn't. You've only got to think of Mr Rochester and Heathcliff. Sweet Jesus, listening to you makes me all the more glad I'm not involved in the heterosexual rat-race. It sounds a real pain in the butt, mentally as well as physically.' Elaine said ironically, and put her arm round Sarah, who leant closer to her.

'Men are only needed for their sperm,' Sarah agreed, her small hands playing with the tiny ball buttons that fastened Elaine's short bodice which she wore under a vividly hued sari. Since returning from Goa, they had both adopted Eastern dress for leisure wear. 'And there's enough frozen in fertility centre banks to keep the human race going for generations. They've outlived their usefulness in that direction. Soon we'll be able to clone ourselves anyway, and robots will take away the need for so much muscle. Think of cyber-sex, too.'

Kim sighed. She found this topic depressing, though if she thought about it hard enough she realised that she had been conditioned from infancy to expect love and romance, marriage and children. They were all related to the male. Now, remembering the pleasure Elaine had given her, she began to reconsider.

She had met several of Elaine's lesbian friends who had become mothers using a syringe, impregnating themselves with the help of their partners. The sperm was supplied by carefully selected donors who were also gay but also wanted children. These couples shared the children between them, and this arrangement seemed to work out, no more or less successfully than when conception took place through the old method.

Her brain hurt. Jack had bombarded her with information which she would once have found outlandish, and now Elaine and Sarah were doing the same. It was just too much. She swigged down her wine and held her glass out for more.

'A hangover won't make it go away,' said Sarah sagely. 'You've got to face up to these issues, Kim.'

'Do I really have to? Life was simple once, when there was just Oliver and me.'

'And you were willing to settle for this, until Jack offered you alternatives. Bad boy though he is, he's made you start to question, to think, to explore unknown territory,' Elaine remarked. 'Stay here tonight.'

'I'll have to now. I shouldn't drive. But I must call Oliver first. I can sleep on your couch.'

'You're welcome,' said Sarah.

Kim phoned Oliver, the brief conversation depressing her even more. She could tell he was displeased. Whatever she did seemed to be wrong. Neither he nor Jack were satisfied with her behaviour.

Following the sound of low, murmuring voices, she wandered into Elaine's bedroom. She and Sarah lay entwined on the wide divan, a muddle of slender limbs and bodies that strained against one another. The air was incense-fragrant, and the exotic throb of the tambour, and the riffs of the sitar, made the fine down rise on Kim's skin. It was as if she had walked into another world, a world inhabited by lovely women, where everything was geared for their delight – sights, sounds and smells – a tactile world, soft as silk.

They looked across at her but did not stop caressing. Both were lean as boys, naked among the discarded saris and heavy jewellery. Kim neared the couch, unable to stop watching them. She could feel the sap of pleasure spilling from her, her desire gathering momentum as she saw that Sarah's sex was naked and smooth, without a trace of hair. It tempted the touch, her cleft high and dark, the outer lips protruding. Elaine clasped Sarah round the thighs, holding her haunches in her hands and caressing her slim buttocks. She slid her fingers between them and then, pulling her to her knees, thrust her mouth against her anus and circled the tiny eyelet with her tongue-tip.

Kim remembered Jack saying, 'Have you ever been rimmed?' Now she'd seen it for herself.

Elaine raised her head, her mouth smeared with Sarah's copious juice and said, 'Come here, Kim. There's

232

plenty for all.' But Kim suddenly felt tired. She'd already pushed the boundaries of her sexual life enough for one week and, besides, she didn't want her first full-on lesbian performance to be lacklustre.

'I'm flattered, thanks, but I think I'll leave it to you guys this time,' she said, closing their bedroom door behind her. She needed to think about things. Get her head straight.

Making love with a woman would be different to anything Kim had known before. Different and fascinating, an experience like no other, but somehow – and she was ashamed of this disloyalty to Elaine – she knew it wouldn't be exactly what she wanted.

Was she bred to need cock? Or was it just a habit hard to break? Whatever it was, she knew that when Oliver mounted her or Jack whipped and fucked her, she was utterly satisfied. It felt right. She couldn't say that she'd never repeat her experience with Elaine, but it would never seriously rival her desire for men.

Eventually she snuggled down in her bed in the spare room and swiftly fell asleep. However, when she woke next morning, it was to find Jack occupying her mind. The ghost had not been exorcised. By noon, she couldn't stand it any longer and left Palmer's Emporium to track him down. The church was the obvious place. It was Sunday and unlikely he'd be working. She didn't let him know she was coming. She wanted to catch him out.

London preened under the warm sunshine. The parks had sprung into life, with joggers in tracksuits and idlers in shorts and T-shirts. Girls were baring their shoulders to the sun and the more adventurous men had stripped to the waist, encouraging an early tan. Children ran about, kicked balls or fed the ducks. The latest crop of babies, still swaddled like papoose, gazed up from their smart pushchairs, newborn eyes reflecting the blue sky.

Kim's spirits rose despite herself as she drove. The streets were busy, their shops displaying summery goods. The square was quiet, however, dominated by St

Edwin's. She wheeled round to the side where a driveway had been constructed, along with a double garage. She swung her legs out of the car, and stood on the gravel and listened, then smiled ruefully as the phrase, 'silent as the grave' popped into her mind.

Andy wasn't in the kitchen, but as she pushed open the door leading into the main room, she heard thumps and guttural cries and what sounded like the stamping of bare feet.

She stepped in. Jack was there, all right, but what she saw was far from the sexual scene she had envisaged. He was in fighting gear. His white cotton padded jacket was girded at the waist by a black belt. His legs were covered by the loose trousers of this martial art's uniform. His feet were naked and he was sparring with an older, shorter man similarly dressed, except for a brown belt.

Utterly focused on the contest, neither noticed her come in. She was lost in admiration. This was an aspect of Jack she hadn't seen, though she knew that he practised Shotokan karate, trained under a *sensei*, and took it extremely seriously. His fierce masculinity and sensual good looks were enhanced and he was volatile as he fought, every line of his body expressing the warrior. She saw his opponent perform the crescent sweep, a backfist strike, a lunging punch. Jack blocked them all. He seemed hardly to move, yet turned defence into attack, redirecting and parrying the blows.

'*Kiai!*' he shouted and, with a high, lightning-fast kick, brought the other man to the ground.

Jack held out his hand and helped him to his feet. They stepped back and bowed solemnly with traditional, age-old etiquette.

'Hello, Kim,' Jack said and, strolling over to her, kissed her with the air of a man reclaiming a possession.

His every move excited each part of her, his closeness thrilling through every molecule in her body. He smiled and unfastened the complicated knotting of his belt, then took off the top of the *gi*. His chest hair was matted and wet. The drawstring of the loose trousers had slackened to just below his navel. The long, thick finger of his penis lay against his left thigh. He smelled pungent, of exertion and energy and expensive deodorant which couldn't mask the odour of fresh sweat.

'I was at the shop. I thought I'd drop in on my way home,' she faltered, her eyes going from him to the stocky man who was towelling his dark, straight hair.

'Yes,' Jack said, and turned to his sparring partner. 'This is my sister. Kim, meet Giles.' Then he added dismissively, 'Andy's in the sauna, Giles. He's great at giving massages. And thanks for this morning. I was impressed by your *kata* and *mawashi geri*. You'll do well in the competition.'

'Are you entering?' Giles asked, taking the hint and picking up his sports-bag, then making for the door.

''Fraid not. By May I'll be in Japan where I hope for the honour of training with a real master, an eighth dan.'

When Giles had disappeared, Jack took Kim's hand and raised it to his lips. She felt the heat of his lips and some of the sweat from his face touched her skin.

'I don't know why I came,' she said, trying unsuccessfully to free herself. 'This is total insanity, Jack. I'm glad you're going away.'

He held her hand against the slippery warmth of his bare chest, answering with that mockery which she found so infuriating. 'You're coming with me.'

'No. I'm not. I'm staying with Oliver and forgetting that any of this ever happened. Why don't you find yourself a regular girlfriend?'

He laughed and moved his hands to her breasts. 'You think I should shack up with some sensible broad? Settle down and marry her, so you can pat my children on the head and have them call you auntie?'

'Something like that,' she stammered, though the vision cut into her like cold steel.

As an answer, he propelled her to the arched door of

the crypt, saying, 'I haven't shown you the alterations, have I? Come along.'

'I don't want to,' she muttered sullenly, though memories set her ablaze.

'It's much improved,' he replied, unlocking the door. 'So desirable, in fact, that Imogene's renting it out while I'm abroad.'

'To live in?' Kim couldn't believe Imogene would exchange that damp vault for her luxurious apartment.

'As a dungeon, darling. Her friends will go mad about it. Quite a profitable venture.' He led her down the stone stairs into the place that still filled her with dread.

It was gloomy, but Jack had had the rubbish removed, the stone walls brushed, and electricity and radiators installed. In the eerie glow of red spotlights, Kim could see a whipping-post, chains and pulley-blocks, and all the other paraphernalia associated with savage bonds and blissful pleasure.

As if empowered by her thoughts, handcuffs were secured round her wrists in front of her, and Jack pushed her silently to where a meat hook hung down from the ceiling. Her heart was racing, and adrenaline pumping, as he raised her manacled hands and fastened them to it.

He took a pace back to look at her, his naked upper body red as a demon's in that infernal light. Then the air hit her, making her nipples rise, as he unbuttoned her dress, neck to hem, and opened it. He unclipped the front of her bra, so her breasts stood free, then stripped her of her panties. He walked out of sight behind her and she tensed, waiting for his first blow, almost welcoming it as the prelude to his cock plundering her body.

She felt his hands stroking her buttocks, then spreading them, his finger invading her vagina, then her arsehole. 'I've missed you,' he whispered. 'Why have you left it so long?'

'I think Oliver's suspicious,' she blurted out.

'Of little harmless me? Surely not?'

'Not of you specifically, but he may think I'm seeing someone. Don't mark me, Jack. Not this time, please. It was so difficult making excuses not to sleep with him.'

'Then I might just lay the stripes on hard,' he said harshly, and caught her with a smarting blow across the back of her thighs. 'You've got to do it. Leave him, Kim, leave him after the wedding. I've already booked two tickets to Tokyo.'

'Then take Lara or Andy or Sandra.'

'No can do. Andy will care-take this place. Lara will run the office and Sandra's out of the question. It's you I want.'

'Why do you torture me like this? What have I ever done to you?'

'You didn't do anything, but he did.'

'Oliver?'

'No, our father. He pampered you, was there for you, left you a fortune. I didn't get anything, neither his time, nor his love, nor his money.'

His words were accompanied by a series of sharp slaps, and her body betrayed her, her hips gyrating, wanting more, wanting him.

'It's not my fault,' she wailed, then felt him trailing something long and thin up her bottom crease, pressing it between her lips, running it along her crack to tap against her needy clit.

What was he using? Too pliable for a cane. Too stiff for a thong. She imagined the fresh moisture pooling between her thighs was making the thing wet. She breathed in the faint odour of green wood. It penetrated the fusty air and the scent of smouldering pine. Her hips moved involuntarily, and she was ashamed of this blatant betrayal of her all-too-eager pussy and arse.

'I've grown to like your company, Kim,' he murmured throatily. 'You're such a willing pupil, and so embarrassed by it all. It's amusing and exciting and sweet.

Oliver doesn't deserve you. I'm never going to let you go.'

He tapped her bottom lightly and then increased the force, bringing it down across her thighs. 'Don't mark me,' she pleaded again, while her skin tingled and her breasts rose and her clitoris throbbed.

'I'm using a freshly cut bough from the garden. Just think, Kim. It was growing over an old grave until it was disturbed. Reminds me of those rather cute woodland burials. What do you think?'

'I dare not think. Unchain me, Jack. Let me go home.'

He strolled round to the front of her. Now she could see his beautiful face, his hard, blue eyes, and his nakedness. His trousers had gone and his cock jutted towards her in all its aggressive splendour.

She sobbed. Her arms were aching, her toes scrabbling to get a hold on the stone flags. He started to hit her with the whippy branch, tapping her pubis lightly at first, then tapping harder as he progressed down her thighs. She gasped, whimpered, prayed the stripes wouldn't bite too deeply, wished he'd stop, wished he'd go on for ever, punishing this wickedness within her that lusted for him so sinfully.

He clasped her round the waist and drew her nakedness to his, his cock a hard bar grinding against her belly. 'It's a rich feast, isn't it, Kim?' he said, speaking low. 'Almost too much. You're dying to climax, aren't you? Shall I let you? Shall I rub your clit with my finger, or kneel and take it between my lips, tonguing you till you come?'

'My arms hurt. Untie me,' she begged, feeling his breath on her pubes, each hair responding, and she longed to feel his mouth against her wetness.

'Only if you promise to do as I ask,' he said, his eyes glittering.

'You can't force me to leave Oliver,' she cried, her body jerking involuntarily as his finger found her waiting slit. She gasped as he fondled her.

'I'm not forcing you to do anything. The choice is yours. Say you'll come, then your troubles will be over.'

'You are forcing me. You've threatened blackmail,' she moaned, contorting her body to obtain every ounce of pleasure from his touch. 'Those bloody photos. Will you give them all to me?'

'I might, if you're good,' he whispered, rubbing her harder.

Climax took her over, preventing thought, shooting up from her clit to her brain and down through her spine. She slumped against him, sighing her pleasure, and the pain in her arms ceased as he let her down gently, took a small key and unlocked the cuffs. They left indentations on the skin.

She stood on trembling legs, rubbing her chafed wrists and watching Jack. He was on the couch positioned on a low dais against one wall. It was tented with black and crimson drapes, hung with thick, gold cords and covered with throws made from animal pelts.

'Come,' he said, sitting up, his legs slightly apart, his feet placed on the shallow top step. But as she moved forward, he gestured to the floor and she went down on all fours.

The rough paving stones bruised her knees as she crawled over them, but the pain didn't matter. All she could see was Jack's enlarged cock jutting straight out, and his balls beneath, cushioned by the furs. She had climaxed, but longed to impale herself on that solid cock. Desire made her crawl quickly and she crossed the space in between them and angled herself between his legs, while he sat there looking at her seriously.

Staring up into his face, almost asking permission, she placed her hands on his inner thighs to open them further. He eased his pelvis higher, giving her free access to his groin. She fingered his balls, felt their tension, and then took his cock in hand, and guided it to her mouth. First she wound her tongue round the stalk, tasting the sour-sweet flavour of him. Then she took all of it, the

239

last mighty inch, and his hand behind her head forced his helm into her throat. She almost choked, then held still, feeling him throb, the veins pulsing along his length.

She was sure he was going to come, but he moved quickly, pulling out, seizing her under the arms and dragging her on to the couch. He pushed her down, flat on her back, and spread her legs with his knee. In an instant he was ramming inside her. She could feel the throb of his erection through every part of her inner core.

'More, more,' she groaned, and, lifting her legs, wound them tightly round his waist, driving him in further until it hurt.

He said nothing, the pale oval of his face hanging over her. Staring into his eyes, she stopped moving, allowing him to pull his erection in and out of her. Holding her gaze, he increased the pace. She felt him charging towards his goal. His cock jerked and he cried out, then fell across her.

They said nothing, but lay there for a moment, and then he rolled off her. She clung to him and he held her in his arms, the warmth of his body, the softness of the furs beneath them, the ruddy light surrounding her, in this place which had once been the house of the dead.

Chapter Twelve

'Nothing wrong is there, Oliver?' Flyte asked as she opened the front door and let him in. She was surprised to see him. He usually phoned first.

'I don't know,' he said and kissed her cheek absent-mindedly, then paced through the hall towards the living-room. She had never seen him so dejected. He'd obviously come from the office. As he walked, he pulled at the knot of his tie, loosening it, and the collar beneath.

She didn't speak again until she returned from the kitchen with tea on a tray. There was no point in offering him a drink. His car was in the drive.

She found him slumped in an armchair, one hand thrust into his brown hair. 'Do you want to tell me about it?' she said, already guessing, but hoping he didn't know the whole story.

He looked up at her as she handed him a cup, then stirred it slowly and said, 'I think Kim's in love with someone else.'

Now for it, she thought, but kept her voice level as she answered, 'Oh? That doesn't sound like her. She's devoted to you, isn't she?'

'I believed so, once.'

'Then what's made you change your mind?' Flyte

asked, sitting down opposite him, one knee crossed over the other.

'Nothing major, but lots of little things that add up. She's hardly ever at home. Oh, I know she's involved in Elaine's shop and Jenny's wedding, but she never has any time for me nowadays,' Oliver said, putting his cup down on the low table and taking a cigarette pack from his pocket. 'On several occasions I've rung the shop late, but there's been no reply. Once or twice I've come home early, expecting her to be there, but she's left some garbled message with Jenny. She's behaving like a woman having an affair.'

'Ah, Oliver, beware the green-eyed monster.'

Flyte was deeply troubled. She'd guessed this was bound to happen sooner or later, but hadn't been able to formulate a game-plan. Apparently Jack had ignored her warning. He must be very sure of himself, or very determined to get his own way, or – and this seemed likely – hooked on Kim. If this was so, then she felt no compassion; her pity was directed at Oliver.

'I've never been jealous before,' he said slowly. 'She's been free to come and go and I trusted her implicitly.' He looked across at Flyte with an agonised expression, adding, 'Do you know what I've done? I never thought I'd stoop so low, but I found myself going through her things the other day; the dressing table, the bureau, her handbag. Looking for what? A name, a hotel bill, a telephone number, anything that would prove her unfaithful.'

'But do you really want to know?' Flyte ventured, her heart bleeding for him.

'Perhaps not, not the sordid details, anyway. I suppose I'm hoping to be proved wrong, to find that she's innocent. Honestly, Flyte, I don't know which way to turn. This is one of the penalties for marrying a younger woman.'

'That's bullshit. Have you tried talking to her?' A picture of Kim tethered, chained and blindfolded

242

appeared on the screen of her brain, and superimposed on this, the sight of Jack fucking her up the arse.

Oliver's hair became more rumpled as he combed his fingers through it. 'Of course. Though she smiles and is sweetly reasonable, a shutter comes down over her eyes and she lies to me. I know she does. I've even considered following her or employing a private investigator, though this seems terribly melodramatic.'

Flyte sat forward, one elbow resting on her knee, her chin cupped in her hand. 'Have you had a word with Jack?' she said, deciding to drop his name into the conversation.

Oliver's face sharpened, his amber eyes slitted through the cigarette smoke.

'No, I haven't. Might he know something?'

'It's possible. Speak to him. Kim may have confided in him.'

That'll make the bugger squirm, if Oliver turns up demanding the truth about Kim, she thought, and gave a little smile. Oliver could be formidable, an articulate man who didn't mince his words when he was angry. Jack might be a black belt, but Flyte would put money on Oliver if it came to a verbal battle.

'It's got worse since I went away to Brussels,' he continued, almost as if he was not quite hearing her. 'I rang her from there, and said I wanted to talk, but when I got home she moved into a guestroom, and said she was unwell.'

'Haven't you had sex since then?'

'Oh, yes, very passionate sex as a matter of fact, but she wants to do it in the dark. She won't let me see her naked.'

'Maybe she has something to hide.'

He was alerted, as taut as a bowstring, and his eyes were keen and bright. 'What could be so terrible that she needs to hide it from me?'

'The marks of the whip, perhaps?' Flyte chose her

243

words with care, yet there was no avoiding the blunt truth.

'Kim? Into masochism? I don't believe it!' he exclaimed. 'How can you know this?'

'It's only a suggestion. Perhaps she attended a fetish party out of curiosity, and found that it had a certain appeal.'

'She wouldn't,' he growled, but she could see he wasn't convinced. For the first time since she had known him, Oliver was unsure of himself.

'Wouldn't she? I do.'

'You, Flyte? I never guessed you were into S and M.'

'I wasn't when we were together, but a lot of water's flowed under the bridge since then.'

'And is there sex at these parties?'

'Usually. Remember Imogene? You met her at Jack's. She's into the scene.'

'Was it her, then, who introduced Kim to such things?'

'I don't think so.'

'Then who? Is this what she's been doing, being whipped and fucked? Is this where she meets her lover?' He leapt up distractedly, and prowled the room, a man in torment.

Flyte went over to him and placed a hand on his shoulder. 'Listen to me, Oliver,' she said as calmly as possible. 'It could be that you're too kind to Kim. The relationship may have become predictable and boring. Perhaps she hungers for the unexpected, the frightening, the cruel. This turns her on, gets her going. Perhaps you should buy yourself a whip.'

'I could never hurt her,' he said, shaking his head.

'Not even give her a severe spanking for the angst she's causing you?' She went to a drawer in the desk and brought over a pair of handcuffs, some chains and a black, silk scarf. 'Take these with you, and give it a whirl.'

'I can't. I should feel a right berk,' he said with a wry

grin, but didn't return them, his fingers playing over the steel chains.

'Does it matter, if it saves your marriage?' Flyte said, though thinking this a forlorn hope. 'Tell her what a bad girl she's been. Tie her up and chastise her, then keep her waiting for sex. Tease and tantalise her. It'll make you feel better, too, dominant and powerful. You may even grow to like it and make it part of foreplay.'

He moved towards the door, carrying the manacles, then turned and asked, 'And if I do find out she's been screwing someone else?'

'It's up to you. I can't answer that one,' she said, and saw him out into the rapidly darkening evening.

Jack hadn't been able to get hold of Kim, and it was driving him crazy. Whenever he rang Glen House or Palmer's Emporium it was to either speak to someone else who said she wasn't available, or to meet the frustration of an answerphone. He gave Lara hell, taking out his frustrations on both her and Andy, and worked like a fury on the designs for Tokyo, but couldn't get his sister out of his mind.

Oliver was cool whenever they happened to meet. The conversation took the same form.

'How's Kim? Haven't seen her around for a while.'

'She's busy with the wedding. Matron-of-honour, or some such. I'm to be an usher in a morning suit. Top hat and all. Are you coming?'

'I haven't been invited.'

'Well, that's down to the bride-to-be, I suppose, though it seems like the world and his wife will be there. I'm looking forward to meeting Liam's clan. We've ordered enough Guinness to launch a battleship. Give Kim a ring and see if you're on the guest list.'

Jack didn't say that he had tried to get through and failed.

It was late Friday afternoon and the wedding was on Saturday. Jack's flight was booked for the following week. He drove to Glen House. No one answered the bell until he'd pressed it several times. Then he heard the shuffle of footsteps and Oliver stood in the doorway.

'Kim's not here,' he said without preamble. 'You'd better come in anyway. They've all gone off to get ready for the stag-night and hen-night.'

'Without you?' Jack asked unnecessarily. It was obvious by Oliver's sweater and jogging pants that he wasn't planning to go anywhere.

'Without me,' Oliver said, with that faint irony with which he always addressed Jack. 'I consider these to be outworn pagan rituals. The bride and groom's last night of freedom? What a load of shite. These days freedom within marriage is the rule, isn't it? The old-fashioned standards of fidelity have gone to the wall.'

Jack felt suddenly uncomfortably warm. 'I don't know about that. I'm not ready to take on the snaffle,' he said.

'And would you be faithful to your wife if you did, forsaking all others?' Oliver asked blandly, leading him into the conservatory. An operatic tenor voice rang from the speakers, the aria filled with pain, underscored by menacing orchestral chords.

'I don't know,' Jack said untruthfully. He knew he'd never be faithful to one woman, or one man for that matter.

'Whisky?' Oliver asked, and when Jack nodded, poured two measures into tots and added a splash of soda water. 'You like opera?' he continued, the wicker chair creaking as he sat down.

'It's not really my bag,' Jack said, taking the seat on the other side of the round, rattan table.

'You should try it. This, for example, is Verdi's masterpiece, based on Shakespeare's tragedy, *Othello*. It's all about betrayal.'

'I know the play,' Jack said bluntly, gripping the glass in a sweating palm, unable to relax. 'Othello was wrong when he suspected his wife, Desdemona, of shagging Cassio.'

'But how could he know for sure? Weren't all the signs there? Her pleas for him to help Cassio, Othello finding her handkerchief in the young captain's bedroom?'

'Planted by Iago, who hated Othello and Cassio and wanted to bring about their ruin.'

I'll leave just as soon as I can, Jack was thinking. She's not here and Oliver's in a strange mood. All this talk of adultery is going too far. I don't like it.

'How can you know what goes on in another person's mind, however close you are?' Oliver ruminated, refilling his glass.

'But you'd never suspect Kim, surely?' Jack fiddled with his lighter. It wouldn't work and Oliver leant over to light his cigarette with his own.

'Relax, Jack,' he said, coldly watchful. 'You're like a cat on a hot brick. Is it the Japanese trip?'

'Maybe. Yes. That must be it. Sometimes I envy your secure life here, Oliver. You've got it made, you and Kim. I suppose you'll be planning to have kids. You'll want an heir for the House of Buckley.'

'Who knows? Later, maybe. Kim isn't ready yet. But you'd know all about this, wouldn't you?'

'Would I?' Jack replied nervously. There was something quietly menacing about Oliver. My God, he could kill me if he wanted, he thought, suddenly terrified. There's no one about. He could murder me and slip my body into the river. I'd be washed out to sea on the evening tide.

'She's having an affair, isn't she?' Oliver said, his voice devoid of emotion.

'I don't know,' Jack replied, going into automatic-lying mode.

'She's deceiving me, but you're her brother and she'd confide in you.'

'She hasn't said anything about an affair.'

Oliver's eyes were steely as he said, 'I'll get to the bottom of it.'

247

'I'm sure you will, if there's any truth in it, which I very much doubt,' Jack answered, getting up and adding, 'I really must go. Tell Kim I called.'

'Why don't you drop in at the wedding reception? Even if you haven't been invited, everyone will be too pie-eyed to notice.'

'I may just do that.'

'And Jack?' Oliver called from his chair as Jack reached the door. 'You'd better let Kim know I'm on to her.'

'Are you?'

'Oh, yes.'

The Paradise Club wasn't the sort of place Kim usually frequented. In a sleazy backstreet of London's Soho, it had a garish, neon sign and a dusky foyer lined with photographs of young men with rippling biceps posing, in the nearly nude.

'Oh, get a load of that,' squeaked one of Jenny's friends. 'Did you ever see such a package?'

'I hope to get a closer look,' Jenny said, pink with excitement. The great day was almost there.

'So you will,' chorused several of the other women she had invited to the hen-party. 'They bare all here, and they'll let you have a feel.'

Kim was astounded by the change that had taken place among them as soon as they had left their men behind. They were all, without exception, dressed to kill and ready for anything. Was she? Hardly. It wasn't really her thing.

But when they got inside and found their reserved table close to the stage, the atmosphere began to get to her. The room, with its long bar at the back and numerous small tables, chairs and banquettes, was panelled and gilded and dimly lit. House music throbbed from speakers near the low stage from which ran a catwalk. The air was so pheromone-filled, you could almost see it, and the audience was rampant with desire. Even

Elaine and Sarah – who had come along for the laugh – were affected. Hunky stallions might not move them, but the sight of so many lustful females roused almost beyond endurance certainly did.

The beat grew louder. Amid cheers and cat-calls, the evening-suited Master of Ceremonies appeared from the wings. They hooted. They heckled. They told him to 'get 'em off!' They behaved disgracefully, and were having a wonderful time. But this was nothing compared to the uproar when the curtains drew back and the strippers appeared for their first number. The women went wild.

Kim was prepared to be cool, even embarrassed, by such a display of outrageous gyrating, pumped-up muscles and flagrant virility, but she found that their performance was slick and well rehearsed. They moved like the dancers she had always admired. Maybe some of them were fresh from ballet school but unable to find respectable theatre work. Whatever, they were all professionals, and the first set had them dressed as fire-fighters, gradually removing everything from helmets down until only the tiniest jock-straps remained. Then, as the women stamped and roared, these too were whipped away, and a row of cocks jutted towards the near-hysterical spectators.

'Oh, my God!' yelled Jenny, hanging on to Kim. 'I've never seen so many dicks all at one time! Look at that one! It must be ten inches long.'

It was, indeed, an astonishing show. The boys bowed themselves out, then another group appeared, this time barbarians with furry boots, wolfskin cloaks, studded wristbands and leather trousers. Their hair was long and shaggy, their headgear horned, and their suggestive gestures had the audience screaming for more. The choreography had them flinging cloaks away, strutting down the catwalk, the Velcro seams of their trousers giving way at a tug. Jenny screeched as one of the men crouched in front of her, encouraging her to stroke his bulge through the G-string.

The women were standing, clamouring to be allowed to thrust paper money into the dancers' crotches in return for putting a hand under the taut balls and stalwart cocks. A couple of shaven-headed bouncers intervened if the women became too frantic, taking the money and stashing it in the pockets of their dinner jackets.

'Go on, have a feel,' Jenny urged Kim. 'It's worth a tenner.'

But Kim held back, refusing the handsome young man who bent his knees and thrust his crotch towards her face. He was bronzed and beautiful, a perfect example of physical fitness, and her pussy spasmed, a trickle of juice escaping.

'Not like this,' she said, and only he heard her words which were quiet in the surrounding mayhem.

'Meet me round the back. The props cupboard,' he replied quickly, smiling and rubbing the erection straining at his posing-pouch.

'I might,' she replied, thinking: why not? An uncomplicated fuck was all she needed now, ideally with someone other than Oliver or Jack who seemed to think they owned her. Rebellion flared up. She'd prove that she was her own person. No one had the right to tell her what to do.

She tucked her handbag under her arm, thought of the condom inside it, and said to Jenny, 'I'm going to the loo.' She elbowed her way through the crowd towards the rear exit.

There she faltered, but only for a moment.

She couldn't. She wouldn't dare, would she? She would!

Backstage was cramped and crowded. It smelled of young men and fresh sweat. Everyone was so intent on getting to the dressing room and changing for the next number that they ignored her. She found the door marked PROPERTY, opened it and slipped inside. It was dark, and she found the light switch. It was a small, cluttered space, but big enough for what she had in mind. Footsteps echoed outside and her barbarian came in.

He was bigger close up, and even more handsome under his greasepaint than she had imagined. He turned the key in the lock, saying, 'I usually get paid for this.'

'In your dreams!' she said savagely, and grabbed him, her hand instantly inside his jock-strap.

'Christ!' he hissed, amused. 'You're a goer!'

'You'd better believe it.'

Her heart was thudding, her sex wet. She wanted this boy, wanted to be immoral, to show that she, too, could do as she liked. Now was the moment to feed at the altar of this dancer's sex. The bonds that tied her to Oliver and Jack were weakening.

They didn't kiss. It was a swift encounter. He lifted her and placed her on top of a small table, then pressed between her legs. Her skirt rode up. He dragged her panties to one side and found her clit, rubbing it hard. She absorbed his energy, his desire, and came abruptly. Recovering instantly, she seized his cock, finding it already latex-covered, and guided it into her. He rode her quickly, panting and shoving, reaching his climax in a few seconds.

Someone banged on the door, and a voice called, 'Get out of that tart's snatch, Danny. You're on in five minutes.'

He grinned down at her, tucked his cock away and left.

Kim followed more slowly, savouring what had just happened. She laughed to herself, fluffed up the sides of her hair, and went back to the hen-party.

Everyone was saying, 'What a lovely wedding!'

The sun was shining. The ceremony in the small, local church had gone without a hitch. The bride and groom had been driven to the reception in a horse-drawn carriage. The caterers had been on the go since dawn.

251

Flowers were massed everywhere. The wedding presents were on display in the hall, and the huge marquee
had been decorated in pink and silver by Elaine. Hearts
and fertility symbols were everywhere.

Kim felt the responsibility of it keenly. As Polly was
quick to point out, 'It's almost a rehearsal for the day
when your own daughter gets married.'

Polly's latest pregnancy was beginning to show. Kim
harked back to the night of the swimming party. Had
Polly forgotten about contraception in the heat of the
moment?

There were so many people to talk to: Jenny's parents,
Liam's Irish relatives, innumerable guests. Kim escaped
from the tent once the meal was eaten, the cake cut and
the speeches over. Now the guests could settle down to
the champagne. Soon the newly-weds would leave for
Venice and everyone could let their hair down and really
start to party.

Kim couldn't control her anxiety. She was half expecting Jack to turn up. Jenny had been apologetic about not
inviting him. 'I feel I should, him being your brother
and all, but I hardly know him, and there's so many as
it is,' she had said.

Oliver hadn't mentioned this omission. They didn't
speak of Jack any more, and this made Kim more
apprehensive. She had the gut feeling that Jack was
planning something. Those damn photos, she kept thinking. He's never handed over the prints and negatives.

Glen House looked magnificent, a perfect setting for
such an occasion, and Kim leant against the stone balus-
trade, enjoying the spring sun and taking time out. She'd
been up since seven o'clock, and hadn't left the strip
club till three in the morning. The memory of her
barbarian lover was like a secret heat within her, but she
had no desire to meet him again. She felt both ashamed
and proud of herself. It was all right. No one knew.

Then, glancing across the lawn towards the boat-
house, she saw Jack. It was too late to hide among the

guests. Before she had even decided to run, he was upon her. 'Why have you been avoiding me?' he demanded.

Once again, it was a conversation that had never really stopped. 'You know why,' she said. 'We broke the rules. It was a ghastly mistake.'

'Oh, I see,' he sneered. 'You've had your fun, put a little sparkle into your marriage, and now that's it.'

'I didn't ask for this,' she replied. 'It was your idea.'

'And you just came along for the ride?' he said, and slid an arm round her waist.

'Jack, don't,' she pleaded, hoping she wasn't about to cry and ruin her make-up. Her duties weren't over till Jenny came down in her going-away outfit.

'I need you as a brother.'

'That's not enough,' he said, and despite Oliver and the boy at the club, she couldn't help the ache in her breasts, the longing in her pussy, weak and desirous in his presence. 'You've got to disentangle yourself from Oliver. We have this final chance. I fly on Wednesday.'

'No, no,' she cried, pulling away from him and running blindly, holding up her layered, silk skirt, losing her wide-brimmed picture hat, her satin shoes already soaked by the wet grass.

She could hear him pounding after her, and headed for the river. She thought she'd shaken him off, but a quick glance round showed that he was gaining on her, his face hard, his eyes like blue ice. She could feel the adrenaline surging through her, driving her on. She reached the uncultivated part of the garden and could hear Jack crashing through the undergrowth and calling her name. He sounded furious, and excitement gripped her gut. The trees closed around her and she hid behind one of the biggest. If only it were full summer and the branches thick with leaves. But it wasn't, and he found her.

She turned to face him, and her hand flew out, fingers wide as they clawed at his cheek. Bright beads of blood joined that of sweat.

253

'Bitch!' he snarled, and grabbed her. She heard the rip as one shoulder-strap broke and, stepping back, she caught her heel in her skirt hem. Her expensive dress was ruined, and this made her angrier.

She fought him savagely, but he pinned her down on the earth, his lips crushing hers, his body heavy and hot against hers, fly unzipped, his cock ready for action. She could feel herself yielding, that old magic working between them, then looked across the glade. Oliver was framed between two saplings. He didn't speak, merely came over and, seizing Jack by the scruff of the neck, hauled him off.

'You've both got some explaining to do,' he said sternly, and marched towards the house. Bruised and bloody, Kim limped behind him, with Jack bringing up the rear, fumbling to return his semi-inflated cock to his trousers.

No one noticed the trio cross the lawn and enter through the kitchen. In the study, Oliver handed Jack a tissue, saying, 'Better do something about that scratch. I don't want you bleeding all over my carpet.'

Kim waited, seeing her life passing before her eyes, remembering the closeness she and Oliver had shared, how they had talked of being in love and spending the rest of their lives together. All their dreams and aspirations: a villa in Spain: a palm-thatched hut in the Caribbean; children.

And she had thrown it all away.

For what? For a forbidden liaison, an addiction stronger and more potent than any drug.

Oliver didn't look at her. His shoulders straight, hands locked behind his back, as he stared out at the wedding guests strolling in the sunshine, and Polly's children scampering about with a lively contingent of youngsters from Dublin.

'For Christ's sake. Say something!' Kim shouted, unable to stand the silence.

He turned and shot her a scathing glance, and she felt like the meanest tramp with her dress torn and muddy, bits of twig tangled in her hair, her mascara running and her lipstick smeared by Jack's kisses.

'What do you expect me to say?'

'You know about us, don't you?' she said.

'Do I, my dear? What is there to know?' he replied quietly.

'I'm the man she's been seeing. Would you like to hear the details? Shall I give you a blow-by-blow account?' Jack said, arrogant as ever, in spite of the tissue held to his cheek.

Oliver stared at him coolly, then answered, 'I'm aware that you and Kim have an unusual relationship, but I've decided that I don't want to discuss it. There's always too much talk about everything. It's over now, and you'll be leaving London.'

'Not for ever,' Jack said threateningly.

'No, but when you return, things will be different, I assure you. If you try it on again with her, I'll open up the whole can of worms, and you'll never get any decent work again.'

'Is this what you want, Kim?' Jack demanded.

She could hardly bear to look at him. 'Yes,' she murmured, light-headed with fatigue and stress.

'Are you sure?' he insisted, taking a step closer, but finding Oliver barring his way.

'Yes. Go now, Jack, please,' Kim said.

'Really?'

'You heard the lady,' Oliver said, and his arm came round her in a protective way which she was sure she didn't merit.

Jack turned on his heel and marched off, but as she leant into Oliver she couldn't help thinking about the unfinished business between her and her brother.

Would it ever be really over?

'I've come for the photographs,' Kim said, walking through the chancel and into Jack's office.

He looked up and smiled. 'Oh? And what makes you think I'd let you have them?'

'It's over between us. I'm back with Oliver and it's better than ever. At least I can thank you for that. You've made me appreciate what's important,' she answered, head up, confident that she looked stunning in a tangerine-coloured top and a pair of palazzo pants.

'Really? So you're back to being the dutiful wife?' he said sarcastically. 'No chance of a quickie then?'

'None at all. Give me the prints and negs and I'll go.'

'Does Oliver know you're here?'

'That's not the point.'

'So he doesn't know. And you're trying to kid me that things have changed?'

He came over to her, and, with an impudent finger, touched her right nipple as it strained against the cotton. Kim went rigid, denying the pleasure coursing down her spine. It wasn't to be, and could never be again.

She pushed his hand away, saying, 'The photos?'

He casually appraised her, and she hated this, hated the knowing way in which he read her very soul, hated his confidence and his hauteur.

'I won't give them to you,' he said, with a tigerish smile.

'Please, Jack,' she begged, losing her nerve and beginning to panic.

'What does it matter? Oliver knows we've been screwing.'

'He didn't want the details, remember? He's been so forgiving. He's never mentioned it again. He mustn't see those prints. It would finish him.'

'Darling, I don't know which I like best. When you're blazing away like a hellcat, or begging,' he commented slowly, and she could see he was enjoying himself hugely. 'I won't give them to you, but you can watch while I destroy them.' He took a foolscap envelope from his desk.

'Let me see. Are they all there?' she shouted, fierce

with him, and angry at the way he had turned her life topsy-turvy.

'Do you doubt my word?' he said, pained, and withdrew the pictures and negatives, holding them out so that she might examine them. She handed them back and he started to feed them into the paper shredder.

'Thank you, Jack,' she breathed on a sigh of relief. 'Let's continue to think well of each other.'

He watched the evidence of their affair reduced to strips, and light from the stained-glass church windows gave him an undeserved halo. 'I may keep you to that, sister,' he said. 'Now, goodbye. I've a lot of loose ends to tie up before my flight.'

Kim walked away from him, blinded by tears. He was totally unscrupulous, a man without morals or principles, and yet, were it not for circumstances, who knew what might have happened. One thing she was sure of: she'd never again experience such deep emotions and physical passion as she had felt for him.

She parked in the car-port at the back of the emporium. Elaine and Sarah were viewing a house with an eye to a new commission, and she was in charge for the afternoon. She was busy, yet her thoughts kept straying to Jack. He was a lost cause, and she knew it all too well, but –

Half past five and it was time to close. She set the security system and let herself out into the yard. She was about to press the central-locking device on the car when she heard someone behind her.

'Don't scream,' a guttural voice said, and she felt a heavy hand at the back of her neck before her sight was obliterated by a silk scarf.

She was frogmarched forward, and pushed down across the slippery bonnet of the car. Her arms were wrenched back and the coldness of a chain bound round them. She wasn't sure of the voice, the touch, or the smell of her assailant. Was it Jack, or a total stranger? If it was the latter, then she could be in grave danger.

Hands under her hips, he lifted her, then yanked at the fastening of her trousers, and pulled them roughly down, her panties, too, exposing her buttocks. She struggled and tried to squirm away, but the sudden, savage blow of a hard hand across her bottom made her stop resisting.

'Jack, is that you?' she cried, her tears rising behind the scarf, her rump warming, the heat spreading to her pussy.

There was no reply, just the feel of ungentle fingers probing into her crack, exploring each fold and orifice. She could hear the man breathing heavily, and she stiffened as the air cooled her naked rump when he withdrew. There was a pause, a moment of pure terror. What was he about to do? Then, as a lash cut into her, her body slid across the bonnet and she bucked and yelled. She felt numbness in the first instant of impact, followed by burning, beautiful agony.

'Is this what you want?' the harsh voice whispered. 'Is this what it's all about? And this!' A swish and a thwack and the bite of pain, and Kim lay limp, moaning.

'Oh, no! No! Please.' And her voice held a keening, sexual quality, the cry of an animal on heat.

The stranger went on whipping her, and she was mindless now, her body melting into a pool of anguish and desire. This was the moment when Jack had thrown away the punishing rod and taken her. Would he now do the same? Was it him subjecting her to such bitter chastisement?

She couldn't believe that he was done with the whip, but heard it clatter as it dropped to the floor. There was a pause, when she hung between consciousness and oblivion, her skin flaming, her arousal every bit as intense.

Now he was on her. She felt a hard cock driving into her slick, wet opening, jabbing against the neck of her womb, heedless of her discomfort. He was intent only on his own gratification, pumping, thrusting, using her brutally, and with each inward stroke his clothing chafed her tender welts and she screamed. His hand clamped over her mouth and his pelvis powered his cock, like an imperative that must be obeyed. She wanted to climax, too, lifting her hips, feeling the rap of his hardening balls against her perineum, but unable to bring pressure on her clit. And he came, shooting his semen into her with a punishing force.

He slumped across her and she knew it wasn't Jack. This man was smaller, and she could feel his hair tickling her face and smell his cologne and guessed that were he to free her hands, she would recognise his cock by the feel of it, so familiar, so dear to her.

'Oliver,' she whispered.

'Yes,' he murmured, and softly kissed her tear-streaked cheek.

'But why?'

He undid the chains, unbound her eyes, and helped her to her feet. He looked different, harder, once again the man of power with whom she had first fallen in love.

'I don't have to explain anything to you,' he said. 'Accept it, my dear. Jack has gone. You have a new master now.'

Do I? she thought, but though she coiled herself against her husband, inside she was upheld by steel. All right, I'll play this game, enjoy it, too, and get all I can out of it, but Jack has taught me how to be selfish in my pleasure. I'm strong now, ready to explore new avenues of sensation. For this, at least, I have cause to be grateful to him.

'If you're so masterful, then I suggest you take me home, Oliver,' she whispered. 'The honeymoon couple are still away and we have the house to ourselves. No one will hear if I scream and beg for mercy.'

It was almost time for Andy to drive him to Heathrow airport, and Jack cast a final glance over his luggage. There wasn't a lot. He liked to travel light. They were leaving earlier than necessary, for he had a mission to accomplish before boarding the plane.

He stalked across the room to where an oil painting concealed a wall safe. Shifting it to one side, he manipulated the complicated locking mechanism, opened it, and pulled out a package, then closed the safe up and replaced the picture. He glanced at the contents of the package and smiled. Yes, this would lie snug and safe in his deposit box in the vaults of his bank while he was away.

His smile deepened, and he glanced over the material in his hands. Kim in the crypt, naked, suffering, chained to the bars. It was his favourite. He replaced the photographs and the negatives in the envelope and sealed it, then slipped it into his case. She thought he had destroyed the evidence, and he'd let her believe that, but Jack never completely let go of anything which he considered to be rightfully his. In this instance he had made sure he had a complete duplicate set.

He paused on the threshold of the church, looking round his property, warmed by the knowledge that he had the damning material in his briefcase. There was no doubt about it. He'd be back. The devil always looks after his own.

BLACK LACE NEW BOOKS

Published in September

OUT OF BOUNDS
Mandy Dickinson
£5.99

When Katie decides to start a new life in a French farmhouse left to her by her grandfather, she is horrified to find two men are squatting in her property. But her horror quickly becomes curiosity as she realises how attracted she is to them, and how much illicit pleasure she can have. When her ex-boyfriend shows up, it isn't long before everyone is questioning their sexuality.

ISBN 0 352 33431 2

A DANGEROUS GAME
Lucinda Carrington
£5.99

Doctor Jacey Muldaire knows what she wants from the men in her life: good sex and plenty of it. And it looks like she's going to get plenty of it while working in an elite private hospital in South America. But Jacey isn't all she pretends to be. A woman of many guises, she is in fact working for British Intelligence. Her femme fatale persona gives her access to places other spies can't get to. Every day is full of risk and sexual adventure, and everyone around her is playing a dangerous game.

ISBN 0 352 33432 0

Published in October

THE TIES THAT BIND
Tesni Morgan
£5.99

Kim Buckley is a beautiful but shy young woman who is married to a wealthy business consultant. When a charismatic young stranger dressed as the devil turns up at their Halloween party, Kim's life is set to change for ever. Claiming to be her lost half-brother, he's got his eye on her money and a gameplan for revenge. Things are further complicated by their mutual sexual attraction and a sizzling combination of secret and guilty passions threatens to overwhelm them.

ISBN 0 352 33438 X

IN THE DARK
Zoe le Verdier
£5.99

This second collection of Zoe's erotic short stories explores the most explicit female desires. There's something here for every reader who likes their erotica hot and a little bit rare. From anonymous sex to exhibitionism, phone sex and rubber fetishism, all these stories have great characterisation and a sting in the tail.

ISBN 0 352 33439 8

To be published in November

VELVET GLOVE
Emma Holly
£5.99

Audrey is an SM Goldilocks in search of the perfect master. Her first choice is far too cruel. Her second too tender. But when she meets Patrick – a charismatic bar owner – he seems just right. But can she trust the man behind the charm, or will he drag her deeper into submission than she's prepared to go?

ISBN 0 352 33448 7

BOUND BY CONTRACT
Helena Ravenscroft
£5.99

Samanta Bentley and her cousin Ross have been an illicit item for years. When Ross becomes involved with the submissive Dr Louisa, Sam senses that Ross's true passions aren't compatible with her own domineering ways. Then she reads the classic novel *Venus in Furs*, which inspires her to experiment with being his slave for a month. When Dr Louisa shows up at Ross's country hideaway, there are surprising shifts in their ritual games of power and punishment.

ISBN 0 352 33447 9

If you would like a complete list of plot summaries of Black Lace titles, or would like to receive information on other publications available, please send a stamped addressed envelope to:

Black Lace, Thames Wharf Studios,
Rainville Road, London W6 9HT

BLACK LACE BOOKLIST

All books are priced £4.99 unless another price is given.

Black Lace books with a contemporary setting

PALAZZO	Jan Smith ISBN 0 352 33156 9	☐
THE GALLERY	Fredrica Alleyn ISBN 0 352 33148 8	☐
AVENGING ANGELS	Roxanne Carr ISBN 0 352 33147 X	☐
COUNTRY MATTERS	Tesni Morgan ISBN 0 352 33174 7	☐
GINGER ROOT	Robyn Russell ISBN 0 352 33152 6	☐
DANGEROUS CONSEQUENCES	Pamela Rochford ISBN 0 352 33185 2	☐
THE NAME OF AN ANGEL £6.99	Laura Thornton ISBN 0 352 33205 0	☐
SILENT SEDUCTION	Tanya Bishop ISBN 0 352 33193 3	☐
BONDED	Fleur Reynolds ISBN 0 352 33192 5	☐
THE STRANGER	Portia Da Costa ISBN 0 352 33211 5	☐
CONTEST OF WILLS £5.99	Louisa Francis ISBN 0 352 33223 9	☐
THE SUCCUBUS £5.99	Zoe le Verdier ISBN 0 352 33230 1	☐
FEMININE WILES £7.99	Karina Moore ISBN 0 352 33235 2	☐
AN ACT OF LOVE £5.99	Ella Broussard ISBN 0 352 33240 9	☐
DRAMATIC AFFAIRS £5.99	Fredrica Alleyn ISBN 0 352 33289 1	☐
DARK OBSESSION £7.99	Fredrica Alleyn ISBN 0 352 33281 6	☐
COOKING UP A STORM £7.99	Emma Holly ISBN 0 352 33258 1	☐

SEARCHING FOR VENUS £5.99	Ella Broussard ISBN 0 352 33284 0	☐
A PRIVATE VIEW £5.99	Crystalle Valentino ISBN 0 352 33308 1	☐
A SECRET PLACE £5.99	Ella Broussard ISBN 0 352 33307 3	☐
THE TRANSFORMATION £5.99	Natasha Rostova ISBN 0 352 33311 1	☐
SHADOWPLAY £5.99	Portia Da Costa ISBN 0 352 33313 8	☐
MIXED DOUBLES £5.99	Zoe le Verdier ISBN 0 352 33312 X	☐
RAW SILK £5.99	Lisabet Sarai ISBN 0 352 33336 7	☐
THE TOP OF HER GAME £5.99	Emma Holly ISBN 0 352 33337 5	☐
HAUNTED £5.99	Laura Thornton ISBN 0 352 33341 3	☐
VILLAGE OF SECRETS £5.99	Mercedes Kelly ISBN 0 352 33344 8	☐
INSOMNIA £5.99	Zoe le Verdier ISBN 0 352 33345 6	☐
PACKING HEAT £5.99	Karina Moore ISBN 0 352 33356 1	☐
TAKING LIBERTIES £5.99	Susie Raymond ISBN 0 352 33357 X	☐
LIKE MOTHER, LIKE DAUGHTER £5.99	Georgina Brown ISBN 0 352 33422 3	☐
CONFESSIONAL £5.99	Judith Roycroft ISBN 0 352 33421 5	☐
ASKING FOR TROUBLE £5.99	Kristina Lloyd ISBN 0 352 33362 6	☐

Black Lace books with an historical setting

THE SENSES BEJEWELLED	Cleo Cordell ISBN 0 352 32904 1	☐
HANDMAIDEN OF PALMYRA	Fleur Reynolds ISBN 0 352 32919 X	☐
THE INTIMATE EYE	Georgia Angelis ISBN 0 352 33004 X	☐
CONQUERED	Fleur Reynolds ISBN 0 352 33025 2	☐
FORBIDDEN CRUSADE	Juliet Hastings ISBN 0 352 33079 1	☐

------ ✂ --------------------

Please send me the books I have ticked above.

Name ....

Address ....

....

....

.... Post Code ....

Send to: **Cash Sales, Black Lace Books, Thames Wharf Studios, Rainville Road, London W6 9HT.**

US customers: for prices and details of how to order books for delivery by mail, call 1-800-805-1083.

Please enclose a cheque or postal order, made payable to **Virgin Publishing Ltd**, to the value of the books you have ordered plus postage and packing costs as follows:

UK and BFPO – £1.00 for the first book, 50p for each subsequent book.

Overseas (including Republic of Ireland) – £2.00 for the first book, £1.00 for each subsequent book.

If you would prefer to pay by VISA, ACCESS/MASTER-CARD, DINERS CLUB, AMEX or SWITCH, please write your card number and expiry date here:

....

Please allow up to 28 days for delivery.

Signature ....

------ ✂ --------------------